Egret's Loft Murder Myste

Unnatural Causes

The Dead Men's Wife

Serial Seniors

Raven's Wing Murder Mystery Series

Strange Winds

Cursed Ground

CURSED GROUND

A Raven's Wing Irish
Murder Mystery

T.E. HARKINS

CHARLES
FORT
PRESS

This is a work of fiction. Names, characters, places, and incidents either are the product of the author's imagination or are used fictitiously. Any resemblance to actual persons, living or dead, events, or locales is entirely coincidental.

Copyright © October 2024 by T.E. Harkins

All rights reserved. No part of this book may be reproduced or used in any manner without written permission of the copyright owner except for the use of quotations in a book review. For more information, address: teharkins.author@gmail.com.

This book is dedicated to Mia.

I can't wait to see the amazing places life takes you!

PROLOGUE

The early morning air filled Kevin Donnelly's lungs with a crisp coldness. Just last week, the weather girl on television had promised more sunny days on the horizon. But the temperature, as Kevin walked across the quiet, empty construction site, felt more Baltic than Balearic.

Not that he was surprised the weather girl was wrong. He didn't trust anything he heard on television. Or read in the newspapers. Or was told by people he probably ought to trust.

No.

As far as Kevin was concerned, the whole world was out to sell him things he didn't want or need. And he was rarely in a buyer's mood.

After all, he hadn't built a billion-euro empire by doing what other people thought he should do.

If it had been up to them, he'd never have broken ground on this—his greatest and most lucrative project. Everyone in the nearby village had warned him not to build here. Said he'd be invoking the wrath of the faeries.

He'd gotten a good laugh out of that.

As if he'd let old folklore and silly superstition impact his business decisions.

Those villagers didn't know him at all. Which was probably for the best. They'd like him even less if they did.

But he hadn't dragged his slightly pudgy butt out of bed at five o'clock in the morning to worry about such inconsequential concerns. He came here because he had a job to do before the crew arrived in a few short hours.

So, he figured he'd best get to it.

He zipped his Helly Hansen parka just under his chin, then pulled a flashlight out of his pocket and aimed it at the ground in front of him.

Mud from the previous day's rain slurped at the soles of his Canada Goose boots as Kevin walked across the lot to where a pair of diggers rested, their claws curled under like the misshapen arms of a Tyrannosaurus rex.

He climbed into the cabin of one of the excavators and fired up the engine. The stench of diesel fuel flooded the tiny glass-encased cab. Kevin breathed deeply, appreciating the intoxicating aroma he associated with his success.

It had been a while since Kevin operated one of these machines. As the boss, he usually had the luxury of farming out jobs like this to the hired help. After a few minutes of reacquainting himself with the equipment, Kevin flipped on the headlights and shifted the machine into gear.

Steel tracks plowed through the mud as Kevin drove toward a large, shallow hole that would be filled with concrete in a few short hours.

Kevin steered the digger to the hole's edge and fidgeted with the levers to extend the long arm.

Then, he began to dig.

Once started, it took him less than ten minutes to dig a hole deep enough to suit his needs. Then, he reversed the machine so that its weight wouldn't collapse the edge of the hole.

He climbed out of the digger, bracing himself against the frosty

April air. As he trudged through the mud to his Land Rover, he thought about the steaming, hot cup of cappuccino that his much younger wife would prepare when he returned home.

It wouldn't be much longer now. Then maybe he could stop worrying and enjoy the fruits of all his machinations over the past few months. All he had to do was bury the duffle bag that had been stashed, as welcome as a stinking pile of trash, in his trunk overnight.

He hefted the bag onto his shoulder, surprised again by the weight of the thing.

As quickly as he could, he lumbered back across the vacant lot. His shoulder ached when he finally dropped the bag onto the ground, where it landed with a soft thud.

Despite the cold, sweat beaded on his forehead, and he brushed it away from his receding hairline with the sleeve of his jacket. He allowed himself a few minutes to collect his breath before getting on with his task.

He was leaning against the side of the digger, imagining the spectacular structure that would soon dominate this empty space, when he heard a noise.

At first, he dismissed the sound as wildlife. A rabbit or fox had probably pulled a runner from the neighboring woods.

Then he heard it again.

A kind of grunting that sounded vaguely human came from inside the hole where he'd just been digging.

Maybe the faeries are coming for me after all, he thought.

He wanted to dismiss the notion, but the thought lodged in his mind carried on memories of his mother reading him bedtime stories about the mythical Tuatha Dé Dannon.

An ancient Irish tribe rumored to have possessed godlike abilities, the Tuatha Dé Dannon were driven underground by the race of people who would eventually populate Ireland. Centuries later, the legend persisted that members of the long-lost tribe would occasionally emerge from the Underworld as fearsome faeries to torment anyone who offended them.

Don't be such an eejit, Kevin ordered himself. *You'll get nowhere with all this fantasy and nonsense. You've got mightier fish to fry.*

His sense of reason restored, Kevin pushed himself off the digger and rose to his full height.

"Whoever you are, you're trespassing on my land," he roared. "Show yourself, and maybe I won't call the Guards."

The pre-dawn countryside fell silent. Kevin strained his ears and squinted into the darkness. But he neither heard nor saw anything.

He took a step closer to the hole.

"I mean it now. My offer has an expiry date, and I won't be hesitating to press charges if you don't show yourself to me right quick," he warned, though he had no intention of following through on the threat.

He received no response. With rising annoyance, Kevin stepped forward a few more feet.

"You've no business here, and I want you gone," he called out. "I'm going to count to three, and if you're still here when I stop counting, there'll be hell to pay."

Still, he heard nothing.

"Three," Kevin began counting.

Something rustled beneath his feet.

"Two."

He thought he caught a flash of movement out of the corner of his eye, and the soft tinkle of faraway laughter echoed in his ears.

"One."

Kevin took a step forward and the earth seemed to turn to jelly beneath his feet.

Then, before his eyes, he saw lights rising from the ground and swimming across his field of vision.

He didn't know it at the time, but it was the last thing he would ever see.

CHAPTER 1

I'm lying next to the pool back home in Florida. My eyes are closed, but I can hear the water splashing.

Ireland had been so cold over the past month I feared I might never be warm again. But now, the heavy air feels weighted with a humidity that's almost too hot. The wind feels balmy as it caresses my face, and in the draft, I catch a subtle hint of…peanut butter!

I open my eyes to find myself in my little cottage in Ballygoseir, with rain hammering at the window and Fergal snuggled up next to my side, breathing contentedly into my face. When he sees that I'm awake, his tail begins to beat a steady rhythm against the mattress, and he licks my face with his sticky tongue.

"Ah, Fergal!" I moan. "I thought you ate all the peanut butter outta your Kong last night. Did you save some for this mornin'?"

At the mention of the tasty treat, Fergal launches himself off the bed, grabs the red rubber toy off the floor, and looks up at me expectantly.

"Oh, no. You're not gettin' anymore. Not until after I've had some coffee anyway," I tell him.

For a brief moment, he looks deflated. But his disappointment never lasts long. Before I know it, he's back on the bed, licking my face and sending me into a fit of very unladylike giggles.

Even though I'd been dreaming of Florida, it feels right to still be here at Raven's Wing, the cottage my mama bought in Ireland. It's been a few weeks now since I arrived in the land of my ancestors and, other than initially getting caught up in a murder investigation, I've enjoyed every minute of my time here.

The best part? Getting to spend time with my dad, Ian Murphy. Until recently, he didn't know I existed, and I didn't know who he was, so there's no resentment over all the lost years. We just have lots to catch up on. And, after losing my mama not long ago, Ian and his sister Audrey are the only family I have left.

I just hope I'll be able to stay.

Still groggy with sleep, I'm trying to remember if I'd made any plans for the day when the pay-as-you-go cell phone on my nightstand begins to ring. The clock on the wall tells me it's just past six-thirty in the morning.

Who would be callin' me this early? I wonder. The number of people who have my new number could be counted on one hand—and the only people usually ringing it are my dad, my Aunt Audrey, and Flynn O'Reardon, my boss at the *Glendare Gazette*.

I answer without glancing at the caller ID. "Hello?"

"Good morning to you, Savannah. I'm not after waking you, am I?" Audrey asks, sounding like sleep is just something other people need.

"Not at all," I reassure her while pulling my fiery red hair back into a ponytail. "Is everythin' alright?"

"Sure, everything's fine. But I do have a spot of news I thought you might be interested in."

"Yeah? What's that?" I ask, rubbing my eyes.

"It's about Kevin Donnelly. He had a terrible accident, and he's dead. God rest him."

That catches my attention. Even in my brief time here, I'd heard a lot of stories about the construction magnate—some good, but mostly bad. "Kevin Donnelly? You mean Dad's old boss?"

"The very same! The Guards found his body this morning out at his construction site in Inbetween."

"In between where?"

"No, child. That's the name of the village. Inbetween. They called it that because it's about halfway between Cork and Kinsale. It's thirty minutes or so from here."

"That makes about as much sense as any other way to name a place, I guess," I reason. "Do you know what kinda accident he was involved in?"

I can easily imagine Audrey shaking her head on the other end of the phone. "Sure, it's early doors. I don't have much to go on yet. But I'm hearing that they *think* it was an accident."

"What do you mean they *think* it was an accident? What else would it be?" I hold my breath, hoping she won't say what I think she's about to say.

"Well, I suppose there's always a chance it could be murder…"

"Oh no—" I quickly cut her off "—I'm not about to go gettin' involved in another murder. I've had enough of that sort of business to last two lifetimes! And I thought Ireland was a safe place, without a lot of killin'. You told me that."

"Sure, there isn't. Except for all the mayhem with the drug gangs up in Dublin. But our low murder rate is even more reason to think this was just a tragic accident."

"Uh-huh," I grunt, unconvinced. "And I'm guessin' you think I should head out that way to write up somethin' for the *Gazette*."

"Well, it wouldn't be the worst idea. Given that every man, woman, and child in Ireland knows the name Kevin Donnelly, it's bound to be a big story either way," Audrey says. "I was also wondering if your father had heard the news yet. Is he about?"

"I haven't seen him this mornin'." Throwing back the covers, I get out of bed and walk to the bay window overlooking my driveway. My father, Ian, has been staying with me for the week while some work is being done on his house in the nearby village of Glendare. "His car's not here, so he musta gone out earlier."

Audrey sighs. "That's too bad. I was hoping to pass on my condolences."

"Your condolences?" my voice reflects my skepticism. "You and I both know my daddy won't be rushin' out to send flowers to the funeral home."

"Maybe so, but they knew each other a long while. And it's not like Ian will be celebrating the news when he hears it."

I raise an eyebrow, which, of course, she can't see. "Not meanin' any disrespect, but are you sure about that?"

"Sure, I know they've had their moments. But you best be careful who you go saying things like that to, child," Audrey scolds me. "We wouldn't want people getting the wrong impression."

"No, of course not," I reply, chastised. "Personally, I think the man is lower than a snake's belly for the way he treated Dad in the end."

"You won't hear me disagreeing on that point; sure, you won't. But it's not right to be speaking ill of the newly departed."

"I'm sorry. You're right." *Even if he does deserve it*, I add silently to myself. "Well, I best be gettin' ready to head out. Seein' as how I have a story to write and all. Thanks for the heads up, Miss Audrey."

"No bother at all. Be careful on the roads, wet as they are from the rain. And do give me a holler if you hear anything interesting. I'm having tea with Deirdre later, and I'd love to pass along some gossip she doesn't already know."

It's funny because it's true. There's nothing the people in this village love more than one-upping their neighbors with inside information.

"I'll do the best I can, Miss Audrey. But don't go gettin' your hopes up for anythin' juicy. Like you said, it's probably nothin' more than a terrible accident."

"That's right, just a terrible mishap," Audrey agreed. "I'm sure that's all it'll end up being."

Deep down, I don't think either of us really believe it.

CHAPTER 2

The first thing I notice when I step outside half an hour later is that the rain has tapered off to a drizzle.

I don't remember ever having spent so much time thinking about the weather, not before my extended trip to Ireland anyway. Where I grew up in the South, there were only two seasons: sunny and hurricane. Here, it feels like there are three seasons in every day. The only one of the traditional four missing is summer, which, I'm starting to suspect, doesn't exist in this part of the world.

Come to think of it, I don't think I've ever seen the sun here without also seeing at least one rainbow. But there's little chance of seeing one of those today. Gray clouds extend across the horizon like blackout blinds on a hotel window.

Gravel crunches under the soles of my Vans sneakers as I stride toward the used Honda CR-V Ian picked up for me at an auction two weeks ago. It had more miles than he would have liked, but it was the only car on the lot with an automatic transmission. And there's plenty of room for Fergal in the back.

On my way out the door, my Irish wolfhound makes it abundantly clear that he's unhappy about being left behind. But he's not the sort of dog I could take into a china shop, let alone a potential crime scene.

That doesn't stop me from feeling guilty. We've developed a habit of starting our days with long walks through the woods near my cottage—a practice I've been forced to abandon this morning. I shudder to think about what the place will look like when I return.

But I can't worry about that now. I have a job to do.

After typing the location into the GPS, I back out of the driveway and begin the thirty-minute journey to Inbetween.

I've been on the road for less than five minutes when my phone rings, and I see Jamie Reilly's name pop up on the dashboard touchscreen. Jamie is the son of Audrey's neighbor and the only local policeman, or guard as they call them in Ireland, stationed in Ballygoseir.

Audrey also thinks he's kind of sweet on me.

I groan as a second wave of guilt washes over me. It had completely slipped my mind that we'd agreed to meet for coffee this morning.

"Good mornin', Jamie," I say after answering his call.

"Good morning to yourself," he replies. "It sounds like you're in the car. That's good. I just arrived at the Gilded Heron and wanted to make sure you hadn't overslept."

"Naw, I didn't oversleep. But I'm not gonna be able to meet you for coffee, after all. I'm sorry."

"No bother," he says, but I can hear the disappointment in his voice. "I take it you got a better offer?"

"No, it's nothing like that. I have to work today. I'm writin' a story about Kevin Donnelly's death."

"Kevin Donnelly, you say?" Jamie sounds surprised. "I haven't heard a word about his passing. Do you happen to know how he died?"

It surprises me that Jamie, being a police officer, doesn't know about it yet but my aunt did. Then again, before Audrey retired, she worked for Ireland's intelligence service, so she has some pretty high-placed sources.

"They're thinkin' it was an accident," I tell Jamie. "That's all I know right now."

"Does your auld fella know?" Jamie asks, referring to my dad.

"Not that I know of. Why?"

"No reason," he attempts to lie, then thinks better of it. "Sure, it's no secret they had a bit of history. Donnelly chose not to press charges, but everyone knows it was your father who broke his nose a few weeks back."

"Yeah, well. The way I see it, Donnelly had it comin'." There's a warning in the tone of my voice. I have no choice but to defend my dad. After all, the fight had been, indirectly, my fault.

"I wouldn't doubt it. The man had a bit of a reputation for nasty business dealings," Jamie says. "Well, I suppose I should get going meself. I'll have to find another volunteer to cover my shift at the community shop today. Once news trickles down this way, I'm sure I'll be getting a call to go deliver the death notifications."

"Why would they call you for that?" I ask, wondering why the guard in a remote coastal village would get involved in the murder of Ireland's most famous real estate developer. "Does Donnelly have family in Ballygoseir?"

"That he does," Jamie confirms. "He and his first wife had a fine house out on the old head. She got it in the divorce, so he moved away. She still lives there with their two daughters."

I commit that tidbit to memory. Depending on how things go in Inbetween, I might need to interview the family for my article. "Sorry again to be cancellin' on you so last minute."

"Don't mention it," he assures me. "If the Guards were half as well informed as the local journalists, I'd have been the one canceling on you. I will take a rain check, though."

"Given how often it rains 'round here, I'm sure we'll find a way of makin' that happen."

"Mind yourself on the roads. They're murder on a wet day," he warns. "It'll be much nicer once the new motorway is built. But sure, that won't do you a bit of good today."

"I'll be fine. But thanks."

Jamie hesitates a moment. "Until later, so."

"Catch you later," I reply and quickly hang up the phone so I can focus on the road.

Even if Jamie hadn't gotten a call from the guards in Inbetween, it strikes me as odd that Audrey didn't tell her friend and neighbor Deirdre, Jamie's mother. Normally the gossip spreads much faster around Ballygoseir.

But the news will be all over Ireland soon enough. I have the radio on to make sure I hear the reports when it breaks. But the misty miles pass, down the winding and narrow roads, without any word of Donnelly's untimely demise. Until, just as a vague outline of the construction site comes into view, a breaking news alert comes through my car's speakers.

"We've just received word that Kevin Donnelly, billionaire construction magnate, died this morning under what the Guards are calling suspicious circumstances. His body was discovered earlier today on the site of his latest project outside Inbetween. A source close to the investigation says they are preparing to question a person of interest. We'll have more..."

The radio announcer continues speaking, but I'm no longer listening.

Suspicious circumstances? A person of interest? This is sounding like anything but an unfortunate accident. Exactly the sort of thing I didn't want to get involved in.

But I've come this far. And as I pull onto the construction site I notice that no other journalists have arrived yet. The only people milling around are a handful of Guards erecting a tent out in the field next to a digger and a few curious locals in the parking lot. I suppose I might as well see if I can get a scoop for the *Gazette*.

I can just barely make out the silhouette of a person in the back seat of a Garda vehicle a short distance away. That has to be the person of interest the radio had been talking about! And, with a bit of luck, I might be able to ask them a question or two before the guards can run over to stop me.

My phone begins to ring as I shift the car into park. It's Audrey, probably wanting an update on what I've been able to find out. Since I don't know anything yet and don't want to miss an opportunity to learn more, I decide to call her back later.

Exhaling deeply, I throw open the door of my Honda and walk quickly toward the Garda vehicle's rear occupant, preparing questions in my head as I go.

Less than ten feet away, the person seems to sense my approach. They turn toward me, and our eyes meet. Then my heart seems to stop beating.

The person of interest in the suspicious death of Kevin Donnelly... is my dad!

CHAPTER 3

"Dad? What in the heck is going on?" I demand through the closed window of the Garda vehicle.

"Savannah! What are you doing here?" he asks, then shakes his head when the realization hits that it really doesn't matter. "Never mind. I know how this must look. But so you know, I didn't touch a hair on Kevin Donnelly's skull. I swear it."

I'm tempted to point out that he's not being entirely truthful. He did break the man's nose a few weeks back. But this hardly seems the time to be splitting hairs—no matter whose skull they're attached to. "But why are you here? And why are you locked in the back of a cop car?"

"Sure, I can explain everything—"

"And what exactly do you think you're doing?" a man's voice interrupts.

Without taking my eyes off my father, I respond with annoyance, "I'm talkin' to my dad. Do you mind?"

"Actually, yes. I do. You're interfering with an official Gardai investigation," the man informs me in a voice laden with warning. "Step away from the vehicle. I won't be asking you again."

Reluctantly tearing my eyes away from my father, I turn to face the person who dared to butt in on a private conversation. Standing a short distance away is an extremely attractive thirty-something man with a jaw sharp enough to cut glass and a cleft in his chin that a woman might be tempted to run her thumb across. Then, recognition dawns. I've met him before. "You're the detective from Cork. The one who was down in Glendare last month exhuming a body."

"The name's Detective Brian Mulhaney." His dark brows turn downward toward the bridge of his aquiline nose, then lift when he seems to recognize me. "And, if memory serves, you're the Yank that was making a nuisance of herself during my last murder inquiry."

"How many times do I have to tell you? I'm not a Yank. I was born in Alabama. I'm a redneck."

"And how many times do I have to tell you to step away from the vehicle?" he fires back. "I'd have no problem with locking you up right alongside your auld fella if it comes to that."

"Alright, alright," I hold my hands up and take an exaggerated step away from the vehicle. "Happy now?"

"Not nearly," he reaches into the pocket of his puffer jacket and pulls out a notebook. "May I ask what brings you to these parts this early of a morning? Did you come here looking for your auld fella?"

"No, I did not," I respond curtly, conscious that anything I say may be used against my father.

He scribbles something in his notebook. "Then why are you here, Miss…?"

"Jeffers. Savannah Jeffers. I'm a journalist. I heard Kevin Donnelly had been in an accident, so I came to check things out."

"And how did you receive word of this alleged accident? Did your father call you to say he was involved in an incident with the deceased?"

I straighten my shoulders. "He most certainly did not."

"Then how did you know?" he asks again, staring me down with his caramel-colored eyes. "We had a media blackout up until about ten minutes ago. So please tell me, how did a reporter from America hear about what had happened before any of the local press?"

I can feel the proverbial ice beneath my feet getting thinner. I don't want to get Audrey into trouble with her high-placed contacts, but I don't want to lie either. I hedge my bets by saying, "I have sources."

He raises one perfectly groomed eyebrow. "Do you, now? You must be one hell of a journalist. Here for such a short while and already getting inside information about a possible homicide."

"Homicide?" My heart sinks as I say the word. "So, it wasn't an accident. You think someone killed Kevin Donnelly?"

"No, I don't know that for sure. It's still an active investigation, like," he quickly backpedals. "If you have any further questions, I'll have to refer you to the Garda Press Office."

"Can you just tell me why my dad is sittin' like a criminal in the back of your car? You can't possibly be thinkin' he killed Kevin Donnelly."

"Why not?"

"Because…" I search my brain for a reason to give Detective Mulhaney, other than offering the weak defense that I'm related to the suspect. That's not likely to buy me much credibility. "It's just not possible. My dad just wouldn't do somethin' like that."

"Do any of us really know what another person is capable of?"

"Don't go gettin' all philosophical on me," I protest. "If you want to go down that route, I could argue that I don't know what *you're* capable of. Maybe you killed him!"

Detective Mulhaney draws back in surprise at the wild accusation. "That's absurd. What reason would I have to kill Kevin Donnelly?"

"How would I know? You're the one that hypothetically killed him. Why'd you do it?"

The vein in his neck starts to pulse erratically. "I didn't do it! This whole conversation is completely ridiculous. I'm a detective. This is my murder investigation."

I seize on the information he let slip. "Aha, so Donnelly *was* murdered?"

Detective Mulhaney opens his mouth, and then quickly closes it. When he finally does speak, his voice is calm but irritated. "Would you ever go away? I have a job to do. And the longer you're bugging me for answers, the longer your dad will be sitting in the back of that car."

"Are you arrestin' him? Or just takin' him in for questionin'?" I press.

"One of the uniforms will be driving him up to Cork shortly. I'll question him when I'm done here," he says in a clipped voice. "Why?"

I raise my voice so my father can hear me inside the car. "I don't want anyone tryin' to question him until he has a lawyer in the room with him."

"Alright, enough with the amateur dramatics," Detective Mulhaney says. "Now, would you please leave so I can do my job?"

I hold up a finger, stalling for time so I can think. "Just one more question—"

Detective Mulhaney hangs his head and whispers, "Lord, give me patience."

Ignoring him, I continue. "So, you're thinkin' Donnelly was murdered, but you're not a hundred percent sure because, if you were, you'd just come right out and say it, which is also why you're not arrestin' my dad yet. But you do want to question him. And since he's in the back of your car, and because you haven't asked me to give him an alibi, I'm guessin' you want to talk to him because he was already here when you arrived."

The muscles in Detective Mulhaney's jaw clench. "You said you wanted to ask me something. Is there a question anywhere in my future?"

"I was just gettin' there," I assure him. "I'm wonderin' how the Guards knew to be here. Correct me if I'm wrong, but I'm thinkin' someone must have tipped you off that somethin' was after happenin'. So I guess my question is, who made that call?"

Detective Mulhaney's face remains stoic. It's impossible to know from his expression whether he'd already thought of that himself. "Once again, all I can tell you is that media inquiries should be directed to the Gardai Press Office. Now, if you're done wasting my valuable time, my colleagues have set up a barricade and, at the moment, you're on the wrong side of it. Please remove yourself from the area, or I will be forced to arrest you."

Without waiting for me to respond, he pulls out a walkie-talkie and orders one of the uniformed officers to drive the suspect to the station.

Before walking away, I spare one final glance at my father, who offers me a weak smile. I smile back, but it's a half-hearted attempt at best.

Because, as much as I may have rattled the detective by asking about a possible tip-off, I'm feeling more than a little uneasy myself.

What *was* Ian doing here on Donnelly's construction site?

And, having only met him a month ago, how can I know with a hundred percent certainty that my dad isn't a cold-blooded killer?

CHAPTER 4

"Is my dad a murderer?" Those are the first words out of my mouth when Audrey answers her phone.

I'm sitting in my car with the engine running for warmth, but my skin feels clammy, and my hands are shaking. Outside, I watch as the cop car carrying my father drives away.

Audrey sighs. "You've heard he's being questioned, so. I did try calling to warn you before you got there."

"You didn't answer my question," I point out. "This is all startin' to feel a bit overwhelmin'. I don't know whether to go home or go crazy. So I need you to tell me, plain like, if you think he coulda killed Kevin Donnelly."

"No, of course not," Audrey emphatically states. "I mean, unless it was self-defense. If Kevin Donnelly attacked him first, like, I suppose it *could* be possible."

My heart beats painfully against my chest, and my mind feels like it's riding a Tilt-A-Whirl. "I'll be honest. I don't know what to think. My dad told me he could explain everythin', but—"

Audrey cuts me off. "Were you able to have a word with him, so?"

"Just for a minute before that detective from Cork interrupted us."

"Please tell me you didn't let on to the Guards that you're doubting your own father's innocence," Audrey pleads.

"Heck, no. I wasn't born yesterday! In fact, I was tryin' to point out to them why they have the wrong man. But this is your brother. You've known him all your life. I need *you* to tell me that he didn't do this. I mean, why was he even here this mornin'?"

"Sure, I've no idea why he was there. He didn't say a word to me about going to Inbetween today. And I never would have sent you there if I thought this was what would happen," Audrey says. "But if he says he can explain, then I'm certain he can."

I want her words to bring me comfort. But Ian is still, for all intents and purposes, a stranger to me. And, in the little time I've known him, he doesn't have the best track record of self-control. "You know they'll find out about him breakin' Kevin Donnelly's nose. That's not gonna look good."

"I wouldn't be disagreeing with you on that," she admits. "Which is why I've already hired a big-shot lawyer, Cormac McGill, and I'm on the road to Cork myself. One of my contacts told me where they're taking your dad."

It's a relief, at least, to know that Audrey believes in her brother enough to galvanize the troops so quickly in his defense. "How did Kevin Donnelly die, anyway? Do you know?"

"Do you see a digger out there?" she asks.

"Yeah. Why?"

"Apparently, he was run over by it—an awful way to go. You can only hope death came quickly to the poor man. God rest him."

Immediately after the grisly image appears in my head, I try to push it away. "Is that why they thought it was an accident at first?"

"Accidents like that do happen on occasion. Workers leave the diggers running when they get out of the cab and then inadvertently end up under the tracks."

"So why did they change their minds about it bein' an accident? Did they find somethin'?"

"That I don't know. But I'm sure we'll find out soon enough," she assures me. "Are you still out at the construction site?"

"Yeah," I say, staring with new interest at the excavator in the field. "The Guards set up a barricade, so I'm sittin' in my car. Should I drive to Cork and meet you?"

Audrey remains silent for a moment as she thinks. "No. Stay where you are. See if you can find out any more information from there. I'll be in touch as soon as there's anything to report from my end."

I'd like to argue with her. The last thing I want is to be on my own right now. But she's right. The only way to get answers—for me and for my dad—is by asking questions. "Yeah, alright."

"Good. And Savannah, try not to worry overly much. Sure, we'll have this all sorted in no time."

It could be my imagination, but I think I detect a hint of uncertainty in her voice. Then the line goes dead. She's hung up on me.

Alright, Savannah, I tell myself. *Let's see what we can find out.*

From behind the safety of my windshield, I look around in search of a target. Most of the curious onlookers fled after the guards set up the barricade, but I notice two women—a blond and a brunette roughly my age—with baby carriages. They're standing off to the side, talking to one of the uniformed officers.

When he strolls away, I make my move, walking quickly across the paved parking lot. As I approach the pair, I hear the brunette say to her friend, "As awful as this business is, Mary is bound to be delighted with the outcome."

The other, a large blonde woman with green eyes and a menacing expression, quickly chastises her, "Watch your tongue, Emma! You can't go around saying things like that. What if someone were to hear you? Mary doesn't need the guards showing up at her door."

The brunette casts her eyes downward. "I'm sorry, Saoirse. I didn't mean any disrespect. I was just hoping something good might come out of this terrible business."

"As are we all," the woman named Saoirse replies.

A twig snaps under my sneakers, betraying my presence. Both women turn to face me.

Caught unprepared, I freeze momentarily. "Good morning, ladies.

Sorry to interrupt, but I heard someone was murdered here. Do you know anythin' about what happened?"

The large blonde woman, Saoirse, assesses me. "Sure, we know you're a journalist. And that you're the daughter of the prime suspect. Why would we be talking to you?"

Damn it!

News travels even faster here than it does in Ballygoseir. I didn't even think that was possible. But I suspect Detective Mulhaney might have had a role in making sure the locals know who and what I am.

"You're right," I admit. "I am a reporter, but I won't be workin' this story. As you quite rightly pointed out, my dad is bein' questioned. That's a conflict of interest. I just want to understand what my dad's bein' accused of. I wanna help him if I can."

Saoirse's eyes narrow. "It doesn't sound like you're from around these parts. Where's home?"

"Originally, Alabama. But I came here from Florida after my mama was…after she died." They don't need to know my mama was murdered. That might make them more suspicious of me. "I found out I had family in Ballygoseir. So, I've been stayin' there for a little while."

"Florida?" the brunette replies with appreciation in her eyes. "I've always wanted to go to Miami. The beaches look divine."

Saoirse shoots the other woman a look that tells her to shut her mouth. Then she returns her icy gaze to me. "Being from America, you're probably used to this kind of violence. As for us, we're still trying to wrap our heads around it. Murder's just not a done thing around here."

It would only inflame the tension to point out that in the month I've been in Ireland, this is the second murder that has personally impacted my life. So, I keep my mouth shut on that point. "I totally understand. And, if you knew Kevin Donnelly, I'm truly sorry for your loss."

"It's hardly a loss," Emma blurts, drawing a murderous glance from Saoirse. She quickly adds, "God rest him."

I look from one woman to the other, drawing a conclusion. "People around here didn't like him very much, did they?"

Emma opens her mouth, but Saoirse cuts her off. "We really should be on our way, Emma. It's fierce cold out this morning. The babies will get a frightful chill if we don't get them indoors soon."

Not even trying to hide her look of disappointment, Emma agrees. "I suppose you're right. And I could do with a little nap before Jack comes home, looking for his lunch."

With a brusque and dismissive goodbye, the two women walk away from me toward the road.

It's a shame I wasn't able to get any details about the murder out of them. I have a feeling they know a lot more than they were willing to say. But they did give me one crucial piece of information.

Kevin Donnelly made enemies here. Which means someone other than my dad might have had a reason to kill him.

CHAPTER 5

For what feels like the hundredth time in ten minutes, I check my phone to see if Audrey has sent me any updates on what's happening with my dad.

From behind a string of blue and white crime scene tape, I've waited. And waited. For what feels like hours.

Finally, about thirty minutes ago, the forensic pathologist arrived from Dublin. She'd slipped on a white sterile suit and disappeared inside the tent. A few minutes later, the excavator fired up and moved a few feet backward. Since then, nothing has happened.

A small crowd of journalists, the only onlookers remaining at the site, grows impatient.

"This is a bloody waste of time," a reporter with a camera slung around his neck says. "It's not like they're going to tell us anything. It's morbid standing around just waiting to snap a shot of a body bag."

"True, but that photo will be on the front page of every newspaper in Ireland tomorrow morning," another one comments. "It's what the people want to see."

A woman with a portable video camera grunts in derision. "And they think we're the ambulance chasers."

"Hey, does anyone know anything about this fella, Ian Murphy?" a young man barely old enough to grow facial hair asks. "The one they're questioning about the murder."

My ears perk up, waiting to hear what information might be volunteered about my father.

"I hear he got into a fistfight with Donnelly earlier this month. Murphy attacked him for no reason whatsoever," the camera-toting male reporter says.

"One of my contacts told me Murphy has a history of mental illness," a woman holding an audio recording device chimes in.

"I haven't heard that," a sixth reporter joins the conversation. "But from what I'm hearing, he may have been involved in the murder of that American woman down in Ballygoseir last month."

A sharp laugh escapes my lips at the blatant falsehood, and all the so-called reporters turn to stare at me. I'm tempted to call them all hacks and walk away, but the desire to hear what other lies might be showing up in tomorrow's paper is too great.

"Sorry about that," I say. "I had a tickle in my throat."

That does the trick because the muckrakers quickly lose interest in me.

"Whether or not the Guards have had their eye on him before. They're going to throw the book at him for this," an older man with salt and pepper hair says. "You don't go after important people in this country without being made an example of."

"It's not just Ireland where that's the case," the man with the camera around his neck argues. "Sure, the little people never matter as much as the ones with big bank accounts and connections to the decision-makers."

"Amen to that," yet another reporter laments.

Growing bored with the conversation now that they're no longer making wild speculations about my father, I glance over at the stocky Guard stationed on the other side of the tape, keeping the riffraff away from the crime scene. He's shaking his head at a handsome young brunet man dressed in a gray suit and black parka.

Not wanting to draw the crowd's attention, I quietly extricate myself from the mob and move closer to the mystery man in the gray suit. I stop moving when I'm far enough away to avoid suspicion but close enough to hear what the two are saying.

"But they'll have to close the site now, won't they?" the suited man, who appears to be in his late twenties or early thirties, asks.

"Sure, I have no way of knowing that, now do I?" the exasperated officer replies. "That's a decision that'll be made well above my pay grade."

"I told Donnelly not to build here," the suited man, who has a slim but muscular build and a hip, shaggy haircut, says. "The minute he decided to move that fairy fort, he was only inviting trouble onto himself. You don't mess about with fairies. Sure, every child knows that."

"Don't I know it, Aidan," the officer replies, warming to the subject. "But the deed is done, like. I don't think that'll stop someone from taking over the project, now Donnelly's gone on to a better place—God rest him. And the curse would've died with him, one would think."

It strikes me as odd that two grown men are talking about fairies like they actually exist. And what the heck is a fairy fort? If I didn't know any better—which I don't—I'd think it was a theme park ride in someplace like Orlando. But from what the men are saying, it sounds like something far more sinister. After all, the officer just mentioned some kind of curse for moving it.

"Never mind the curse. A man just died here!" Aidan heatedly reminds the officer. "Is there no respect for the dead in this day and age?"

"I don't suppose there is," the officer wearily replies. "But if preventing the shopping mall from being built is what you're after, sure, you'd have more authority to stop it than I would."

"If only that were true," the man named Aidan says. "I'm the council archaeologist, so the village only cares if I find *old* bones. I'd only be able to stop the building here if Donnelly had died a thousand years ago."

The officer shrugs and shakes his head. "Then I'm at a loss for anything useful to tell you. It is surprising, though."

"What's surprising?" Aidan wants to know.

"That ye all didn't find anything when they were digging up the soil to pour the concrete." The officer pauses, removing his flat cap slowly to scratch his balding head. "Since there was a fairy fort here, I would have thought there'd be all manner of ancient artifacts buried here."

"That makes two of us," Aidan responds. "But you know how it was with Donnelly. He greased a few palms, made a few well-placed political donations, and suddenly, the project was fast-tracked. I barely had time to review the schedule of works before the fort was moved and excavation got underway. That's not how things are supposed to work. But then, Donnelly wasn't exactly known for playing by the rules, was he?"

"I only knew the man from reputation, like. But that sounds about right, based on what I've heard," the officer concurs, then leans close to Aidian conspiratorially. "Rumor has it, the Economic Crime Bureau had him in their sights a few years ago. Wanted him for bribery, apparently. Then word came from on high that they were to stand down."

Aidian's eyes widen. "You're joking me!"

"I wouldn't tell a lie. The whole investigation stopped cold," the officer spits on the ground. "They say good old Saint Patrick drove all the snakes out of Ireland. But, if you ask me, he missed a few."

"He most certainly did," Aidan agrees.

As I've been listening to their conversation, a new picture of Kevin Donnelly has emerged. My dad had told me that Donnelly had cheated him out of a substantial sum of money. It was the source of their fight a few weeks back. But I'd assumed it was more of a disagreement between the two of them. It hadn't occurred to me that, for Donnelly, breaking the rules and screwing people over was business as usual.

The more I learn about the man, the wider my suspect pool becomes.

But research into that will have to wait. My cell phone chirps with an incoming message from Audrey.

The Garda Síochána, the Irish police, have officially announced that Kevin Donnelly was murdered.

CHAPTER 6

When I was growing up, my mama always used to tell me never to do any important thinking on an empty stomach. At the time, she probably never imagined that advice would come back to me when I was trying to figure out whether my father, whom she'd never told me about, was guilty of murder.

Given the current circumstances, I have a lot on my mind.

So, before getting on the road to meet Audrey in Cork, I decide to stop in Inbetween to grab some sandwiches for us.

After parking at the edge of the village, I walk up the main street—which consists of a museum, a post office, and about half a dozen mom and pop shops—searching for a place to pick up lunch. The quaint shopfronts I pass are well-maintained and welcoming, bearing nameplates like 'Celtic Stitches Sewing Emporium,' 'Irish Rose Couture,' and 'O'Grady's Fine Meats.' But they're all empty of customers, and the signs on the entrances read, "Sorry, we're closed."

I'm wondering if the village decided to shut down for the day following the news of Kevin Donnelly's murder when I stumble upon 'Hannigan's Hideaway Cafe.' Not only is the restaurant open, it's packed to capacity. Every seat is occupied. But since it seems to be the only place around to get lunch, I walk inside.

The cafe buzzes with voices engaged in dozens of different conversations. It's so loud I barely hear the little bell attached to the door begin to ring as I walk in. But everyone else does. All chatter immediately comes to a halt as the cafe occupants turn to stare at me.

Nobody says a word to me or each other.

I've never felt so self-conscious in all my life, and I seriously consider walking right back through the door and finding another, more hospitable place to get food. But my mama didn't raise me to cow to bullies. So, standing up straighter, I stroll over to the counter on the left side of the room, fully aware that all eyes are on me.

"Can I help you with something?" asks a freckle-faced teenage girl standing behind a glass case displaying all manner of mouth-watering pastries.

"Yeah," my voice seems to echo in the silence. "I was wonderin' if I could get a couple of sandwiches to go."

"Ah, so it's just takeaway you're after. No bother," she seems relieved that I'm not planning on staying long. "What would you like?"

The crowd, appeased that I'm here for food, not gossip, return to their earlier conversations.

Not wanting to loiter by the counter after placing my order, I find a place to stand at the back of the restaurant between the doors to the toilets and one that reads "Employees Only." To avoid drawing more attention or suspicion, I pull out my cell phone and open a note-taking app.

The way I see it, the best thing I can do for my dad—and my own peace of mind—is to determine who, aside from my dad, might have wanted Kevin Donnelly dead.

On a blank page, I begin typing.

Angry business partners?

Aidan, the man in the gray suit at the crime scene, implied that Donnelly didn't play fair when it came to business dealings. If I check the local court records, I might be able to find out if any of Donnelly's business associates have filed lawsuits against him recently. Money is always a potential motive for murder.

So is love.

Ex-wife? Current wife?

According to Jamie, Donnelly's ex-wife lives in Ballygoseir. I can probably make a trip out to see her myself. If I take Audrey with me, we can go under the guise of wishing to offer our condolences.

As for the current wife, a quick Google search reveals that she's a gorgeous young blond named Aoife who, if I'm to believe the tabloids, is pregnant with Kevin's first male heir.

The more obvious suspects out of the way, I wrack my brain, trying to think of anyone else who would have had a reason to kill Donnelly.

Rogue police officer?

I know I'm clutching at straws, but the guard speaking to Aidan had mentioned the Economic Crimes Bureau was investigating Donnelly. A diligent officer of the law might not have taken kindly to having the investigation shut down. It's a possibility, however remote, that one of the investigators decided to take justice into their own hands.

Another thought occurs to me, which I quickly type into my phone.

Bribe recipient?

If Donnelly was suspected of handing out bribes, it wouldn't be a stretch to assume there might be blackmail potential as well. A powerful person threatened with the loss of their reputation might be inclined to silence the person who had leverage over them.

Rereading the scant notes I've entered into my phone, I groan. Aside from possibly the wives, tracking down any of these people will be difficult, if not impossible. First, I'd have to find them. If they even exist. Then, I'd have to get them to open up about a secret they were willing to kill to keep.

I slip my phone into my pocket, suddenly hopeless and slightly nauseous.

Glancing at the doors to the toilets, I see a sign that says "Mna" with the silhouette of a stick figure in a dress. I duck inside. Hurrying into one of the stalls, I lower the toilet seat and sit down, trying to breathe.

Then, a sound freezes me in place.

"This is good for us. It has to be," a man's voice bounces off the walls of my stall.

"Shut your hole, you eejit," a dulcet-toned woman's voice hisses. "Do you want to draw the guards onto our heads?"

Wondering where the voices could be coming from, I look up and see a vent a few inches shy of the ceiling. The conversation must be coming from the neighboring room, the one with a sign warning that it was for employees only. I stand on the toilet and put my ear closer to the vent.

"Sure, it's just the two of us in here," the man replies. His voice is raspy, the kind of coarseness that only comes from decades of heavy smoking. "And neither of us are going to the guards!"

"Best keep it that way if you know what's good for you," the woman threatens. "No one can ever know what we did. Do you hear me?"

"You think I don't know that?" the man questions.

"Well, you're slinking into my cafe asking for a meeting with me in private like, in front of the whole village. How do you think that looks?" she raises the question but doesn't wait for an answer. "Unless you want to end up in jail, you'll act like nothing happened and keep your gob shut. Are we understanding each other?"

"Yes, Mary," the man agrees.

Mary? I think. *Why does that name sound familiar?*

Then, I remember. The two young mothers out at the construction site had mentioned a Mary. The less hostile of the two, the brunette, said Mary would be delighted about Kevin Donnelly being dead. This could be the Mary she was referring to.

"Go through the kitchen on your way out so no one sees us coming out of here together," the woman named Mary instructs the man. "I need to go attend to my customers."

Without thinking it through, I flush the toilet and rush into the dining area, wanting to catch a glimpse of Mary.

We emerge through our respective doors at precisely the same moment, coming face to face.

Mary is not at all what I expected. She's short, only coming up to my shoulders. But what she lacks in height, she makes up for in girth. She's so round I can't help thinking she's better suited to rolling than walking. What strikes me most, though, is her face. It's warm and open, and she looks like someone who has a cupboard full of 'world's best grandmother' mugs.

She graces me with a friendly smile, oblivious to the fact that I've just heard her plotting away behind closed doors.

"Excuse me, love," she says before walking past me to chat with one of her many customers.

At the counter, the freckled girl holds up a paper bag, signaling to me that my order is ready. Walking across the room, I risk one more glance at Mary. She's got her hand on a male diner's shoulder, saying something that makes everyone at the table laugh.

Now's not the time, I think to myself. *But I have to find out what Mary is hiding.*

CHAPTER 7

"Miss Audrey!" I call out to my aunt when I arrive at the Cork Garda station later that afternoon.

She glances up from her phone, pushing a pair of reading glasses onto the top of her shoulder-length strawberry white hair. "You were able to find the right place, so."

I plonk myself into the plastic seat beside her and hold out a paper bag. "I brought you a sandwich."

"Thank you, love," she says, accepting my offering. "Though I'm afraid I don't have much of an appetite at the moment."

"Yeah. Me neither." The sandwich I bought for myself sits uneaten in the passenger seat of my car. "Where's the lawyer? Is he here yet?'

Audrey nods. "He was already here when I arrived. He's with your father now."

My eyes scan the small lobby, lingering briefly on the only other person within earshot—an older male desk sergeant who's shopping online for fishing rods. I lean closer to Audrey. "Have they told you anythin' yet?"

"I've had no word on your father if that's what you're asking," she admits. "But I do know why the guards changed their minds about Kevin Donnelly's death being an accident."

"Why?" I'm asking before she can even pause for breath.

"As you know, they'd thought he left the excavator running when he jumped out of the cab. Then, he was just in the wrong place when the thing started moving. The lower half of the poor man was completely flattened by the tracks. God rest him."

I taste bile in the back of my throat as the gruesome image takes shape in my mind. I swallow it down. "And now? What're they thinkin' happened?"

"They're thinking someone hit him with something very heavy and very sharp. There was a big hole in the back of his skull," she tells me. "And though an unfortunate man may very well stumble into the path of a moving digger, he'd hardly cosh himself in the back of the head before he did it."

"So, whoever killed him ran him over to make it look like an accident?"

"Exactly. And the guards seem mighty convinced your father is the guilty party," Audrey bluntly states. "Though, if you were to ask me, your auld fella would have far more sense than to run over the wrong half of the body."

She makes an interesting, if graphic, point. If the killer had run over Kevin Donnelly's top half, the evidence of a crime would have been literally and metaphorically squashed. The guards would have no reason to think it wasn't an accident. Which means we're either looking for a killer who's incompetent or one who wants everyone to know what they're capable of.

"Did Detective Mulhaney tell you all this?" I ask, annoyance sharpening the edges of my tongue. The only thing he'd told me was to get lost.

A crease appears between Audrey's eyebrows. "Mulhaney? Is that the gorgeous young man assigned to investigate Donnelly's murder?"

My eyes roll so far back that if my mama were still alive, she'd be warning me they'd get stuck that way. "He might be easy on the eyes, but, Lord, does he try my patience."

A strange twinkle appears in Audrey's hazel eyes. "Does he now?"

"Don't you go reading into anythin'," I half-heartedly warn her. "All

I'm sayin' is that the man would make a bishop mad enough to kick in a stained-glass window."

"Well, he's certainly gotten under your skin," Audrey observes.

"And you're startin' to as well," I tease her. "But you haven't answered me. Who told you about the hole in Donnelly's head?"

"It wasn't Mulhaney if that's what you're after. I heard it from a little birdy."

I should have assumed Audrey's source was still feeding her information about the case. And I'm secretly glad Mulhaney didn't tell her more than he was willing to say to me.

"Hey, Miss Audrey, do you think your little birdy could get some information about a woman named Mary who runs Hannigan's Hideaway Cafe in Inbetween?"

"Sure, my little feathered friend could probably tell you what the woman ate for lunch six years ago on this very day," Audrey says. "But do you mind telling me why I'd be asking?"

I quickly summarize the conversation I overheard at the restaurant.

"Very interesting," she says, deep in thought. "And you don't happen to know who the man that she was talking to was?"

"Naw, I didn't see him. He snuck out the back. But from his voice, I'd bet he's over fifty and has a two pack a day habit."

Audrey shakes her head. "Sure, you could be describing half the men in Ireland. But I suppose it's a start. Let me see what else I can find out about this Mary character. Did you hear anything else while you were down in Inbetween?"

"I heard an earful about Donnelly. From the sound of things, the man was crooked as a barrel of snakes. The guards wanted him for bribery, but someone shut down the investigation. Do you think you can find out anythin' about that?"

"I can certainly try." Audrey types something into her phone. "Anything else?"

"Not really." Then, I remember something that struck me as odd. "But there were a couple of people talkin' about fairy forts and curses. Do you know anythin' about that?"

Audrey swats the air with her hand as if she's taking a swing at an imaginary fly. "Don't mind any of that. It's just superstitious nonsense."

"What is a fairy fort anyhow?"

"They're circles of stones that, if you believe the tall tales, are magical portals into a realm inhabited by the old gods," Audrey explains. "There are thousands of the things spread all across Ireland. Legend has it anyone who disturbs a fairy fort suffers a tragic fate—illness, injury, even death."

It now makes sense to me why people were mentioning them. "Donnelly moved one of 'em to build his shopping mall."

"That he did. But it seems to me, from what you were able to find out in one day, he had more to fear from the living than he did from the fairy folk. And I've a feeling we're only glimpsing the tip of the iceberg," Audrey reasons. "We'll need to get a better view of the whole thing if we want to help your father."

"Where are you thinkin' we should start?"

"Funny you should ask." A hint of a smile appears on Audrey's face. "I've been giving it some thought as I've been waiting. And I kept coming back to the same question. Where do you go to hear the absolute worst about a man?"

I nod, understanding. "His ex-wife."

"Did you know that Ayleen Donnelly lives a mere ten minutes from Ballygoseir? Why, she's practically a neighbor. And the poor woman just suffered a terrible shock."

"It'd only be right to pass on our condolences," I finish Audrey's thought, grinning. "And we gotta go in person."

"Savannah, dear, I couldn't agree with you more."

Before we have more time to plot our strategy, the door leading into the bowels of the Garda station burst open. A man in his early forties wearing an expensive suit and a butter-wouldn't-melt-in-your-mouth expression confidently strides out.

Audrey rises from her chair to greet him, then pulls me up to stand beside her. "Cormac, this is Savannah, Ian's daughter. What news do you have for us?"

"It's a pleasure to meet you, Savannah." He shakes my hand. "Well, I'm happy to report that your father is being released…for now. He'll be out shortly. But I did have one question for the pair of ye."

Audrey's body tenses. "Well, what is it?"

Cormac leans toward us so the desk sergeant won't hear what he's about to say. We move closer, hanging on to the words he's yet to speak.

"Do you happen to have a spare change of clothes for Ian?" he asks. "The guards insisted on keeping all his clothes as evidence. And sure, after the day he's had, you wouldn't want him having to walk out of the station with his arse hanging out for all of Cork to see."

CHAPTER 8

*I*n less time than it would take me to Google a place to buy men's clothing, Audrey is back in the Garda station lobby with a charity shop bag clutched in her hand.

She passes the bag to the desk sergeant, and ten minutes later, my father appears in the open doorway wearing baggy gray sweatpants, a blue rugby jersey, and a sour expression.

"Seriously, Audrey. A Leinster jersey? You know full well I'm a Munster supporter," he complains.

"Would you quit your squawking? Sure, you know nobody in Cork would be giving a Munster jersey to a charity shop! You can take the bloody thing off when you're home. At least there's a shirt on your back while we walk to the car."

"I might prefer wearing nothing at all," he moans.

Audrey holds up a finger in warning. "If you're not careful, I'll leave you here altogether."

That draws a chuckle out of Ian. "You wouldn't dare. You love your little brother far too much for that. Thank you, by the way, for getting me out."

"We have Cormac to thank for that." Audrey rests a hand on

Cormac's arm. "We're ever so grateful for your help. And please, pass along my best to your father. Tell him I'll ring him soon."

"I'm sure he'd love to hear from you. But right now, we should be thinking about getting Ian out of here without having to run the gauntlet of reporters loitering outside," Cormac brings us back to our present reality. "The detective has graciously permitted Ian to leave through the back door, but it would be best if a car were waiting for him on the other side."

"I'll go," I volunteer. "My car's just 'round the corner. I can be outside the back door in two shakes of a dog's tail."

"Let me walk out first, Savannah," Audrey gently orders. "As a decoy, like. While all the journalists are trying to ask me questions, you sneak out to your car and collect your father. I'll meet the pair of ye back at the house."

After one more round of thank you's to Cormac, we put our plan in motion.

And it works. Audrey is able to distract the reporters long enough for me to run to my car in complete anonymity. I'm still breathing heavily from the quick sprint when Detective Mulhaney ushers my father out the station's back door.

Now that he's letting my father go, however temporarily, I'm much less annoyed with him.

"We'll be in touch soon, Mr. Murphy," Mulhaney says with one hand on the open passenger door. He leans down briefly to give me a nod, saying, "Miss Jeffers."

Then, the car door slams shut, and Mulhaney disappears back inside the station. My dad and I are alone in my car with nothing between us but an ocean of unspoken uncertainty.

"You doin' alright?" I ask, not knowing what else to say.

He runs a hand through his reddish-white hair. "Let's weigh things up, shall we? I'm suspected of killing a man who, to be honest, I'm not sorry is dead. I've spent the better part of the day being grilled by an upstart half my age. And now I've had to slink away from the Garda station wearing the jersey of my team's most bitter rival."

"So, your average Tuesday, then?" I quip.

His easy laughter makes me loosen my grip on the steering wheel.

We sit in silence for a few minutes as I navigate my way out of the city.

"You want to know what the worst part of today was?" my father eventually asks.

"Wearin' that jersey?" I tease.

"Hardly. It was seeing the look on your face when I walked into that lobby," he says, suddenly serious. "We're only just getting to know each other, and now you're having to ask yourself, 'Is my father a murderer?' It's not the impression I was hoping to make."

I don't know how to respond. I mean, I really *want* to believe he's innocent. But he's right. There's still so much I don't know about him, like, for starters, what he was doing on Donnelly's construction site early this morning.

My voice is shaky when I ask, "You wanna tell me what happened?"

"Donnelly was already dead when I got there," Ian insists. "I pulled onto the site and saw his car. But he wasn't in it. Then I heard the digger. The engine was on, but it wasn't moving. So I walked over and turned it off. That's when I saw him. And I knew there was no way he was still alive."

"But you didn't call for help, did you?" It's a hunch, but one that would explain his current situation.

"No. My phone was in my truck. I ran back to get it. But just as I was climbing in to reach the phone, a pair of guards turned up, accusing me of trying to flee the scene. So, they stuffed me into the back of their car and, sure, you know the rest."

"What were the guards even doing there? Did somebody call 'em?"

"If they did get some kind of tip off, that isn't the sort of information the guards were willing to share with me," he says.

"It just seems strange they came by right after you found the body. You didn't see anybody or anythin' else?"

He sighs. "If anyone was there, I didn't see them."

Something doesn't seem right. I can't believe the timing was a coincidence. But there's a more pressing question I've wanted to ask

Ian since I saw him in the back of the Garda car. "What were you doin' out in Inbetween this mornin' anyway?"

"Kevin texted me early this morning. He said he wanted to meet," Ian explains. "I was a bit torn about whether or not to go. But in the end, I hoped that if I went, we might be able to come to some arrangement about the money he owed me. I really wanted to be able to give it to you."

While I appreciate the gesture, I wish he'd never gone to see Donnelly. I'll find a way to solve my current financial problems, one way or another. But by trying to help me, Ian has put himself in a tight spot. The guilt feels suffocating.

"Do you know of anyone else who mighta wanted Donnelly dead?" I ask, hoping he'll be able to serve me up an alternative suspect on a silver platter.

"Loads of people. The man had some knack for making enemies," Ian confirms what I've already heard. "But I could make a list long enough to fill a novel and it wouldn't make a bit of difference."

"What do you mean?"

"None of them were at the construction site when Donnelly's body was found."

As much as I want to tell him he's wrong, deep down, I know he's not.

And it hits me then. If we don't find out who killed Donnelly, my dad is going to jail for the rest of his life.

CHAPTER 9

*A*udrey's car sits idling in my driveway when my dad and I arrive back at Raven's Wing.

As I step out of my Honda, I see Fergal's big, happy head through the living room window. He's wagging his tail so vigorously that his entire body sways. The poor guy has been trapped inside all day, hungry and probably needing a potty break.

As I'm approaching the front door, Audrey rolls down her window. "Before you settle in for the evening, we should drive over to Ayleen Donnelly's place and pay our respects."

I hesitate, looking from Fergal to my dad and back to Audrey. "You wanna go now?"

"No time like the present," she replies. "And it'd be best if we're there and gone before the family sits down for their supper."

"But Fergal'll be needin' to go for a walk," I protest.

"Sure, I'll take the beast out for a wander through the woods," Ian offers. "To be honest, I could do with a bit of air. And, given the present circumstances, I don't think my presence would be much appreciated on your condolence visit."

"It's all sorted, so," Audrey says. "Let's get a move on, Savannah.

Ian, we'll be back in an hour or two. And then, I expect to hear all the details of what happened today."

Not daring to question Audrey's orders, my father enters the house while I climb into Audrey's car. She's already pulled onto the road before I even have time to buckle my seatbelt.

The aroma of cinnamon and butter fills the car's interior.

My stomach begins to rumble. "Somethin' smells real good in here. Did you stop at a bakery or somethin'?"

"I did one better. I called Deirdre from the road and asked her to throw a batch of her scones in the oven. We can't very well show up to a house of mourning with our hands hanging, now can we?" It amazes me how Audrey always thinks of everything.

"How well do you know Miss Ayleen?" I ask, wanting a better sense of the environment we're about to walk into.

"Let's put it this way: she's not the kind of woman you'd be calling up to have a proper chin wag, but she is someone you'd ring if you were looking for a donation to a local charity."

"It sounds like what you're sayin' is that people like her money a heck of a lot more than they like her," I cut to the chase. "Am I readin' that right?"

"Not entirely," Audrey disagrees. "Ayleen is a lovely woman, and she can be great craic. But after divorcing Kevin, she stopped coming down to the village. She holed herself up in her great, big house with her daughters and started keeping herself to herself. But she made it clear she still wanted to support the village however she was able."

"When'd she and Kevin get divorced? Was it a long time ago?"

Audrey frowns, thinking. "It must be about two years ago now."

"Is that when Kevin took up with his new wife?" I ask.

"It was," Audrey confirms. "In your typical mid-life crisis cliché, Kevin traded in the mother of his children for a woman less than half his own age. I can't say for certain, but rumor in the village has it the new wife was the friend of one of his daughters."

"That's tacky as all get out." Sympathy flares up in me for Ayleen, but I can't let it cloud my judgment. "But it's also a pretty darn good motive for murder."

"Probably best, though, we don't bring up the subject on our visit." Audrey turns the car up a small, paved road that quickly carries us above the forest line. As we emerge from the dense woods, a panoramic seascape reveals itself. The only structure marring the barren but beautiful landscape is a massive steel and glass edifice that seems to soak up the dark blues and grays of the sky above and the ocean beyond. "We're nearly there."

My first thought is that the house seems out of place. All the houses in the village possess a kind of rustic, old-world charm. This mansion-sized home seems garish and soulless by comparison. But after a moment's reflection, I change my opinion. The building's sharp lines and cold glass are a perfect reflection of the harsh environment it inhabits.

The long, paved driveway provides no cover as we approach the house, so I'm half expecting someone to be waiting for us when Audrey and I knock on the front door. But no one seems aware of our arrival.

Looking through a glass panel next to the door, I see lights on in the back of the house and hear music and laughter coming from inside.

"It doesn't sound to me like there's a whole lot of mournin' goin' on in there," I say to Audrey.

Audrey shrugs. "People grieve in different ways, I suppose." She raises her hand and raps sharply on the front door.

Again, there is no answer.

"Maybe we should try the doorbell?" I suggest.

When Audrey nods, I push the buzzer. Almost immediately, the music inside is switched off. The house falls silent until we hear the faint clacking of high heels across the tiled floor. A lock turns, and the door opens to reveal a stunning, auburn-haired woman in her fifties.

"Audrey," she says, recognizing my aunt. "I hope you haven't been waiting long. We weren't expecting visitors tonight."

"We hope this isn't a bad time, Ayleen," Audrey rests a hand on the other woman's arm. "We heard the awful news about Kevin and wanted to come over to pass on our condolences. And we brought you some scones."

Ayleen glances down at the foil-covered confections and then looks back at us. "That's mighty kind of you, Audrey. Sure, it came as a terrible shock to me and the girls. But I don't suppose anyone's ever prepared for the kind of news we got today."

"No, I don't suppose anyone is," Audrey agrees. "But look, we don't want to disturb ye in your grief. We just wanted to come by and pay our respects."

Ayleen seems torn between her eagerness to see us depart and her inclination to extend hospitality by inviting us to stay. We don't have to wonder for long which path she will choose.

"Where are my manners, leaving you standing out there in the cold?" Ayleen plasters a bittersweet smile on her lips. "Please, come in."

"If you're sure it wouldn't be an imposition," Audrey says as she steps into the front room. "And may I introduce you to my niece, Savannah. She's on an extended holiday from America, but we're hoping to convince her to stay on permanently."

"It's a pleasure to meet you, Savannah." Ayleen leans in to kiss me on the cheek, and I would swear I smell champagne on her breath. "Come on into the kitchen. We'll be more comfortable in there."

Ayleen leads us down the hall into an open-plan kitchen and living room with floor-to-ceiling windows opening onto a patio overlooking the ocean. Two attractive blonde women, roughly the same age as me, are busying themselves in the kitchen. One boils the kettle while the other secrets some dirty champagne glasses away in the dishwasher.

When we enter the room, Audrey walks up to each girl and hugs them. "Caitlin. Deborah. I wish we were meeting under happier circumstances. I am so sorry for your loss."

"Thank you for coming, Audrey," the taller of the two, Caitlin, says.

"And girls, this is Savannah," Ayleen introduces me. "She's here all the way from America."

"Really?" Caitlin's blue eyes light up. "I've always wanted to go to America!"

Deborah glares at her sister. "Well, lucky you. Now you can."

A look of warning passes from Ayleen to her youngest daughter.

Caitlin breaks the awkward silence. "Can I make you ladies a cup of tea?"

"That would be lovely if it's not too much trouble," Audrey replies.

"No bother," Caitlin replies. "Can I get ye anything else?"

Audrey shakes her head. "Not at all. And we won't be imposing on you for long. And, sure, there's no easy way of bringing this up, but I'm sure you've heard on the news that it's my own brother they're questioning in connection with Kevin's murder."

Ayleen raises her hands to stop Audrey from saying more. "Audrey, please…"

But Audrey charges ahead anyway. "Now, I know you've no reason to believe me, but I want to assure you, Ian had nothing to do with this nasty business."

"Thank you for saying that, but it's really not necessary," Ayleen tries to assure her.

"No, it is. I'm sure over the next few days, you'll be hearing a lot about Ian, so I wanted to come up here to say that my brother doesn't have a malicious bone in his body. He certainly wouldn't have done anything to tear apart your family."

Ayleen's face fills with color, and her voice comes out sharper when she responds. "I'd really prefer not to talk about this at the moment."

Tension builds in the room, making it hard to catch my breath. Caitlin and Deborah seem just as uncomfortable as I'm rapidly becoming.

But, despite the dirty look I shoot her, Audrey refuses to be deterred. "You know how the media can be. What is it they're always harping on about these days? Ah, yes, the fake news. Well, saying Ian had anything to do with this sad business would be the worst sort of fake news."

"I'm sure that's true," Ayleen replies. "Now, why don't we all have one of your scones? They smell delicious."

"In a minute," Audrey puts her off. "Sure, I know Kevin had his faults, as all men do. But he was a good husband and a loving father, and he didn't deserve what happened to him. He deserved to have—"

"That pompous prick deserved everything he got!" Ayleen's voice echoes through the room. Seconds later, stunned by her own outburst, Ayleen sinks into a nearby chair.

Caitlin, Deborah, and I stare at the floor, unsure where to look. Audrey never takes her eyes off of Ayleen.

"My mum didn't mean any of what she was saying. It's been a long day, and the doctor gave us all sedatives earlier," Caitlin finally speaks up.

Deborah gets in her sister's face. "That's not true. She meant every word of it."

Caitlin's face turns a bright shade of crimson. "No, she did not."

"Enough!" Ayleen exclaims. "Look, Audrey, in all honesty, we were celebrating before ye arrived. The three of us mourned losing Kevin years ago when he left our family to start building a new one with his child bride. And lately, he's given us nothing but grief and heartache. So, good riddance, I say. And I won't feel bad about *not* feeling bad that he's dead."

Audrey spends the next few minutes apologizing for upsetting the family before a resigned-looking Caitlin ushers us out.

Once we're back in the car, I turn to Audrey. "You did that on purpose, didn't you? Pushin' Ayleen like that?"

"Well, we could have wasted the next two hours pretending to mourn the woman's cheating ex-husband, but I'm tired, and I want to go home and wash the day off of me." Audrey starts the car. "And we got what we came here for."

"Yeah? What's that?" I ask.

Audrey looks at me, smiling. "A few more names to add to our suspect list."

CHAPTER 10

Garda Jamie Reilly is a man who likes routines. Bright and early every Wednesday, he stops for breakfast at the Gilded Heron.

So, at seven o'clock the following morning, with Fergal snoring at the foot of the bed, I quietly climb out of bed and put on a pair of jeans, a Gym & Coffee hoodie that Audrey bought me, and my favorite pair of Vans sneakers. Then, I drive down into Ballygoseir.

As expected, Jamie is sitting at the table by the window, drinking coffee.

"Savannah? Well, this is a surprise." Ever the gentleman, Jamie stands up to greet me. "Will you be joining me?"

"Don't mind if I do." I pull out the chair opposite Jamie and we both sit.

He takes a sip of his latte. "As much as I'd like to think this is purely a social call, I think I know you better than that by now."

My lips part in a smile. "Your mama didn't raise no fool, that's for sure."

He blushes and rolls his eyes at the same time. "Alright, so. What it is you're after?"

"I was hopin' to ask you a few questions about your visit to Ayleen

Donnelly's. You told me you were headin' out there yesterday to give the death notification, right?"

"That's right." He eyes me suspiciously. "But I won't be able to tell you much. It *is* an active investigation, as you well know."

"Yeah, yeah," I dismiss his ethical concerns. "All I want to know is, did Ayleen seem surprised when you told her that Kevin was dead?"

"Oh, no!" his short, blond curls bounce as Jamie shakes his head. "There's no way I'm answering that!"

"Why not?" I demand.

"Because it's one very small step away from asking me if I think she killed him!"

"No, it's not," I say, though he's pretty much spot on.

"Right. And suppose I were to say, 'Well, Savannah, now you mention it, she didn't seem one bit surprised that an excavator drove over her husband.' What would you be thinking?"

Honestly, I'd be thinking that she probably had something to do with it. But that's precisely what he wants me to say. So, I have no choice. I lie. "I'd just be wonderin' if she heard it on the radio or somethin' like that."

"Bollocks!" Jamie's outburst draws a disgusted look from a female octogenarian wearing thick glasses and a large cross around her neck. "Begging your pardon, Mrs. McCleary."

Mrs. McCleary tsks loudly before turning back to her newspaper crossword puzzle.

When Jamie speaks again, it's in a whisper. "I can't believe you think I would use my position with the guards to point an accusing finger at a grieving woman the day after her husband passed away. God rest him."

"Ex-husband," I point out. "And, trust me, she's not grievin'."

Jamie's mouth falls open as he processes my apparent insensitivity. "Sure, that's an awful thing to say."

"No, I mean, I know she's not grievin'. She told me and Audrey as much last night when we stopped by," I explain. "I'm serious. She was celebratin' with champagne."

That mollifies Jamie. A little bit, anyway. "Still and all, would it kill you to show a little more respect for the dead? Please tell me you're not planning to put anything about that in your news article."

"I'm not writin' an article about the murder."

His eyebrows shoot up. "Oh, really? Then why were you telling me just yesterday that you were?"

"That was before my dad was the lead suspect," I hiss back at him.

A look of bewilderment crosses his face. "What's that now?"

"How do you not know this already?" I struggle to keep the frustration out of my voice. "Gossip spreads faster around here than a virus. Heck, I can't go for a walk without having ten people in the village callin' me up askin' if I need a ride. Yet you don't know they're thinkin' my dad is responsible for the most publicized murder in Ireland. Do you not listen to the news?"

"Yesterday was supposed to be my day off. So, when I finished at Ayleen's place, I went fishing," he defends himself.

"Well, while you were out fishin', I was tryin' to figure out whether my dad's a murderer or not. So, it'd be real nice if you could help me out and just answer my question."

Jamie's expression softens. "I'm sorry about your father being accused and all. For what it's worth, I've known him all my life. He's a good man. Not at all the sort of man that would go around killing people."

That seems a relatively low bar for basic human decency but, at this point, I'll take it. "Thank you."

"Regarding your question about Ayleen, I can't help you much. She seemed surprised enough when I passed along the news, but, sure, she could have been faking it for all I know." He pauses, sympathy pouring out from his steel-gray eyes. "But you should know, the Guards are under a lot of pressure to put this case to bed. I'm not trying to upset you, but if they're thinking your dad is good for the murder, I honestly don't know how much further they'll look."

I try—and fail—to hide my disappointment. "I understand. Thanks for tellin' me."

"Look, I'll do what I can to help you. I can ask around at the station and try to make sure they're following all the leads that come in,"

Jamie tries to reassure me. "And it might not be a terrible idea to talk to some of the folks from Inbetween. There was a bit of a dust-up a while back when Donnelly announced plans to build his shopping mall."

I lean forward in my seat. "What kinda dust-up?"

"Someone set Donnelly's car on fire."

"No way. Really? Do you know who did it?"

"Nope. The whole village closed ranks. No one would say a word about it," he tells me. "And seeing as Donnelly was able to collect on the insurance, it seemed pointless to waste resources on a victimless crime."

"Except the man whose car caught fire is now dead," I point out. "Isn't it possible whoever torched Donnelly's car was tryin' to kill him? That plan failed, so they tried again with an excavator."

"It's as good a theory as any, I suppose," Jamie admits.

I push my seat back in preparation to stand. "Well, I best be headin' off."

"Where are you going?" Suspicion laces his words.

"Inbetween. I need to find out who set Donnelly's car on fire," I tell him. "The guards might've already written my dad off as a killer. But I need to know what happened."

Without giving him time to try and change my mind, I stand up and step toward the door. His hand on my wrist stops me.

"Jamie, please don't try to talk me out of this."

"I wouldn't dream of it. And it wouldn't do any good if I tried," he smiles. "I just wanted to say you should start by talking to a woman called Mary Hannigan. My friends who work up that way say she knows everything that goes on in the village."

While I appreciate his advice, he needn't have bothered. Ever since he mentioned the incident with Donnelly's car, I've been wondering how much Mary knows about what happened. And whether that's the thing she was worried could send her to jail…or if it's something far worse.

CHAPTER 11

Preoccupied with thoughts about how best to approach Mary Hannigan, I don't notice Colin O'Rourke walking toward me until I practically step on his feet.

"Whoa there, girl," he chuckles as I step back in surprise. "Did you not hear me calling out to you?"

Colin, the owner of the only hotel in the village, is a few years older than me. Most eligible women around these parts would describe him as a good catch—with his teal eyes, dark hair, and rugged physique. But he and I have a complicated history. I find him to be naïve, superstitious, overly familiar, and entirely too charming for his own good.

"Sorry, Colin. My head was a million miles away," I explain.

"No bother. I hope wherever your head was, it was warmer than it is here today," he jokes. When I don't respond to his attempt at humor, he adopts a serious expression. "But sure, no one could fault you for being a little scattered under the circumstances."

"What 'circumstances' are you talkin' about?" I ask, not wanting to give him the satisfaction of thinking he knows how I feel about anything.

"Your da being accused of murder. All the auld fellas were going on about it last night in the hotel bar." Seeing the thunderous look on my face, he quickly tries to reassure me. "No one thinks he did it, of course. Everyone knows it was the fairies getting revenge for moving their fort."

It's a wonder to me that he can say that with a straight face. "That's honestly what you're thinkin'? That a bunch of vindictive pixies killed the richest property developer in the country because he moved a coupla stones? Bless your heart. Is your six-pack missin' a few beers?"

Rather than being offended, Colin acts like I'm the one who's short a pint or two. "A couple of stones? You think that's all they are? Have you not heard the tales of people losing everything after disrespecting the fairy folk?"

I plant my hands on my hips. "Yeah? Give me one example."

"Sure, there are so many. I don't know which one to choose." Colin pauses, then, seconds later, snaps his fingers. "I've got one that an American might appreciate. Do you know what a DeLorean is?"

Confusion creases my forehead. "You mean like the car in *Back to the Future*?"

He smiles. "All Americans know that movie. But what you probably don't know is that the cars were built just outside Belfast."

I steal a glance at my watch. "What does this have to do with fairy forts?"

"When John DeLorean was building his factory in Dunmarry, there was a lone hawthorn tree on the site. The local workmen all warned him to leave the tree alone. See, Hawthorn trees have been sacred since druid times. The fairies dwell at the base of them as their guardians, like. But John DeLorean was an American funded by the Brits. He paid the legends no mind and bulldozed the tree himself."

"And he died right after?" I assume.

"No, he lived another twenty years or more."

"Oh, for cryin' out loud, Colin! What in the heck is the point of this story, then?"

"The company went bankrupt after only a few years," he says. "He messed with the fairies, and they got their revenge."

"Or people just didn't like his cars," I reason. "All due respect,

Colin, the guards think my dad killed Donnelly, not a bunch of angry fairies."

Before Colin can respond, I hear Jamie's voice behind me. "I hope I'm not interrupting. Don't worry. I didn't hear what you were chatting away about. I know the pair of you like your secrets."

I know Jamie's dig is aimed at Colin. The two of them are constantly bickering when I'm around. It's been common practice since Colin and I solved a recent murder in Ballygoseir, but didn't pass along our discovery to the Guards right away because we'd been illegally trespassing at the time. Everything ended well, so I wish Jamie would just get over it already.

"We weren't talkin' about anything secret, Jamie," I try to assuage him.

"No secrets here." Colin holds his hands up in a parody of being arrested. "We were just chatting about the murder up in Inbetween. It's been all over the news. Do you know, a while back, I went out with your one that's married to Kevin Donnelly."

"You dated Aoife?" Jamie asks. "Though I probably shouldn't be surprised. I doubt there's a woman within fifty miles you haven't gone out with at least once."

"It was just a few dinners and a movie, like." Colin's face is flushed. "But that's a fine thing for you to be saying, Jamie Reilly. Don't think I've forgotten that you once broke my sister Neve's heart."

"We were fourteen!" Jamie defends himself. "Do you really want to go digging up ancient history? I could bring up the time you—"

"Enough!" I interrupt them. "Y'all can compare conquests later. Colin, what can you tell me about Aoife? Is there anythin' I should know about her, seein' as how I'll want to chat with her at some point?"

Jamie sighs heavily but doesn't bother trying to talk me out of it.

"She's pleasant enough. But she does have a taste for the finer things in life. Those dinners set me back a fair bob," Colin admits. "Anyway, it didn't last long. After a few dates, she told me she'd found someone else. And that was that."

"Was that someone else Kevin Donnelly?" I ask.

Colin considers my question for a brief moment. "No, this was back when I spent a year living in Dublin. That would have been about five years ago. I don't think she got cozy with Donnelly until a few years later."

Remembering something Audrey said, I ask, "Do you know if Aoife was friends with one of one of Donnelly's daughters?"

"That sounds about right," Jamie chimes in. "I heard me mum gossiping to her friends about how Kevin was running around with one of Deborah's university friends. That couldn't have been more than three years ago. There was a big party in the village before Deborah went off to study at Trinity College. And she brought Aoife with her on her first trip back home."

Something, I'd wager, Deborah has regretted every day since. "Do either of you know where Aoife lives now?"

"She's probably up in Fermoy," Jamie says. Then, upon seeing my blank stare, he adds, "It's about half an hour north of Cork. Donnelly bought a massive house up there along the river. Lives next door to that American fella made famous for his Irish dancing."

"The one that performed at Eurovision back in the '90s?" Colin asks. "My mum made Neve and me watch a video of that when we were kids."

I don't know what they're talking about, and I don't care. Donnelly's neighbors don't interest me. All I care about is finding the killer.

And I'm only going to be able to do that by finding out who wanted Kevin Donnelly dead. And why.

CHAPTER 12

"No, no, no!" I scream seconds after opening the front door to my cottage.

Fergal is charging at me with his tongue hanging out of his mouth and his tail threatening to take out the legs of a console table in the hallway. In his excitement to see me, there's no stopping the enormous wolfhound. Leaning on his back legs, he throws his front paws onto my shoulders, knocking me backward onto the floor.

"Ya big beast. What am I gonna do with you?" I laugh despite the pain in my backside.

Fergal licks my face and replies with a short, happy bark.

I push him back slightly so I can sit up. "I know. I snuck out on you this mornin' without takin' you for a walk. It's my own fault, right?"

Too late, I realize my mistake. At the mention of the word 'walk,' Fergal races down the hall in search of his leash. There's no getting out of it now. I'll need to take him out before I can leave again for Inbetween.

As I plant my hands on the floor, preparing to stand up, I feel paper underneath my fingers. Shifting for a better view, I see someone has pushed an envelope through my letterbox. The return address reads Office of the Revenue Commissioners.

The smile vanishes from my face.

I already know what I'll find inside—a bill for thirty thousand Euros that I don't have to pay the inheritance tax on this cottage. My mama paid for the house when she was alive, but now that she's gone, I'm stuck paying for the privilege of inheriting it.

If I can't come up with the money, I'll be forced to sell the little cottage I've come to love.

That debt motivated my dad to confront Kevin Donnelly two weeks ago. He was trying to get money Donnelly reneged on paying him so he could give it to me. When Donnelly laughed in his face, my dad broke his nose.

It's also the reason my dad now stands accused of murder. If it weren't for me, he would never have been trying to meet Donnelly at the construction site yesterday morning.

The guilt threatens to overwhelm me until I hear my mama's voice in my head. *Throwin' yourself a pity party won't do squat. Get off your butt and go do somethin' about it.*

And that's precisely what I plan to do…right after I take Fergal for his walk.

After throwing the bill, unopened, onto the front table, I attach Fergal's leash to his collar, and we step out into the cloudy but miraculously dry day.

We cross the narrow road and enter the woods. The dense canopy from the oak and birch trees blocks out the sky in a thick veil of green leaves. Once we're a safe distance from the road, which, to be fair, is rarely used, I let Fergal off his leash and let him run free.

As he darts off into the thicket, I pull out my cell phone and dial Audrey's number.

She answers on the first ring.

"Are you only just now waking up?" Audrey asks.

"No, ma'am. I've been up for hours," I tell her. "But I haven't seen my dad. Is he with you?"

"He said he had some business to attend to in town," Audrey says before quickly adding, "But don't go asking me what sort of business.

He wouldn't tell me. Sure, what do you expect? Women are always left to get men out of the trouble they find themselves in."

"Speaking of, I ran into Colin in the village this mornin'. Did you know he dated Aoife, Donnelly's new wife?"

"I did not. Though it's no surprise. That one's been said to have a way with the ladies," her tone is suggestive. "But funny you should mention Aoife. I came across some rather interesting news about her this morning."

"What's that?"

"Kevin Donnelly had scheduled a meeting with his solicitor for the beginning of next week. According to one of my contacts, Donnelly was looking to change his will."

That piques my attention. "Change it how?"

"Apparently—" she draws the word out to heighten the suspense, "—he was going to change it to leave all his worldly possessions to his unborn son. And Aoife was going to be named as the trustee."

I feel a twinge of disappointment. "Well, I guess that rules her out as a suspect then."

"The very same thought crossed my mind," Audrey remarks. "That if she were going to kill her husband, she would have waited until after he changed the will. But what if she didn't know the will hadn't been changed yet?"

I should have known Audrey would hold an ace up her sleeve. "Alright, Miss Audrey. What aren't you tellin' me?"

"Merely that Donnelly was supposed to have the meeting on Monday. He had to cancel it last minute, like, but he didn't say why. Just asked to reschedule for the following week."

Aoife rockets back to the top of my suspect list. "Well, if she did kill him for the money, she's in for a surprise, isn't she?"

"Precisely. Which is why I think we should pay her a visit sooner rather than later," Audrey says. "I have a doctor's appointment around lunchtime, but I can meet you in Cork in the afternoon to drive out to her house."

No longer thinking about Aoife, I ask, "Why do you need to see a doctor? Is everythin' alright?"

"Sure, I'm grand," Audrey insists. "My GP referred me over to get some medication for my blood pressure. I'd cancel, but I've already been waiting three months for this appointment. I can't stomach the thought of trying to get another one."

I'm not entirely convinced. "If you're sure you're okay…"

"Would you ever stop? I'm fine. Old bodies just need a tune-up every now and again. What are your plans for the morning, so?"

"I was plannin' to head to Inbetween. I want to see if I can find out any more about why Mary is worried about bein' arrested. Your source didn't know anythin' about that, did they?"

"Nothing that's of any use to us, unfortunately," Audrey laments. "The woman seems to be a right pillar of the community. She owns the local cafe. She's the Director of the Inbetween Natural History Museum. And she's reported to be something of an expert on Irish folklore and legends. Universities bring her in occasionally to give lectures on the subject."

An idea springs to mind. "Maybe that's my way of gettin' her to talk to me, by askin' her about the fairy fort." If she's anything like Colin, once she starts talking, I won't be able to shut her up.

"You can tell her you're writing a book about it," Audrey suggests. "If she considers herself an expert, she'd probably love to be acknowledged as one in your book."

"I don't know," I hesitate. "I know it's for a good cause—to prove my dad isn't a killer. But still, I don't want to lie to anybody. And, anyhow, I'm a terrible liar."

"Fair enough. Though you could say you were *thinking* of writing a book. And we have been doing some thinking about telling her you're writing a book. So, technically, it's not really a lie."

I can't help but laugh. "You and your semantics. I tell you what, I'll think about it."

"You do that." I can hear the smile in Audrey's voice. "I'll shoot you the address for where to meet me later. In the meantime, mind how you go."

"I'll be *grand*," I mimic, very poorly, her lilting Irish brogue.

"Darn tootin'," she responds with her own equally lousy imitation of my Southern accent. "But in all seriousness, Savannah, watch your step. Someone has already killed once. Don't give them a reason to do it again."

CHAPTER 13

The salty aroma of frying bacon welcomes me as I step inside Hannigan's Hideaway Cafe later that morning. My stomach rumbles in a noisy reminder that I haven't eaten since last night.

Luckily, there's no line at the counter where the same freckle-faced teenager from yesterday stands waiting behind the till.

All the shops on the main street have reopened today, which may be why there are far fewer patrons in the restaurant. I have no trouble finding an empty table after ordering a sausage roll and a mocha latte.

From my window seat at the far side of the cafe, I have a clear view of the room and the sidewalk outside. What I don't see is Mary. She's not in the cafe's dining area, but the door to the office next to the lady's room is cracked open, and that gives me some hope that this hasn't been a wasted trip.

To give myself something to do as I wait for breakfast, I open the list of possible suspects I created on my phone the day before. It reads 'angry business partners, ex-wife, current wife, rogue police officer, and bribe recipient.' I don't have any new information to add to three of the possibilities, but I start typing out what I've learned about the others.

AYLEEN, *ex-wife:*

- *Celebrated Donnelly's death with champagne*
- *Stood to be disinherited from Donnelly's will (along with her daughters)*
- *Bitter about being replaced by a younger woman*
- *Referred to Donnelly giving her grief following their divorce*

MOVING ON FROM AYLEEN, my fingers hover over the keypad as I think about Aoife.

Aside from learning that she liked nice things and once dumped Colin for another man, all I know about Aoife is that her unborn son was going to inherit all of Donnelly's considerable fortune. But until Audrey and I discover how much Aoife knew about the planned changes to Donnelly's will, I'm reluctant to list that as a reason why she might have killed her husband.

Lost in thought, I'm startled when a stoneware plate and a matching mug of steaming coffee are loudly plopped on my table. Expecting to see the teenage girl from behind the counter when I look up, I get a second shock when I recognize the rotund, smiling face of Mary Hannigan.

"Pardon me for giving you a fright," she says with a smile on her face and a hint of suspicion in her eyes. "You were so focused on whatever it is you were doing that you didn't even hear me wishing you a good morning."

"Sorry, ma'am. I was just, um, making some notes to myself." I quickly exit out of the app on my phone.

"Hopefully, nothing about my little cafe here…unless it's a glowing review." Mary's words are jovial, but with her hands anchored on her ample hips, I find her stance somewhat menacing.

"No, ma'am. I mean…I'm not writing anythin' about the cafe," I fumble to express what I'm trying to communicate while also not saying so much that I reveal my real reason for being here. "But if I did, I'd say your food's so good it makes you wanna slap ya mama."

Mary straightens her spine, growing at least an inch. "Why would you be writing that? I'd never have raised my hands in anger against me own mum! God rest her. And I don't appreciate you saying otherwise."

"No, no! It's just an expression back home. It doesn't mean you'd literally hit your mama," I rush to explain. "It's actually a huge compliment where I'm from."

Mary looks dubious. "It seems to me a strange way to be giving a compliment, like. But sure, ye Americans are a different breed altogether." She looks down at my uneaten food but doesn't leave so I can enjoy it. "What brings you all the way from the New World to our tiny little slice of heaven?"

"I'm visitin' family and doin' a little writin'," I try to thread the needle of telling the truth without being so honest she clams up on me.

"What sort of writing?" Her tone appears light but carries a surprising weightiness, not unlike the feeling I get in my stomach after eating a slice of cheesecake. "There are a lot of journalists poking around these days. I hope you're not one of them."

Finding myself on thin ice in the truth department and not knowing what else to say, I fall back on Audrey's advice. "I'm thinkin' about writin' a book. I studied creative writin' at the University of Alabama."

Her shoulders noticeably relax. "Isn't that lovely? What sort of book will you be writing, so? I'm partial to mysteries, myself. Though I don't like the ones with all the foul language and gory details if you know what I mean."

"I was thinkin' about doin' somethin' on the fairy forts." It's not technically a lie. Any story I do end up writing will have some reference to them.

"Are you now?" A light of interest goes on behind her milky blue

eyes, and she slides into the chair opposite me. "What's your particular area of interest? I'm known around these parts as a bit of an expert on them."

Audrey told me as much, but I do my best to feign surprise. "Really? So you know all about the curses that come from disturbin' 'em?"

"Indeed, I do," she tells me. "I could tell you many a tale of the horrors that befall any poor soul that dares to cross the fairies. Is that the sort of thing you might be interested in?"

"Yes, ma'am. That's why I'm here. I heard that some folks think Kevin Donnelly was killed because he moved one of 'em." After the words spill out, I fear I might have spooked her by mentioning Donnelly's murder.

But she doesn't seem to mind one bit. "And it's right they should be thinking that way. It's long been known that the fiercest of fairies dwelt on the fort out at old man Walsh's farm."

"Old man Walsh?" I ask, picking up my phone to draft a note to myself.

You'd think I just put a video camera in her face the way she warms to her subject. "That'd be Martin Walsh. He's the fella who owned the land before Donnelly bought it to build that monstrosity he called a shopping center. And then, Donnelly goes and moves the fairy fort! But sure, what more could you expect from a man who cheated a poor farmer out of a fair price for his land?"

My ears perk up at the last thing she said. "Cheated him how?"

Mary glances behind her and then leans toward me across the table, her ample bosom disturbing the table's equilibrium. "The land was worth far more than Donnelly offered Martin for it. Not that Martin knew at the time. Plans for the new motorway they're building hadn't been made public yet. But Donnelly knew, of course. And got a prime piece of land for little more than a song."

I lean in closer. "How did Martin react when he found out?"

"Sure, he was furious!" Mary replies. "He filed a complaint with the county council, accusing Donnelly of insider trading or some such."

Complaining to the local authorities is a far cry from murder, but it does seem like Martin Walsh is a man worth looking into. "What happened?"

"Nothing at all. Nobody that could have done something about it dared to lift a finger against Kevin Donnelly, sure they didn't." Mary shakes her head in disapproval. "But here I am going on about Martin Walsh when you're after wanting to know more about the fairy forts."

"I don't mind," I attempt to reassure her.

"But you might be interested in having a chat with Martin. He lives with his sister now. She runs a pottery studio not far outside the village. Before he moved, he was always going on about seeing fairy lights out by the fort at night. Sure, one time, he even claimed to have seen the Goddess Clíodhna. Says he found a half-eaten apple lying inside the fort the very next morning, too." Seeing my look of confusion, she quickly explains. "Clíodhna is a banshee and the queen of the fairies of South Munster. At her side, she's said to have three brightly colored birds who are always eating apples."

"He thought one of Cleo...Clidin..." After two tries, I give up trying to pronounce her name, "The banshee's birds left behind the apple?"

"That he did. And he wasn't the only one—far from it," Mary assures me. "Some people in the village even took to leaving food and drink for the fairies by their windows at night—as an offering, like."

"I'm guessin' Kevin Donnelly wasn't one of 'em," I remark, trying to circle the conversation back around to the murder. "I heard his car caught fire not long before he died. Do you think that had anythin' to do with the fairies?"

Mary's eyes harden. "Where'd you hear about that?"

Not wanting to tell her I heard from Jamie—a Guard—I try to play it off. "It was in one of the news reports." I really hope I'm not wrong.

"Ah. Well, I wouldn't know anything about that." I can tell she's lying, but I don't know why. She seems to mistake my silence as a critique of her fairy theory because she quickly adds, "But it does sound like a bit of fairy mischief, sure it does."

I'm preparing to ask her more about Martin Walsh, but I don't get the chance.

"Mary, what're you talking to that journalist about?" a voice says from behind Mary. I look up and see the tight-lipped blonde from the crime scene.

Mary waves a thick hand in the air. "What are you on about, Saoirse? She's not a reporter. She's writing a book about the fairy forts." She turns to me for confirmation.

I can feel the heat rising in my face.

"Fairy forts, my foot," Saoirse spits out the words. "She's the one I was telling you about. She writes for one of the village papers. And her auld fella's the one they're thinking killed Kevin Donnelly."

The once-soft corners of Mary's face sharpen when she looks at me. "Is that true?"

I'm reminded of a time when I was just a slip of a thing, and my late grandmother caught me eating sweets before dinner. I tried to lie and say I hadn't taken any, but she saw right through me. I suspect Mary has that same ability.

"Yeah, sort of." I don't start strong. "I mean, I have written some articles for the *Glendare Gazette*, and my dad is bein' questioned in Donnelly's murder. But I'm not writin' any news stories about it. I'm just tryin' to find out what happened."

Mary stares at me for what feels like an hour. Then, she picks up my plate and holds it out for Saoirse to take. "Saoirse, dear, can you box this up? Our friend here was just leaving."

Feeling like a scolded child, I don't know what to say other than, "I'm real sorry, ma'am. I didn't mean you any disrespect. I'm just trying to help my dad."

She pauses for a moment in what I hope is understanding, but then she slowly rises from the table and turns her back on me.

Saoirse looks triumphant as she tries to take Mary's arm in her elbow. Mary pushes her away, and the two women move off in opposite directions.

I take my first sip of the now-cold coffee and slip my phone into my bag.

At least the trip wasn't a total waste. It's given me a new suspect, Martin Walsh.

And, if I hurry, I might have enough time to drop in at his sister's pottery studio before meeting Audrey in Cork.

CHAPTER 14

Finding The Spinning Wheel pottery studio had been much easier than I expected.

As luck would have it, I'd seen a flier for the place, nestled amongst a somewhat dusty collection of brochures, in a rack by the door as I was being evicted from Hannigan's Hideaway Cafe. I stealthily swiped a few pamphlets advertising various local businesses while the teen behind the counter was boxing away my uneaten breakfast.

The directions on the back of The Spinning Wheel's brochure led me to this weathered stone building with a bright yellow door that's split in half with the top half hanging open in invitation. The studio, with its sandwich board sign welcoming pottery parties, sits apart from a more modern house tucked in a grove of trees a little further back from the main road.

Enticed by the smell of the food in the little cardboard container on the passenger seat, my stomach rumbles in protest at being ignored for too long. But I don't have time to eat yet, not if I want to finish up here in time to meet Audrey in two hours.

So, with an empty belly, I climb out of my car and cross the pebbled driveway to the studio.

"Hello?" I call out as I approach the sunshine-colored door.

No one answers.

"Is anybody here?" I try again, leaning against the lower section of the door so I can peer inside. The weight of my body eases the door open on rusty hinges, and I find myself in a little front room with racks of shelves displaying beautifully rustic ceramic plates, mugs, and bowls. I recognize them as the same ones used at Mary's cafe.

Through an open door to my left, I can hear the faint hum of an electric motor. I follow the sound and find a thin woman in her late fifties hunched over a spinning pottery wheel, molding a vase with her hands. I observe her in silence for a moment, taking in her long whitish-blond hair tied up in a messy bun on top of her head and her loose, bohemian clothing.

I don't want to interrupt her work, but I also don't want her to catch me staring at her and think I'm some sort of creepy stalker.

"Beggin' your pardon, ma'am." I step into the room. "Your front door was open."

The woman looks up briefly in surprise, and then her lips part in a gracious smile. "As it should be. Artists are always welcome here. But do you mind giving me a wee moment to finish this piece? If I stop now, the whole thing will fall asunder."

"Take your time. Do you mind if I watch?" I sheepishly ask.

"Not at all!" she assures me. "I've been teaching pottery for so long now I'm used to having eyes on me while I'm throwing the odd pot. Make yourself at home, and I'll be done shortly."

With her head, she indicates I should sit at one of the tables set up as student workbenches. I slide into a nearby chair and become mesmerized by the sight of her graceful fingers shaping the wet clay with precision and ease. When she finally switches off the wheel and stands up, I'm half disappointed that the show is over.

"Now, then," she says while wiping her dirty fingers on a rag, "what brings you here on this soft April day? Are you looking for a lesson? Or are you in the market for some new kitchenware?"

"After watchin' you work, I'm interested in both." I don't tell her I lack the money or time for either. After the mistake I made with Mary, I've learned that honesty is probably the best policy. "But I'll

CURSED GROUND

have to take a rain check. I was hopin' I might be able to have a word with Martin Walsh."

"I'm his sister, Mona. What business do you have with Martin, if you don't mind me asking?" Her friendly disposition takes on a hint of wariness.

I hesitate. "Truthfully, I wanted to chat with him about the farm he sold to Kevin Donnelly."

She raises one pale eyebrow. "Now, why would you want to go digging up that ancient history? Unless it has to do with Donnelly's murder, of course. Funny, you don't look like a Guard. What are you, a reporter?"

"I do a bit of reportin' for a paper down in Glendare, yes. But I'm not writin' this story for them. My dad's the one accused of killin' Donnelly," I admit. "I'm just tryin' to find out what happened."

"Your father? Why would an American have any reason to kill Donnelly? God rest him."

"No, my dad's from here. But I only just met him a few weeks ago," seeing the puzzled expression on her face, I consider explaining. But decide against it. "It's a long story."

Sympathy softens the curves of Mona's face. "You poor dear. I'm guessin' you spent your whole life searching for your father, and, now you've found him, you don't know whether he's a good man or a bad one."

I feel tears welling up in my eyes as she cuts to the heart of the situation. "Somethin' like that."

"Well, I wish I could help you. I really do. But Martin's a bit under the weather. He's not accepting any visitors." There's a protectiveness in her voice that makes me wonder if she suspects him of something. "But look, I don't have another class until this afternoon. Why don't I make us a cup of tea, and we'll chat? I'd be happy to tell you anything I know about Kevin Donnelly."

"That'd be real nice, thank you."

She walks to a small table in the corner with a kettle, spoons, and tea bags. Within a few minutes, she's handing me a gorgeous ceramic mug with a slightly distorted rim. "Sorry about the state of the thing. I use my rejects for drinking in the studio. I find it makes my students feel better about their own mistakes."

We sit silently for a minute or two and sip our scalding tea.

"So," Mona breaks the silence. "What is it you're wanting to know about Kevin Donnelly?"

Not knowing what specific questions to ask, I start with the big picture: "What kind of man was he?"

"One doesn't like to speak ill of the dead," she begins, "but he was an awful man. He didn't care about people or any other living thing, for that matter. Only money."

"Did you know him before he bought your brother's farm?"

"We'd seen him around, like. He first showed up in town a month or two before putting in an offer on the farm," she says. "He said he was looking to bid for a job renovating the museum. But sure, we all know there wouldn't be enough money in it for him to be interested. Then he began asking around to see if any land was for sale near Martin's farm. He was told there wasn't. That's when it all started."

"What all started?" I ask.

She takes a long sip from her mug. "Martin's cattle started dying, mysterious-like. The vet couldn't make heads or tails of it. The cows were healthy one day and dead the next. It wasn't long before Martin's suppliers started dropping him. He didn't have the beef to sell them. And then, just as Martin was wondering how he was going to make his mortgage payments, guess who swooped in with an offer to buy the farm?"

"Donnelly."

Mona sighs deeply. "I suppose we should have seen the signs then. But Martin's a trusting old soul. And a proud man. It would have nearly killed him to have to file for bankruptcy. He saw a way out, and he took it. Even if he did sell the lot for far less than it was worth."

Reading between the lines, I hazard a guess. "You think Donnelly poisoned your brother's cows so he could get the property cheap."

"We've no proof of that. I want to make that very clear." Mona's lyrical voice takes on a sharp edge. "Without evidence, Donnelly's lawyers threatened to sue us for defamation, but everyone knew what happened. We just couldn't prove it."

"That's terrible. I'm real sorry," I say with genuine sympathy. My own mama was killed because of someone else's greed. So I can commiserate with the unfairness of it all.

"I was sorry, too. Poor Martin was devastated. He really loved those cows. Though, I'm just grateful he's still with us. For a while there, I thought he might have been poisoned, too."

"What do you mean? Did Martin get sick?"

"Not like a cold or a stomach bug or anything of that sort," she tells me. "He didn't seem right in the head. He started going on about seeing fairy lights out by the stone circle. Sure, he was convinced he was getting visitations from the queen of the fairies."

"You don't buy into all the talk about fairy forts and curses?" I ask, somewhat surprised.

"I do not! Do you think me daft? They're nothing more than fairy tales for the smallies." Her disdain is evident in her voice. "Fairies didn't run over Donnelly with an excavator. A person of flesh and blood did that. And, God forgive me, if they ever do find out who it was, I'd be as like to shake their hand as to condemn them."

The weight of her passion and disgust causes the fine hairs on my arm to stand at attention.

"The way I see it," she continues, "whoever killed Donnelly did the world a tremendous favor."

CHAPTER 15

"You *have* been a busy girl this morning. Though it doesn't sound like you'll be winning any popularity contests," Audrey says without taking her eyes off the narrow backroad we're bouncing down.

Between bites of my much-delayed breakfast, I've been filling her in on my earlier conversations as we make the forty-minute drive from Cork to Fermoy.

"It wasn't *all* bad," I protest. "Mona was real nice. I'm actually thinkin' I should sign the two of us up for one of her pottery classes. Unless she ends up bein' a murderer, of course."

"Oh, no." Audrey shakes her head. "You can leave me out of it. The only pottery throwing I'll be doing is at the wall."

I smile. "You wouldn't."

"Don't tempt me." Her voice is stern, but I think she's joking. "That is interesting, though, about the cows. I don't know this Martin fella, but if he's like most men I know, he'd have been raging if he thought someone killed off his livestock. Too bad you didn't get a chance to speak with him."

"I know. But his sister wasn't lettin' me get anywhere near him." With all the blood rushing to my stomach to digest the food I ate, I'm suddenly feeling sleepy. We've been driving past what seems like the same thick, leafy trees for the past twenty minutes, and I'm starting to wonder if we're going in circles. "Are we almost there yet?"

"The house should be just up the next road," she assures me as she leans forward, searching for a sign. "Here we are. Castlebriar Manor."

Turning off the back road, we pass through an opening in a low stone wall that fences off Donnelly's property. Trees block any views of the house from the road, but once we're a little way down the long driveway, we finally get our first glimpse.

"Heavens to Betsy!" I murmur under my breath.

The enormous mansion's ivy-clad stone walls loom ominously against the overcast sky. The high walls and turrets cast pale shadows on the driveway like ghostly, gnarled fingers reaching out for us. Smoke billows from the chimney, and in the distance, a slow-moving river as gray as the sky meanders past the property.

Audrey stops the car when we're still a fair distance from the house. "Well, it's not the sort of place you'd want to rent out for a wedding now, is it?"

"Maybe if you're the bride of Frankenstein," I volunteer. "Seriously, this place gives me the creeps."

"You and me both," Audrey admits. "It's supposed to be one of the finest houses in Ireland if the magazines are to be believed. Maybe on a sunny day, it looks less—"

"Terrifyin'?" I fill in the blank.

"I was going to say imposing, but your word works, too." Audrey takes a deep breath and then removes her foot from the brake. "Best we get in there before we lose any more daylight."

"Yes, ma'am. This is not the kinda place I want to be when the sun goes down," I agree. "I know it might be a bit late, seein' as we're already here, but have you given any thought to how we're gonna get her to talk to us?"

"Leave that in my hands," Audrey says as she parks the car in front of the massive oak double doors and reaches into the back seat for a bouquet of elegant flowers. "And you should probably let me do all the talking. I've been warned you're a terrible liar."

Audrey smiles and throws open the car door, inviting in an icy wind that sends shivers down my back. Reluctantly, I join her by the front doors as she slams a brass ring hanging from a lion's mouth against a brass plate.

Expecting a formally dressed servant, we're both surprised when a young and very pregnant blonde opens the door. To say she is stunning would be doing a massive disservice to her beauty. The skin of her heart shaped face is as milky as porcelain, and thick, dark lashes frame the most vibrant turquoise eyes I have ever seen. As she observes us, she runs elegant, slender fingers through the golden hair that cascades down her back in soft waves. "Can I help you?"

"Aoife, dear." Audrey grabs the younger woman in a motherly embrace. "I'm so sorry to be here under these tragic circumstances. But I just had to come and see how you're holding up."

The frown on Aoife's face tells me she has absolutely no idea who Audrey is, but she's too polite to admit it. It occurs to me that Audrey was counting on Aoife being too afraid of causing offense to question our presence.

"It's been far too long. I haven't seen you since the wedding," Audrey continues. "But sure, family always comes together in times of need."

Aoife smiles weakly when Audrey eventually releases her. "You'll have to forgive me. I've forgotten your name…"

"That's more than understandable, given all you've been through lately," Audrey brushes it off. "I'm Audrey. Kevin's second cousin twice removed. And this is my niece, Savannah, just over from America on holiday."

I can see from the blank look in Aoife's eyes that she's still not placing us in the context of her husband's extended family. But instead of challenging us, she says, "Won't you please come in out of the cold?"

"Yes, thank you," Audrey accepts and steps into the mansion's chandelier-lit foyer. "But only if you're sure it's not any trouble. We don't want to impose."

"Not at all," Aoife replies politely. "You'll have to excuse the state of the place. I wanted some time alone, so I sent all the housekeeping staff away for the week. Can I get you something to drink?"

"You're in no condition to be looking after us. Just point me to the kitchen," Audrey insists. "I'll get these flowers in water and make us a cup of tea. How does that sound?"

"Yes, of course. Follow me." Aoife leads us through a maze-like assortment of rooms and hallways before arriving in a large, open kitchen. She points to the counter by the sink, then quickly yanks up the shoulder of her dressing gown as it begins to slip. "The kettle's just there."

Audrey nods. "Grand. I'll have a hot brew mixed up for us in no time. You take a seat. You're far enough along that your feet must be barking at you every time you stand upright."

"They are a bit tender," Aoife confesses as she sinks into a chair. Resting her hands on her distended belly, she starts twisting her wedding ring around her finger. "Kevin used to rub them for me every night."

Out of the corner of my eye, I see Aoife glancing at Audrey. It seems like a strange thing to do when she's supposedly thinking about her dead husband's hands on her feet. But it could also be that she's still trying to figure out who Audrey is.

"Sure, you must miss him terribly," Audrey sympathizes. "It was such a terrible shock, hearing that not only was he dead but that he'd been murdered. God rest him."

A lone tear escapes Aoife's turquoise eye. "I still can't believe he's really gone. God rest him. Who would do something like this?"

Audrey turns to face Aoife. "You know yourself, Kevin wasn't always the easiest man to get along with. It was a fierce temper he had on him at times."

Audrey's disparagement of the newly departed takes me by surprise. Normally, she's exceedingly respectful of the dead. I can only assume she's trying to draw information out of the widow. And it seems to work.

"Every now and again. But, at heart, he was a good, decent man."

Aoife says the words, but I'm not entirely convinced she believes them.

"You don't have to tell me!" Audrey exclaims as she sets a dainty porcelain teacup in front of Aoife. "A good man and a good provider. We just have to hope the guards catch whoever did this as soon as possible."

"The guards had someone in custody. I don't know why they let him go," Aoife laments. "But I have offered a reward for any information that leads to a confession or conviction. It's the least I could do for poor Kevin."

"That's mighty good of you. I'm sure he would appreciate it." Audrey rests her hand on the pregnant woman's shoulder. "Do you know anyone who might have wanted some kind of harm to come to him?"

Before Aoife can answer the question, a loud banging comes from upstairs. We all glance up at the ceiling in surprise.

Audrey's face is a mask of concern. "It sounds like there's someone upstairs. Do you want me to call the guards?"

Aoife grabs Audrey's hand. "Sure, there's no need to cause any fuss. I'm sure it was just the dogs. They do get up to mischief when I'm not paying attention."

"Don't I know it," I say before remembering that Audrey told me not to speak. "I just mean that mine is a holy terror when I leave him alone for too long."

Aoife gives me a feeble smile. "I should probably go make sure they're not destroying the house. And I *am* feeling a bit tired…"

"Of course. You need your rest," Audrey takes back control of the conversation. "We'll be on our way, so. Maybe we'll stop by some other time to check in on you."

"That would be nice," Aoife tactfully replies. "I'll walk you out. I wouldn't want you getting lost."

Aoife wastes no time showing us to the door, where she thanks us for stopping by and quickly ushers us out.

"I'm so sorry I brought up Fergal," I whisper to Audrey. "I gave her an excuse to get rid of us before we learned anything."

"Don't trouble yourself, love. We learned plenty," Audrey whispers back.

"Really? What did we—?"

Audrey shakes her head and whispers, "Don't say anything yet. Wait until we're in private. You never know who could be listening."

I think she's being paranoid, but I choose not to question her crazy.

Once we're back in the relative warmth of the car, Audrey turns to face me. "Did you see the bruises on your one's shoulder? I caught a glimpse when her dressing gown slipped."

"I didn't see anythin'," I admit, kicking myself for missing such an important clue.

"But you know what it means?" she asks.

"That Kevin was probably beatin' on his pregnant wife?"

"Precisely," Audrey confirms. "I think it's probably safe to add another suspect to your list."

CHAPTER 16

By the time I arrive back at my cottage that evening, I feel like a deflated balloon trying to float on a sea of molasses.

My rear end hurts from endless hours in the car, and my head throbs from the pressure of too much thinking. All I want to do is change into my pajamas, microwave some dinner, and climb into bed. Then I see my dad's car parked at the far end of the driveway.

An involuntary groan escapes my lips.

As much as I want to see him, I don't know if I have the mental energy for a conversation. Not now, when I'm still a little uncertain about whether or not he's capable of murder. Everything he says sends my mind racing for some deeper meaning, trying to connect the dots faster than a cat chasing a laser pointer.

But since he's staying with me for the time being, there's no chance of avoiding him.

As I step out of the car, searching desperately for my second wind, a raven perched high in the giant oak tree that casts shadows over my cottage squawks loudly at me.

"Don't you start on me, now," I warn the outspoken bird. "I haven't eaten in ages, and I'm not above puttin' raven on the menu."

Taking a deep, steadying breath, I open the front door. The rich, peaty aroma of burning wood fills my nose, and the warmth of the turf fire burning in the hearth warms my chilled skin. Riding a momentary swell of contentment, it takes a few minutes to register that Fergal hasn't come bounding through the house to welcome me home.

I rush to the kitchen, worried that something terrible has happened to my beloved wolfhound. But when I reach the door, I stop so quickly I almost topple forward.

My dad is sitting at the table with Fergal on the floor beside him. Fergal's tail whips back and forth in a blur of motion, and he whimpers when he sees me. Yet he remains seated, looking from me to my dad and back again like we're tennis balls at Wimbledon.

Then my dad says, "Go ahead."

Without hesitating for a second, Fergal launches himself from a seated position to a fully upright position, his paws coming to rest on my shoulder. He showers me with a flurry of enthusiastic kisses.

"Alright, buddy," I laugh. "Try not to lick off *all* my makeup!"

"Sure, you don't need it anyway," Ian dismisses my playful complaint.

Once Fergal is back on all four paws, I stare at my dad in wonder. "Have you been trainin' him while I've been away?"

"Someone had to put manners on him. You're a soft touch, and he knows it."

"Yeah, yeah." I roll my eyes. "But seriously, how'd you get him to sit still like that?"

"All it takes is a little time and patience," Ian replies. "Just today, we've learned how to roll over on command and—watch this—Fergal, treat!"

Fergal immediately leans onto his hindquarters and waves his front paws.

I can't remember ever seeing anything quite so adorable.

"Well, stop gawking and give your man a treat," my dad instructs me. "He's still in the reward-based phase of his training."

After plopping a dog biscuit into Fergal's open mouth, I give him a quick scratch behind the ears before walking over and collapsing into the seat next to my dad.

"Long day, so?" he asks.

"You could say that," I confirm. "But what about you? You weren't here when I woke up this mornin'. Where'd you go?"

"I went into Cork to see a man about a loan," Ian tells me. "I'm not saying it will, but if something should…incapacitate me, I want to make sure you're alright to stay here in the cottage."

"No, Dad. You can't be worried about me right now," I implore. "Heck, I've been runnin' around like a decapitated chicken tryin' to clear your name. Shouldn't you be tryin' to do the same?"

He pats my knee. "There'll be plenty of time for that once I know you're sorted. Tomorrow, I have to drop in to see the doctor. The banks won't even consider lending to me until I get a full bill of health. The bean counters want to be sure I can work long enough to repay the debt."

"You really don't need to do that, Dad."

"Well, I'm doing it, so there's no point in saying another word about it." His tone is final. "Oh, and since I had a little time this afternoon, I strung up some lights on the back patio. I was worried about how dark it is when you let Fergal out at night."

"Thanks, Dad. But I wish you'd stop worryin' so much about me," I tell him.

"Nonsense. Dads are meant to worry. It's in the job description." He smiles. "So, tell me about your day. Were you able to learn anything new?"

I groan, sinking deeper into my chair. "Honestly, it's startin' to feel like you can't swing a cat around without hittin' another person who woulda wanted Donnelly dead."

Ian's head bobs in agreement. "He had that effect on people."

"Speakin' of, do you know anythin' about Donnelly's car bein' set on fire?" I ask him. Mary at the cafe had lied when she said she knew nothing about it, leading me to believe there *was* something there.

Back home, where there's smoke, there's generally a barbecue.

"Of course! Sure, it happened the day after I broke his nose. He called me up, threatening to get his lawyers involved. Said he knew it was me blew up his car, and he'd see me in jail for it."

I stare at my dad in disbelief. "Why in tarnation didn't you say anythin' about this before? No wonder the guards think you have somethin' to do with his murder!"

"Calm yourself, girl." His words have the complete opposite effect on me. "I didn't tell you about it because I never heard another word from Donnelly. One of the lads that worked for him told me a faulty battery in his hybrid caused the fire. There was no—oh, what do they call it in the detective novels—foul play. It was just an accident."

I'm skeptical of his theory. After all, everyone thought Donnelly being run over by a digger was an accident at first, too. "What if it wasn't?"

Ian thinks about it for a minute, then shakes his head. "No, it was."

"But what if it wasn't?" I persist.

"It had to have been. Sure, if someone were trying to kill him, using his car wouldn't have been the cleverest way of getting rid of him."

"What do you mean?"

"Meaning, it would have been a miracle if someone planted an explosive in that car, and it actually killed Donnelly." Seeing my confusion, he further explains. "The man never drove the same car twice. He owned a few different automobile dealerships in Cork. He had a habit of taking the newest models out for what he liked to call extended test drives."

If what my dad is saying is true, Donnelly's car catching on fire could have been a coincidence. But I generally don't put much stock in those.

"I hope you're right. 'Cause you best bet the guards'll be givin' that fire another look. I would if their shoes were on my feet."

"You worry too much. It'll all be grand," he tries to reassure me. "Look, if the guards seriously thought I killed Donnelly, I'd be behind bars, not sitting here teaching your old dog new tricks."

I know his confidence is an act. If he really thought he was out of the woods, he wouldn't have made going to the bank such a priority this morning. Still, I appreciate that he's trying to cheer me up when it's his freedom that may be on the line.

"Yeah, I guess." It's the most optimistic thing I can think of to say.

"Come here to me. All of this will get sorted before you know it, and we'll get back to finding a way of keeping you in this house," he insists. "There's no way I'm going to jail. I didn't kill Kevin Donnelly."

CHAPTER 17

"*I*an Murphy, you're under arrest for the murder of Kevin Donnelly."

Detective Brian Mulhaney is standing in the foyer of my cottage when I finally make it down the stairs, still dressed in the clothes I had worn the night before.

After chatting with my dad last night, I'd gone to my room and collapsed onto the bed. I woke to someone knocking loudly on the front door. Without so much as brushing my wild, red hair, I'd made a beeline for the front hall with Fergal at my heels. But I arrived too late.

A muscular uniformed Guard standing next to Detective Mulhaney is slapping handcuffs on my dad's wrists and telling him he has the right to seek the advice of a solicitor.

Blinking away the last remnants of sleep, I try to clear my head, which currently feels like a bowl of grits left out in the rain—mushy, lumpy, and desperately in need of a stir.

"What's goin' on? Why are you arrestin' my dad?" I demand to know.

Seemingly amused by my disheveled state, Detective Mulhaney

smiles. "Apologies for calling in so early in the morning. But as I just stated, we're arresting Mr. Murphy for murder."

I run my hands self-consciously through my hair, trying to smooth any flyaways. "But you just let him go," I argue. "Did y'all get some new information?"

The detective shakes his head. "That's not something I'm able to talk to you about."

As I try to absorb all the possible implications of my dad's arrest, one thing jumps out at me. "Does that mean you're not lookin' at any other suspects?"

"I don't know how things work in America," Detective Mulhaney's tone sounds slightly condescending, "but when we arrest someone here in Ireland, it's generally because they're the one we think committed the crime."

"For the record, I don't appreciate your sarcasm," I surprise even myself for scolding him. My mama always used to say I was too timid for my own good, but these men in Ireland really bring out the wildcat in me. "But just to clarify—and a simple yes or no will do—are you looking at any other suspects?"

Detective Mulhaney's face is as stony as the rocks in a fairy fort. "No."

"Well, that makes about as much sense as teets on a bull!" The words slip from my mouth. "Do you have any idea how many people had a reason for wantin' Donnelly dead?"

Color rises on the detective's cheeks. "And can you tell me how many of them were found trying to flee the crime scene?"

"I already told you I wasn't fleeing. I was looking for my cell phone to call you lot," Ian calmly corrects him.

"And do you always start up your car before making urgent phone calls?" Detective Mulhaney presses him.

"Sure, it was a frosty morning. I was just turning on the heating," Ian replies.

Worried that my dad shouldn't say anything without his lawyer present, I attempt to steer the conversation back to my original point.

"Have you even bothered talkin' to Ayleen, Donnelly's ex-wife? Did you know she and her daughters were about to be cut out of his will?"

Mulhaney's sidekick, a beefy, young guard, who looks like he only recently graduated from Garda College, turns to his superior with a questioning look.

Through gritted teeth, Detective Mulhaney tells me, "I can't comment on an active investigation."

It's obvious I'm only angering the detective at this point, but I can't stop myself. "What about Martin Walsh? Have you asked him about his dead cows?"

"Dead cows? What do they have to do with anything?" The young guard blurts out in confusion.

Detective Mulhaney rounds on him. "That'll be all, Garda Sullivan. Take Mr. Murphy out to the car. I'll follow you shortly."

Watching my father being marched out of my cottage like some common criminal stokes the fire burning in my blood. "Do you even want to solve Donnelly's murder? Or are you just lookin' for the most convenient way of closin' the case?"

Once we're alone in the house, Detective Mulhaney takes a menacing step toward me. Fergal, who I'd been too busy to notice was in the room, takes a step forward, placing his massive body between me and the detective.

I know it's inappropriate, given the circumstances, but I can't help thinking Mulhaney's even better-looking when he's angry.

"Miss Jeffers," he says, glancing down at Fergal, "I appreciate that you're trying to help your father, but I'd advise you to mind how you go. You're coming dangerously close to interfering in official Gardai business."

I refuse to back down. "Well, if you're not gonna try to find the *real* killer, somebody has to! I bet dollars to donuts you haven't even questioned Aoife, Donnelly's wife. Did you see the bruises on her shoulder? Who do you think did that?"

Indignation flares behind his eyes. "Please tell me you did not interrogate the dead man's wife!"

Feeling slightly ashamed, I feel the need to defend myself. "Of course not. We just dropped by to pay our respects."

"We?"

Darn it! I hadn't meant to bring Audrey into this, but that horse just bolted out of the barn. "Me and my aunt. We took flowers and made her some tea."

"Good Lord in heaven," Detective Mulhaney sighs in exasperation. "There are two of you off trying to play detective?"

"No, just me. Audrey wasn't with me when I talked to Mary Hannigan. Do you know her? She runs the local cafe. Anyway, I think she's got somethin' to hide. I overheard her talkin' in the backroom to some guy about—"

Detective Mulhaney interrupts my verbal rant. "You need to stop. Hasn't anyone ever told you that curiosity killed the cat?"

"Lucky for me, I'm more of a dog person," I quickly retort.

"I'd say you're more like a badger," he says. "I don't think I've ever met a more relentless and infuriating woman."

I stand up a little taller. "I'll take that as a compliment."

He shrugs. "Take it however you like. But, for your own good, don't go chasing after imaginary suspects. People around these parts don't take kindly to wild accusations. I wouldn't want you getting hurt."

"What's that supposed to mean? Are you threatenin' me?"

"Not at all. I just don't want you swanning around making enemies of the locals because you're too afraid to face the facts." There's a look on his face that almost resembles concern.

I take a deep breath to keep my voice steady. "What facts? You won't tell me why you're arrestin' him. As far as I can make out, all you got on him is that he was there when the body was found."

A minute passes in silence. Then another.

Bored by the inactivity, Fergal wanders off in search of his breakfast.

"You just met your father recently, didn't you?" Detective Mulhaney eventually asks.

"How do you know that?"

He smiles. "I'm a detective, remember?"

I'm tempted to roll my eyes, but I stop myself. "Fine. But what does that have to do with anythin'?"

There's a kindness in his eyes that I haven't seen before. "I'm merely pointing out that you don't know him that well. Sure, few of us know the people we love, even after being around them our whole lives. It is admirable how you're coming to your auld fella's defense. But I'd hate to see that kind of loyalty misplaced."

The little voice of doubt that I've been trying to silence for the past two days starts shouting inside my head. Detective Mulhaney might not realize it, but he's legitimized all my own concerns about my dad. He's made them real. And even worse, he seems convinced he's right.

Butterflies gnaw at my stomach when I ask, "What aren't you tellin' me?"

"I really shouldn't be telling you this," he hesitates. "But I suppose you'll find out sooner or later."

"Tell me what?"

He seems to take no pleasure in informing me, "We found Donnelly's blood on the shirt your father was wearing. He claims he was just checking for a pulse but, I'll be honest, it doesn't look good."

CHAPTER 18

"*L*et's see..." I say, scanning the menu with laser focus. "I'll take the Steel-Cut Apple Oats to start, followed by scones with clotted cream, and then I'll have the full Irish breakfast. But can I substitute the black pudding for extra sausage? And I want my bacon well done."

The waitress, a sweet teenage girl named Cara, scrambles to keep up with my lengthy order. "Well done," she repeats.

"Very well done," I emphasize. "The more burnt, the better."

Cara wrinkles her nose in distaste but says nothing.

"And any chance the chef can make biscuits and gravy?" I ask, longing for the savory Southern breakfast staple.

This time, Cara can't disguise her horror. "You want gravy on your biscuits?"

Only then do I remember that biscuits here in Ireland aren't anything like the ones I used to get back home. Here, they're cookies. Putting gravy on them sounds about as disgusting as licking the bottom of a shoe after a mud-wrestling competition.

"Never mind," I say, closing the menu. "May I also get some orange juice? Thank you."

Cara finally stops scribbling and then stares at her notes about the feast I ordered. "Are you expecting anyone to join you?"

I can feel the blush rising in my cheeks. "Naw, just me. It's been a rough coupla days. I'm eatin' my feelin's."

The young waitress nods, but her eyes tell me she thinks I might have gone insane. The way I'm feeling, she may be right.

I'd called my aunt Audrey right after Detective Mulhaney hauled my father off to the station. She said she had some calls to make, but that I should stop by her cottage in an hour.

Unable to sit still for that long at home, I'd come to the Gilded Heron for breakfast.

Ten minutes after arriving, as I'm taking my first bite of oatmeal, Kevin Donnelly's younger daughter, Deborah, walks into the cafe's lobby.

"Good morning, Cara. How's your da? I heard he'd been down with the flu." She speaks to the waitress with the ease of an old friend.

"He's in good form now, thanks for asking," Cara replies with a smile. "Just as well, too. I thought he would drive me mum mad if he stayed in bed another day."

"Well, I'm glad he's feeling better." Deborah's voice cracks slightly as she speaks. "Is it alright if I take my usual table?"

"Of course. Go right ahead in, and I'll be with you shortly," Cara tells her.

Deborah begins walking toward a seat by the window and freezes when she sees me sitting at the neighboring table. She nods her blonde head in acknowledgment of my presence and then sits down with her back facing me.

I push the bowl of oatmeal away from me, no longer feeling hungry. Deborah, like me, probably came here to escape thinking about her father. Seeing me probably brought it all rushing back. That could be why her shoulders are shaking slightly, racked by silent sobs.

Without thinking, I grab a clean napkin, walk to her table, and kneel beside her. She looks at me through red-rimmed eyes but doesn't accept the napkin I'm holding out to her.

"I would ask if you're alright," I tell her, "but I know you're not. My mama was murdered a few months back. I still miss her every day. I'm real sorry that you're havin' to go through it, too."

Deborah squints her eyes. "It's Savannah, right? You're the one came by my mum's house the other day?"

I nod, feeling slightly guilty. The main reason we stopped by was to pump her mother for information that we hoped could keep my dad out of prison.

She doesn't blink as her weepy blue eyes assess me. "Word around the village is *your* dad was just arrested for killing *my* dad. Is it true?"

It shouldn't surprise me that she already knows. In this village, news travels faster than a greased pig at a county fair. There's no point trying to sugarcoat things. "Yeah, it is."

A single tear runs down her pale cheek. "Did he do it?"

"I don't think so," I tell her honestly. But the memory of what Detective Mulhaney said about blood on my dad's clothes forces me to admit, "But I don't know for sure."

She reaches for the napkin in my hand, finally taking it. "We always want to believe the best about our auld fellas, don't we? Whether they deserve it or not."

"Truth be told, I don't know what my dad deserves," I admit. "We only met about a month ago. My mama never told him about me, and I didn't know who he was."

"Sorry you had to grow up without a father." Her face conveys genuine sympathy. "Though, to be fair, I don't know whether it's better having no father or one who's constantly letting you down."

My knees are starting to cramp from kneeling next to her chair. "Do you wanna join me? I ordered enough food to feed a hungry bear fixin' to hibernate for winter."

She seems unsure, her shoulders tensing in indecision. Then, her muscles relax, and she nods her head. "Why not?"

We take our seats just as Cara arrives with my plate of sweet-smelling scones.

"Dig in," I tell Deborah as I cut open one of the freshly baked treats and smother it with jam and clotted cream. Since it's been a rough week for both of us, I attempt to steer the conversation away from our recent troubles. And because the only thing I know about her—not related to her father's murder—is where she went to school, I decide to ask about that. "So, tell me a little bit about yourself. I hear you went to Trinity College?"

If my intention had been to ease the tension, it doesn't seem to work. She replies with a curt, "Yes, I did."

"Nice. What were you studyin'?"

Deborah runs her butter knife over her scone, evening out the jam. "Ancient history and the classics."

"Wow! That sounds interestin'. I'm a big fan of Sophocles, myself. I'm partial to the Greek tragedies, but I don't mind peppering in a little Aristophanes now and again for some comedic spice."

She stares at me in amazement. "Me too! My focus was on the Greek Hellenistic Period, specifically tracking the societal impacts of the infighting after Alexander the Great's death. Did you study Greek playwrights at your school in America?"

"Naw, I studied creative writin'," I tell her. "But I love to read. My mama used to joke that I'd rather read the ingredients on a cereal box than turn on the television. I've never met a book I didn't learn somethin' from."

"I feel exactly the same way," Deborah agrees. "But sure, I do wish history books didn't have to be quite so dry. The past should feel alive and relatable, not convoluted and buried under bland and sluggish language."

I nod. "That's so true! A lot of them are so borin'. Maybe you should write your own—one that's interestin' and not just loaded down with a bunch of dates and locations."

"You're not the first person to suggest that," she blurts, then the enthusiasm melts off her face. "Aoife used to say the same thing."

I hesitate, wondering if I should change the subject. But, unfortunately for the proverbial cat, my curiosity gets the better of me. "Aoife was your friend, wasn't she? Before she married your dad."

"Sure, Aoife was my first roommate at college, and we had a couple of the same classes. I was new to town and didn't know anyone. She was from Dublin, so she knew all the best pubs and was invited to all the hottest parties. We had so much fun," a subdued smile flickers across her face. "Then I invited her home for winter break."

"We don't have to talk about any of this if it's makin' you uncomfortable," I tell her.

"You know what? It's actually kind of refreshing to talk about it without being blamed for splitting up my parents."

"I don't mean to pry, but how long was it before you suspected somethin' might be goin' on?"

"Between my dad and Aiofe? At the time, I had no clue. But thinking about it later, which I've had plenty of time to do, I should have known right away. When I introduced them, she mentioned all of these construction projects that he was working on—almost as if she'd Googled him before coming to the house."

"Maybe she was just tryin' to be nice?" I suggest. "When I was young, my mama always made me take flowers for my friends' moms when I went to sleepovers."

She shrugs. "Yeah, I suppose. But then, I woke up on her first night at the house, and she wasn't in the spare bed we'd set up in my room. I went downstairs to make sure she was alright. I saw her in the kitchen, and it looked like she was flirting with my dad."

"Did you say anythin' to her about it?" I ask.

"Of course, as soon as we got back up to my room!" Deborah exclaims with half a bite of scone still in her mouth. "But Aoife denied that she was flirting. She said my dad was old. That it'd be gross to even think about hitting on him. She said I had some weird daddy issues to even be thinking like that."

"And you believed her?"

"I did. But more than believing in her, I believed in my dad," Deborah says. "He wasn't always a good man, but he was good to me. And I really thought our family would come first, no matter what. But, like I said, I should have known. That's what my mum keeps reminding me, anyway."

"It wasn't your fault," I try to reassure her. "I don't mean to be rude, but it kinda sounds like Aoife made a move on your dad so she could get rich."

Deborah sighs. "Well, I hope she enjoyed it while it lasted."

Thinking about the changes to Donnelly's will that Audrey told me about, I wonder if Deborah knows that her dad was planning to change his will but never got the chance. There's only one way to find out. "What do you mean?"

"Not long before he died, my dad asked to take me to lunch," Deborah says. "He said he realized that what he'd done to the family was wrong and that he would always make sure we were taken care of."

"Well, that's good he wanted to make sure you were okay," I say supportively while hoping she never finds out that he was planning to leave everything to his unborn son.

I nearly fall out of my chair when Deborah says, "That's why he decided to write Aoife out of his will."

CHAPTER 19

*E*ven though it's technically Spring, smoke billows from the chimney when I pull up outside Audrey's cottage later that morning.

She must have been keeping an eye out for me from the parlor window because she's standing in the open doorway by the time I traverse the short path to her house.

"Any news about my dad?" I ask before even giving her time to wish me good morning.

"Nothing yet, I'm afraid. But Cormac is headed over to the Garda station. He said he'd call me as soon as there's any news," Audrey assures me. "How are you holding up?"

"Well, I just ate enough comfort food to make my waistband cry for mercy," I admit. "But other than that, I'm feeling pretty awful. How 'bout you?"

"Sure, it's not exactly a banner day now, is it? But the important thing is, we can't lose hope." It's not a motivational speech. She's giving an order. "Now come in out of that cold before you catch your death."

Audrey ushers me into the parlor, where I sit next to the fire, warming my hands. I long to kick off my Vans sneakers, curl up in the armchair under one of Audrey's knitted blankets, read a book and pretend that none of this is happening.

But, even though she's my aunt, I still don't know Audrey well enough to abandon the manners my mama drilled into me when I was young. Nor do I have the luxury of ignoring the fact that my dad needs my help.

"Miss Audrey, do you mind me askin' who told you that Kevin Donnelly was plannin' to leave all his money to Aoife's son?" I ask.

She hands me a steaming mug of peppermint tea. "I don't mind you asking, but I won't be able to give you any names. I have to keep my sources confidential, like. But, rest assured, my source heard it from someone close to Aoife."

"That's real interestin' because I ran into Donnelly's daughter Deborah this mornin'. He told her was gonna take care of *her* and that he was writin' *Aoife* out of the will," I tell her.

"Is that so?" Audrey considers the contradictory stories. "As I see it, there are two possibilities. One, someone isn't being honest about what Donnelly told them. Or, two, Donnelly was lying, telling people what they wanted to hear."

"Yeah, but if he died before he changed his will, it's gonna be real hard to figure out what's what," I observe. "When will the family get to see the will?"

"Not until after the funeral," Audrey says. "But you raise an interesting point. Based on what I'd heard, we thought the new will was the reason someone wanted Donnelly dead. But we don't know what's in the original one or who it benefits. We'll have to find a way to remedy that."

"Alright. But until we figure that out, what should we be doin'?" I wonder aloud. "I mean, we have to do somethin'. The guards are convinced my dad killed Donnelly. They aren't gonna be lookin' at any of the other suspects, which means we have to."

"You're absolutely right," Audrey says. "If we want to clear Ian, we have to give the guards some kind of proof that he didn't do it. And the best way to do that is to figure out who did. You've been making a list of suspects, haven't you?"

"Yeah. You know most of 'em already. There's the wife, the ex-wife, the cafe owner, the farmer," I rattle them off. "I'm sure there are others, too. Donnelly seemed better at making enemies than friends. And then there's the business with his car bein' set on fire. It might be connected in some way."

"And let's not forget the call tipping off the guards about the murder," Audrey reminds me. "Someone else knew Donnelly was dead before Ian could even call for help."

"I don't suppose that call woulda been recorded?"

Audrey shrugs. "There's no way to know for sure. All calls to emergency services are supposed to be recorded. That's not to say, though, that they always are. But it's worth asking about—in unofficial channels, like. I don't think Detective Mulhaney will be too eager to help us."

"No, he definitely won't," I say, remembering the look on the detective's face when he told me about the blood they found on my dad's shirt.

"Right, so. I'll see if I can track down a recording of that call and try to get a copy of the police report related to Donnelly's car fire. Those might give us some clues," Audrey reasons. "But we need to start whittling down the suspect list. And the best way to eliminate people is by finding out who has an alibi."

A long sigh escapes from my lips. "That's not gonna be easy."

"True," Audrey acknowledges. "Donnelly was killed early in the morning. Most people would have still been asleep. Aoife and Ayleen were probably sleeping alone. But we don't know for sure."

"It shouldn't be too hard to find out if Ayleen's seein' anyone. Not the way news travels in this village," I point out.

Audrey nods. "Fair enough. But we still need to find out about Aoife. And do you know if Mary from the cafe or that farmer, Martin, have partners that could vouch for their whereabouts?"

Nothing springs to mind. "No idea. But I'll see what I can find out. I was thinkin' of goin' up to Inbetween again today. See if anybody'll talk to me. Unless you need me to be doin' somethin' else?"

"Nothing I can think—"

CURSED GROUND

Across the room, Audrey's phone bings. She walks over to the dining table and checks the new message.

"Actually, there is something we'll both need to do later." She looks over at me, her eyes doing some kind of evaluation. "Do you happen to own any dresses?"

I glance down at my customary jeans and Madewell hoodie. "No. Why? Is there somethin' wrong with what I'm wearin'?"

With her voice, Audrey says, "No." Her eyes give me a different answer. "But if you're going to a wake, you might need to step it up a little bit."

"A wake? What's that?"

"It's an old Irish tradition," Audrey informs me. "When a person passes, the family brings the body home for a couple of days before the funeral. Mourners come to pay their respects, and family members stay up all night, 'waking' the dead."

"Y'all bring dead bodies *into* the house?" The words slip out of my mouth before I can stop them. "I'm sorry, Miss Audrey. I didn't mean no disrespect. It just sounds creepy to me."

"No need to apologize, dear," she assures me. "I know that other cultures tend to sanitize death. But sure, what can we do? It's just our way."

Clips of zombie films start playing behind my eyes, but I force the mind movies away. "Back to the point, you were sayin' that we're goin' to Donnelly's wake?"

"Precisely," Audrey confirms. "The notice was just posted on RIP.ie."

I smile, thinking she's making a joke. It takes a minute to realize that she's not. "That's a real website?"

"It most certainly is!" Audrey exclaims. "There are two certainties in Ireland—that you'll pay a crippling amount of taxes when you're alive and when you die, you'll end up on RIP.ie. Sure, a fair number of people check it more often than they read the news."

I guess it makes sense. Toward the end, my grandma back in Alabama spent a lot of time perusing the obituaries looking for news of her friends. "So, when is this wake? How long do I have to buy a dress?"

"I'd like us to be there this afternoon when it'll be the most crowded," Audrey says, checking the watch on her wrist. "That means you have a few hours to find a frock before we need to be heading out to Aoife's place."

A ripple of unease courses through me. Not only because I have to wear a dress, but also because it occurs to me that there's a very good chance that, if my dad didn't kill Donnelly, whoever did will be at the wake.

And they won't be happy about Audrey and me trying to unmask them.

CHAPTER 20

My palms are sweating, and there's a good chance I might be sick.

I've stared down real danger before. In the past few months, I've come face-to-face with two murderers and lived to tell the tale. My mama, if she were still alive, would tell me I'd grown into a real tough cookie.

But now, staring down racks and racks of frilly dresses while listening to old Enya tunes through scratchy overhead speakers, I feel absolutely terrified. A beach coverup is the closest I've come to wearing a dress in years. I have no idea what might be suitable for a house party where the guest of honor is a corpse.

"Is there anything I can help you with?" a thin, gray-haired woman with big gold earrings and an even bigger smile asks.

Since there are no clothes shops in Ballygoseir, I'd decided to kill two birds with one stone by coming to Inbetween to find a dress and, hopefully, some leads. That's how I ended up inside Irish Rose Couture, across the street from Hannigan's Hideaway Cafe.

"Yes, ma'am. I need a dress to wear to a wake," I tell her. "It's my first time goin' to one, and I'm not real sure what'd be appropriate. I'm not a dress kinda girl."

She pauses a second to take in my accent and casual attire. "You're not from around here, are you?"

"No, ma'am. I'm American, but I have family over here."

"Of course you do, dear. We get a lot of your kind in these parts. Come to trace your roots, have you?" Then, her face flushes in embarrassment. "Pardon me, you said you were here for a wake. My condolences. I hope it wasn't someone close to you."

"Thank you kindly, but no. I never met him. He was a family friend." Sensing this might be my way to get in on the local gossip, I add, "You might know him. Kevin Donnelly."

Her kind blue eyes bulge in surprise. "Kevin Donnelly, you say? Sure, everyone in the village knew him. That's a horrible business altogether."

I rifle through some hangers on the rack, trying to act casual. "Did you see him around much?"

"Sure, we *saw* him a lot, usually speeding down the road in one of his fancy cars." From her voice, it's evident she disapproves. "But he didn't spend time in any of the local shops. I suppose it wouldn't have been proper, seeing as how he was hell-bent on putting us all out of business."

"You mean because of the mall he was fixin' to build?" I press for more details.

"More like a temple of cheap consumer goods made in overseas sweatshops," she replies, not disguising her disgust. "There's no way a shop like mine—with well-made clothes sold at a fair price—could compete! Sure, if that monstrosity does get built, I'd wager I'll be out of business in six months."

This shop owner, whose name I don't even know, is in danger of ending up on my suspect list. "Really? That's terrible. Isn't there anythin' you can do to stop it?"

"A bunch of us tried," she insists. "We went to the local council with our budget projections and everything. We told them that if people were to stop coming into the village because it was handier to stop at a shopping center off the new road, we'd all be in for hard times."

That sounds like a motive for murder to me. "What happened?"

"Donnelly got his lawyers involved. Sure, he had more money to fight it than we did. God rest him. In the end, the council said we were just standing in the way of progress," she lets out a mighty harumph and shakes her head. Seconds later, a smile is back on her face. "But listen to me, blathering on about my troubles. You came in here to buy a dress."

After a whirlwind five minutes in which she proceeds to load my arm with half a dozen dresses, she hooches me into a dressing room and pulls the curtain closed.

"You let me know if you need a different size in any of those," she instructs me from the other side of the brocade barrier.

I look at the dresses hanging on hooks on the wall and exhale deeply. Stripping off my jeans and sweatshirts, I pull the first dress—a black one with pastel flowers—on over my head. It's so tight in the shoulders my arm smacks loudly against the wall as I struggle to squirm into it.

"Everything alright in there?" the shop owner asks.

"Umm…I'm not sure this flowery one is my size. I can't get it past my shoulders," I admit.

She hesitates momentarily before asking, "Did you unzip the side? Under the armpit."

"There's a zipper on the side?" Why on Earth would anyone put a zipper there?

"Try unzipping it and see if that makes things any easier," she advises.

With one arm in the sleeve and the other caught up in the skirt's fabric, I can't reach the zipper. "I'm not sure I can. I think I might be stuck."

"Oh, dear," she says, clearly concerned that I might ruin her merchandise. "Why don't you lean out, and I'll see if I can help you remove the garment."

"Yeah, okay." Mortified, I lean my torso out from behind the curtain, and she lifts the dress over my head and pulls. Following ten seconds of grunting and tugging, she somehow manages to yank off the dress, taking some of my hair with it.

"There we go," she says, eyeing the garment for holes. Finding none, she sighs in relief. "If you're not accustomed to wearing dresses, perhaps you might find the green one a little simpler to get into."

Looking at the remaining dresses, I lift the one that's emerald green. It's open in the front, and there are two long strands hanging down to the floor. I put it on like a robe, then tie the ends together in the front, and stare at myself in the mirror. It's very loose, but I guess it looks alright...when I'm standing still. As soon as I move an inch though, my bra and underpants peek out from the loose folds of fabric. There's no way I can wear this in public!

"How are you finding that one, so?" the shop owner wants to know.

"Uh, I think it might be the wrong size," I tell her. "It's kinda big. And should I be wearin' something underneath it?"

"Let me take a look." Without warning, she yanks the curtain open and stares at me. "Huh, you weren't joking about not wearing dresses."

"No, ma'am." I look down at the ill-fitting garment. "Am I doin' somethin' wrong?"

She looks at me with a tenderness that I imagine she usually reserves for misguided young children. "My name is Rose, as in Irish Rose Couture. It's much nicer than ma'am."

"Yes, ma'am—I mean Rose. My name's Savannah."

"It's a pleasure to meet you. And now that we're on a first-name basis, I feel more comfortable doing this." She yanks the tie loose, and the dress falls completely open. Before I can protest, she slips one long strand through a hole in the left side and wraps both ends around my body before tying them together in a neat bow at the front. "There we are. Now, what do you think?"

I turn toward the mirror, and my breath catches. The potato sack I'd been wearing moments earlier has transformed into a figure-hugging piece of art that makes me feel like a model in a hair commercial. "It's real nice."

"The color is stunning with your complexion," she flatters me, making me blush. "And it matches your eyes."

Unable to bear the humiliation of trying on any more dresses, I decide this one will be more than adequate. "I'll take it. But can you cut off the tags so I can wear it out of the store? I might not be able to get back into it if I take it off."

She chuckles but seems relieved that the other four dresses she selected for me will be spared my fumbling. "Not a bother. Grab your things and meet me at the counter."

I quickly fold my jeans and sweatshirt while trying to think of a way to bring the conversation back around to Kevin Donnelly's murder.

"It is crazy to think somebody was murdered not far from here," I clumsily begin. "Y'all must be scared the killer might go after somebody else." I'm hoping the news of my father's arrest hasn't spread yet.

"Oh no, the Guards took someone into custody just this morning," Rose replies, dashing my hopes that she might spill the bean about her top suspects. "Someone he worked with, apparently. I'm a little ashamed to admit, but before the arrest, I was half thinking the killer was someone here."

Jackpot! "Really? Who did you have in mind?"

"It's silly, really," she practically giggles as she hoists a pair of scissors and takes aim at the price tag at the back of my neck. "But I thought the woman who owns the cafe across the street might have been in league with the museum curator to do away with Donnelly."

So, I'm not the only one who thinks Mary's hiding something. "Why did you think that?"

"It's nothing, really. More like the plot of a Hollywood movie than anything that would happen in real life." She snips the tags from the collar of my dress. "But after Donnelly's body was found, I couldn't help remembering that I'd seen Mary and Domhnell sneaking out of the museum late at night about a week before the murder. I was here, doing inventory. But it seemed a bit odd that they'd be there so late. They were acting real mysterious-like and Domhnell was carrying something that looked heavy."

She has my rapt attention. "Could you tell what it was?"

"I have no idea. Sure, it was dark and a fair ways away down the road. But the guards have their man, so it was all just in my imagination. No more scary movies for me," Rose laughs as she sets the scissors on the counter.

She may be right. It could be nothing. But it could also be a clue that might help free my dad. Which means I have to find out more about this Domhnell who works in the museum.

Not now, though. A clock on the wall tells me I have to leave soon if I'm going to meet Audrey at Aoife's house in time. I just have to settle up with Rose before heading back to my car.

Rose, however, has something else in mind. "Before you go, what are we going to do about those shoes?"

CHAPTER 21

"You're wearing runners with a dress?" They're the first words out of Audrey's mouth when we meet up outside Aoife's house.

Glancing down at my Vans, I'm hoping she's just not of the generation that thinks it's hip to wear casual shoes with business attire. "It's a trend. I saw it online."

Which is true. In an attempt to justify not torturing my feet with a pair of heels, I'd scoured the internet searching for photos of women wearing sneakers with dresses. There had been loads of them.

But Audrey still sees through my bluff. "You drew the line at wearing a dress, didn't you?"

"Yes, ma'am," I admit. "But it really is a thing. I swear."

"I doubt anyone here will see it that way," Audrey rebuffs me. "But sure, you're American, so your bizarre attire will just seem normal to them. Shall we go in?"

Feeling slightly self-conscious, I follow Audrey into the imposing manor house.

A large crowd of mourners are gathered in the front room. Some of them are crying, some of them are laughing, and all of them have drinks in their hands. Except Aoife, who's sitting next to a closed casket, weeping. When I cry, my face gets splotchy, my eyes shrink, and my nose runs. Aoife, on the other hand, looks like a porcelain doll with holy water dripping out of her eyes.

A shiver races through my body, and I notice that one of the windows is fully open.

"Do you think anyone'd mind if I closed that window?" I whisper to Audrey. "It's cold enough in here to freeze the balls off a pool table."

"Don't you dare!" Audrey stares at me in horror. "Sure, if you close it, the soul of the departed won't be able to find its way out."

I'm tempted to laugh but the serious expression on Audrey's face stops me. "I'm sorry, I didn't know." I glance around me to make sure nobody else heard me when something else catches my eye. "Does that have anythin' to do with why all the mirrors have black sheets on 'em?"

"It is," Audrey confirms. "Sure, nobody wants the poor man's soul trapped here for eternity."

I can't shake the feeling that, at some point in the life of this house, someone must have forgotten to open the windows and cover the mirrors for the dead. And not just because it would be the ideal filming location for an arthouse horror movie, but because it feels like I'm being watched everywhere I turn.

"Did you happen to see a washroom when we were here last?" I ask Audrey quietly. "It was a long drive, and I didn't have time to be makin' any pit stops."

"I believe I spotted one along the right corridor, two doors down on the left," she tells me.

Her answer takes me by surprise. "How the heck did you see that? We didn't even go down that way."

"I always make it a point to keep my eyes open." It would feel like a lecture if she weren't smiling. "But you know what? I could probably do with a 'pit stop' myself."

I shake my head at her horrible attempt at a Southern accent. "Very funny, Miss Audrey. Would you mind leadin' the way since you know where you're goin'?"

"Alright, so. Follow me." Audrey slips back into the hallway,

CURSED GROUND

walking past several rooms before making a sharp right turn down a narrow hallway. As we approach the bathroom, a man emerges from a room farther down the hall. We watch as he locks the door.

Then he turns, taking a small step back and putting his hand over his heart when he sees us. "Lord, you gave me a fright. What are you ladies doing back here?"

"Sorry we startled you," Audrey tells him. "We were just looking for the toilet."

"Well, you're in the right place. It's just there." He points to the exact place Audrey said it would be. "I'll leave you to it, so."

As he walks away, I step toward the bathroom, eager to relieve my bladder. But Audrey stops me.

"Come with me. We don't have much time," she whispers before taking my arm and pulling me toward the door the man recently exited.

"What're we doin'?" I whisper back. "I really need to go."

"That was Donnelly's lawyer—the one he was supposed to be meeting with about the will," Audrey informs me while using a small piece of metal that she pulled out of her pocket to pick the lock. "According to my source, he's the only person—aside from Donnelly and the butler—who has a key to this office. We might find something useful in here."

I look nervously down the hall, ensuring no one is watching us. "So, what? We're just breakin' in? We can't do that."

The lock opens with a faint click, and Audrey turns to face me. "Do you want to help your father or not?"

My heart races. "Alright, but only for a minute. If we get caught, we could end up in jail with him."

Audrey pushes the door open and, with one last look down the hallway to make sure the coast is clear, we step into the office. She locks the door behind us.

Donnelly's study is distinctly masculine, with mahogany paneling on the walls and bookshelves lined with leather-bound books. Fire crackles in a fireplace to our right, and on our left, there's a large oak desk stacked with papers and an antique desk lamp.

"There must be a copy of the will in here somewhere," Audrey says. "You check the desk while I try and open the safe."

"How do you even know there's a safe in—"

Before I can finish my sentence, Audrey has pulled at the corner of a painting next to the fireplace. It swings open, revealing a touchscreen safe built into the wall. I've got to hand it to my aunt. She might be retired, but she still gets first-class intel.

"Alright, there's a safe. But do you know his passcode?" I ask.

"You let me worry about that," she tells me. Now hurry up and see if you can find anything on his desk."

My hands shake as I rifle through the pile of contracts, blueprints, and newspaper clippings. I don't see anything that looks like a will, but a clipping toward the bottom of one of the stacks grabs my attention. It has a black-and-white image of a man in his mid-sixties with hooded eyes and a scraggly beard. I begin to read, but Audrey interrupts me.

"Well, this is very interesting," she says from across the room where I can see she's managed to get the safe open.

Dropping the clipping, I step around the desk and walk over to her. Without pausing to wonder how she cracked the safe's code so fast, I ask, "Did you find the will?"

"No, but this may be even better." Pinched between a pair of tweezers, she holds out a crumpled piece of paper.

I KNOW WHAT YOU DID.
MY SILENCE WILL COST YOU €100,000.
THE CLOCK IS TICKING.

AT THE BOTTOM is a series of numbers that make no sense to me.

Audrey anticipates my unspoken question. "It's the routing number to a bank account."

"Donnelly was bein' blackmailed," I state the obvious. "Do you have any idea what he was bein' blackmailed for?"

Audrey seems as mystified as I am. "How would I know?"

"The same way you knew where the safe was and how to crack the code," I reply, slightly annoyed by everything she's not telling me. I also still really need to use the bathroom.

"I suppose you have a point. But I don't know anything about this. I would tell you if I did," she assures me. "Do me a favor. Take a picture of this on your phone. Someone may know it's in here, and we don't want them to find it missing."

I snap a quick photo and peer into the safe. "Is there anythin' else in there?"

Audrey shrugs. "I haven't had the chance to look through everything. There's a lot to go through and not much—"

She abruptly falls silent as the office's door handle begins to rattle. Someone is coming! It's probably the lawyer coming back to check on us since we never reappeared.

Frozen in place, I imagine myself in handcuffs.

Then Audrey's hand grabs my wrist, and she drags me to the window as the office door creaks open.

CHAPTER 22

Seconds after Donnelly's office door opens, Audrey and I hear the lock catch as the door closes behind whoever has entered the room.

The bad news is we can't see who came in. The good news is they can't see us either.

When Audrey heard the door handle rattling, without a moment's hesitation, she'd pushed the painting back into position to hide the safe and pulled me behind a pair of velvet damask curtains that brush the floor. A ledge on the windowsill allows us to sit facing each other with our knees drawn into our chests and our feet touching.

The intruder's footsteps echo through the room, causing my heart to beat frantically against my chest. I'm terrified we'll be discovered, and it doesn't help that I still haven't had a chance to use the washroom. But when I glance at Audrey, she looks completely relaxed, as if she's wondering what she should make for dinner.

We hear papers rustling on the other side of the heavy curtains and then half a dozen sharp ripping noises. The fire crackles.

Realizing the intruder is probably burning some evidence, I lean forward, preparing to jump out and stop them from destroying more potential leads. Audrey's hand on my leg stops me. She shakes her head and puts her index finger in front of her lips.

The intruder is on the move again.

We listen as the footsteps become more distant until we hear a faint click as the door closes softly behind them.

Jumping up from the ledge, I race to the wall safe, which now stands open. Flipping quickly through the papers inside, I realize the letter Audrey had just shown me is now missing.

"The blackmail note's gone!" I exclaim, walking quickly to the door. "We need to find out who that was. If they knew it was here and came to destroy it, they must be involved."

"Stay put, dear. We can't risk anyone knowing we're in here," Audrey orders me calmly from the ledge, where she's stretching out her legs and wincing. "And I need a minute to stretch my legs. My body isn't as flexible as it used to be."

"I'm sorry. Are you alright?" I walk over and offer my arm to help her descend from the ledge.

"Sure, I'm grand. But thank you for your help." She pats my arm. "Now, do your aunt a favor. Look into the fire and see if there's anything that didn't burn."

Kneeling, I peer into the fire, its flames warming my face. Antique andirons hold up the burning logs, and the floor beneath them has been recently swept. The lack of ashes makes it easy to spot a small torn fragment of paper. "I think I found something."

"Careful now, mind yourself," Audrey says as I pull up the sleeve of my dress, preparing to reach into the fire. She grabs a poker from a rack next to the fireplace and hands it to me. "Try using this."

Going slowly so I don't damage the evidence, I gently guide the small piece of paper away from the fire until it's safe enough to pick up. "I don't think this is the same thing we were lookin' at before."

Audrey leans closer. "The printing is too small. What does it say?"

The edges are burnt, leaving only two words visible. "Your car."

Audrey's eyebrows draw together. "What about my car?"

"No, that's all it says. *Your car*," I tell her, trying to figure out what it could mean. "Do you think it might have anythin' to do with Donnelly's car being blown up?"

"Perhaps. But I'm not sure how or why," Audrey reflects. "Theoretically, it doesn't make much sense. If someone was trying to kill Donnelly, why would the victim be the one being extorted? And why would the blackmailer risk sending two notes? All the transfer details were on the one we found earlier."

"Maybe Donnelly wanted more information about what he was bein' blackmailed for?" I speculate. From what I've discovered, there could be any number of reasons he was being shaken down.

"That's one possibility," Audrey concedes. "It's a shame we didn't see this note before the stranger came in here and burned it. But sure, that just means we'll have to work a little harder to solve the puzzle. Did you find anything on the desk earlier that might be useful?"

"There was one newspaper clippin' that seemed a bit odd." I walk over to the desk and find the scrap of newsprint right where I'd dropped it. "It's a story in the local paper about Martin Walsh's cows. It says the guards have agreed to look into it, and there's a name circled in red ink. Garda Sergeant Gerry O'Toole. He was quoted in the article."

"That is curious. But I don't suppose it has anything to do with the other notes. If it did, surely the person who burned the blackmail notes would have burned that, too," Audrey reasons.

"Unless they didn't know it was here," I point out.

"Fair point," Audrey admits. "Better take it with us, so, just in case. And now, we should probably remove ourselves from this office. It's starting to feel busier than Kent Station in here."

"Sounds good to me," I say, already striding toward the door. "I need to use the washroom real bad."

Audrey closes the safe and pushes the painting back into place before walking over to join me. She leans her ear against the door, listening for any sounds in the hallway. "Alright, it sounds like the coast is clear. Let's go."

She opens the door to an empty hallway. We quickly exit the office and start walking down the corridor. Before we can reach the bathroom, the door opens, and Donnelly's younger daughter, Deborah, steps out.

"Savannah?" she says, surprised to see me. "What're you doin' here?"

I'm tempted to ask her the same. But my tongue gets tangled as my mind races for an excuse. "We, um…we were just, you know—"

Audrey jumps in to save me, "We wanted to pay our respects. Sure, we know Ian had nothing to do with your poor father's untimely passing. God rest him. So we didn't see a reason not to come."

Deborah seems to accept Audrey's explanation for our presence in the house but not in this hallway. "But what are you doing *here*? Everyone's gathered in the front."

"Same as you," I tell her, bouncing from foot to foot. "I gotta use the washroom."

Deborah isn't buying it. "But you were coming from the wrong direction. What were you doing down there?" She points down the hall toward her father's office.

"Ah, we missed the turnoff and had to double back," Audrey lies easily.

But it occurs to me that Deborah knows this house better than I would have expected. After all, she fell out with Aoife *before* her dad purchased this house. Based on what she'd said earlier, I didn't think the former friends were on speaking terms.

Before I can think of a way of politely asking her about it, another face appears in the hallway. I immediately recognize the brown-haired man from the crime scene. If memory serves, his name is Aidan, and he works as the village council's archaeologist.

"Deborah? I thought I saw you arriving." Aidan comes toward us and embraces Deborah.

She hugs him back. "It's so good of you to come, Aidan."

"Some of the guys from the site wanted to offer our condolences," he explains. "Can't say as I expected to see you here, but fair play for being the bigger person. I'm sure your auld fella would have appreciated it. God rest him."

I squeeze my thighs together, wondering if it would be rude to sneak into the toilet while they're chatting. Audrey softly clears her throat.

"Where are my manners?" Deborah catches the hint. "Aidan, this is Audrey and Savannah. They..." she pauses, probably considering how she should introduce us without saying we're related to the lead suspect in her father's murder, "live in Ballygoseir and knew Dad from when he lived with us."

Aidan doesn't wait for Deborah to introduce him. "Aidan Boyle. Deborah and I have been friends for years, so she assumes everyone who knows her knows me."

Audrey offers her hand and her sweetest smile. "It's a pleasure to meet you, Aidan. Did you know Kevin Donnelly well?"

Deborah and Aidan exchange a look.

"You might say so, though we didn't always get on," Aidan admits. "I'm the archaeologist assigned to oversee local construction projects, which means I have the power to stop work if the digs turn up something of historical significance. Developers don't tend to like the guy who messes up their schedule over a few old broken vases."

"No, I don't imagine that would make you very popular," Audrey commiserates.

After a few seconds of uncomfortable silence, Deborah says, "Well, I should go say hello to some of my dad's friends. If you'll excuse me?"

"Absolutely," I say, a little too quickly. I'm eager for them to leave so I can finally use the washroom. "I mean, we'll be right behind you."

As Deborah and Aidan turn to leave, it occurs to me that Deborah was right outside when we emerged from her father's office. If she'd been using the bathroom, she might have heard or, better yet, seen the person who broke in.

Then, a darker thought follows. What if she was the office intruder who burned the notes? Could Deborah—possibly worried about losing her inheritance—have been blackmailing her own father?

But at the moment, I have more important things on my mind.

As soon as the pair rounds the corner, I rush into the bathroom.

CHAPTER 23

"All I'm sayin' is, I think we might wanna think about addin' Deborah to our suspect list," I whisper to Audrey while loading a plate with mouth-watering savory pies and roasted potatoes. "I don't think we should let the fact that she's a nice person cloud our judgment."

"I disagree. Nice people don't usually resort to murder to solve their problems," Audrey argues in hushed tones so other mourners at the buffet table won't overhear. "And Deborah? Sure, I've known her since she was a smallie. I just don't think she's capable of flattening her own father with construction equipment."

In an attempt to identify potential blackmailers amongst the crowd, Audrey and I had decided to linger a little longer at the wake. So far, we haven't had much luck. None of our primary murder suspects are here, not even Aoife. She seems to have left the front room while we were snooping in her husband's office.

There's a possibility she snuck off to have a private word with Deborah because Donnelly's daughter is nowhere in sight either. Though it's hard to say for sure, the cavernous front room is packed tighter than a Señor Frog's during Spring Break. Which is lucky for me. I'd probably lose my appetite if I had to stare at the coffin while eating.

Someone has turned on music, which a group of mourners take as an invitation to sing and dance.

"I can't believe how many people showed up for this. Are wakes always so…festive?" I ask Audrey as we move off into a relatively quiet corner.

"Sure, this party's only getting started," Audrey tells me, spooning some crispy apple tart into her mouth. "There's an old Irish saying: 'A good funeral is better than a bad wedding.'"

I nearly choke on my meat pie. "You're tellin' me people go to funerals for fun?"

"Not the actual funeral. Those are serious affairs," she corrects me. "But wakes are meant to be a celebration of life. Think of it as one last party for the recently deceased."

"That's kinda nice," I have to admit, wishing I'd known about the custom when my mama died. She always did love a good party. "But that's not why we're here. We got to find out who was blackmailin' Donnelly. Any ideas about how we should go about doin' that?"

Audrey leans closer and whispers, "Just keep your eyes open for anything that looks suspicious."

"Looks suspicious how?" I ask but don't wait for an answer. "I'm sorry, Miss Audrey, but I don't think this is gonna help us find out who sent that note to Donnelly."

"You're right. It won't." She doesn't seem in the least bothered by the realization.

I'm confused. "I thought that's why we stayed. So we could try and find the blackmailer."

"That was a bit of a white lie," Audrey fesses up. "I saw that Grainne McGrath brought her famous apple crumble. Sure, I was only looking for an excuse to stay and have a bite."

"You coulda just told me." No longer on alert, I allow my shoulders to relax. "But then how are we gonna find out who sent that note?"

"I'm going to send it off to my source and have him trace the bank account, of course. Which reminds me, would you mind forwarding me a copy of that photo you took?"

Holding my half-empty plate with one hand, I use the other to text the picture to Audrey. "I just sent it to you."

Audrey doesn't thank me right away. She's too busy scavenging the last remnants of dessert on her plate. "Did you want anything else to eat? I might go for seconds of the apple crumble. You really should give it a try."

Looking at the meat and potatoes slowly congealing on my plate, I decline. "You go on ahead. I'll wait here for you."

"I'll only be a moment," she assures me before walking off in search of more apple crack.

No longer feeling pressured to scope out a suspect, I cast my eyes leisurely around the room. Near one of the side windows, I spot Deborah's friend Aidan resting his hip on the edge of a sofa. He's talking to an older man who resembles a caricature of a university professor in his sports coat with leather elbow patches. I get the impression the men know each other well. Then again, everyone in the room seems to know everyone else—except me.

Feeling slightly self-conscious, my eyes scan the buffet table for Audrey. I find her deep in conversation with a well-dressed gentleman, slightly older than her, who has a thick head of white hair, an easy smile, and a paisley silk pocket square in the pocket of his blazer. There's a lightness to Audrey's movements as the pair chat, and from her body language, I would swear that she's on the brink of laughing.

If I didn't know better, I'd almost be convinced that Audrey is flirting.

She stayed for the apple crumble, my foot!

It looks like there's another mystery to solve, I think to myself. Who is this man that has my aunt acting like a lovesick schoolgirl? It warms my heart to see that he, though equally reserved, seems to be enjoying Audrey's company as much as she is his.

For a brief moment, I experience a flash of protectiveness for my aunt. I even go so far as to mentally size up the older man. He's a full foot taller than me, and even with his thin frame, he probably weighs about seventy pounds more than me. But he's in his late sixties, so there's still a chance I could take him in a fight.

Then I remember who I'm talking about. Audrey is whip-smart, wilier than a coyote, and tougher than the nails on a porch swing during a hurricane. If it ever came to it, my money would be on Audrey taking both me and her gentleman friend out simultaneously without even breaking a sweat.

Not wanting to make things awkward if Audrey catches me staring at them, I turn away in search of a place to leave my plate. Spying a table in the corner with a tub for dirty dishes, I leave the safety of my spot by the wall and walk toward the far end of the room.

As I'm depositing my dinnerware into the tub, I catch sight of two men in a heated conversation near a door that leads into the music room. I recognize one of them as the man Audrey and I ran into in the hallway, Donnelly's lawyer. I've never seen the other, younger man before, but his outfit draws my attention. He's sporting a windbreaker, which already makes him stand out from the crowd of smartly dressed mourners. But it's the logo on the back of the windbreaker that really catches my eye. There's the outline of a sports car and the words 'Rebel County Prestige Autos.'

Could that be one of the car dealerships my dad told me Donnelly owned?

To better eavesdrop on their conversation, I take a few sideways steps in their direction.

"I'm not joking. This needs to be sorted," the younger man angrily insists. "I'm not going down for this."

"This isn't the time or the place." There's the hint of a warning in his voice when Donnelly's lawyer responds. Likely worried about causing a scene, the lawyer glances around…and locks eyes with me.

I give him my most innocent smile, quickly turn around, and start walking away. Looking back, I see the lawyer roughly ushering the other man into the music room.

It's a shame I couldn't listen in on more of their conversation. They're definitely hiding something.

I can't wait to tell Audrey that she was right.

With my eyes and ears open, I did find something suspicious at the wake after all.

CHAPTER 24

I have no idea how I got here. All I know is I need to find a way out.

I'm strapped into one of those vintage vibrating exercise machines —the kind 1950s housewives used because they'd been promised it would jiggle away stubborn belly fat. My teeth chatter and my whole body quakes.

Then, out of nowhere, a winged, glowing fairy appears behind the wheel of an excavator that's driving straight toward me. The exercise machine's thick rubber belt keeps me trapped in place, and I'm about to be flattened by some sadistic sprite.

My eyes fly open, and I find my aunt standing over me in the dark, shaking my shoulders in an attempt to wake me. My heart beats frantically as I search around for any indication this is another nightmare —one of those dream within a dream scenarios. But then I see Fergal sound asleep on the bed beside me.

If this were a dream, I'd imagine him as a much more capable guard dog.

"Miss Audrey?" I mutter, rubbing my eyes. "What time is it?"

She doesn't even bother looking at her watch. "Nearly six o'clock."

In a stupor and without any sunlight to guide me, I assume the worst. "At night? Oh my gosh! Have I been asleep for the whole day?"

"Lord, I should have brought some coffee," she mumbles to herself. "No, dear. It's six o'clock in the morning. You went to bed early last night after we got back from the wake, do you remember?"

It's starting to come back to me now. We'd driven, in separate cars, back to my house. While Audrey made us something to eat, I'd taken Fergal for a walk through the woods. Shortly afterward, with a belly full of Audrey's pan-fried hake and roasted potatoes, I'd collapsed onto my bed and fallen into a deep sleep.

I would have sworn I watched Audrey leave before I passed out. "What are you doing here so early?"

"I tried calling you, but you didn't pick up. So I used my spare key to let myself in," she says as she makes her way over to my closet and starts going through my clothes. "Hurry up, so. There's no time to waste. We should be on the road already."

"On the road where?" I ask, right before getting hit in the head with a sweater Audrey's thrown at me.

"To see your father," she brusquely replies. "Something's happened."

A sickly cold panic settles over me, instantly making me more alert. "Is he alright?"

"I wish I knew myself. All I've been told is that he's in the hospital," Audrey tells me. Her voice holds no emotion, but her words are coming much faster than normal. "But sure, we haven't been called to the morgue, so I suppose that's something to be thankful for."

I grab the sweater Audrey threw at me and pull it on over my pajama top. "Alright, I'll be ready in a sec."

Five minutes later, after letting Fergal out and throwing some food in his bowl, Audrey and I are on the road to Cork.

The thirty-mile journey passes in silence—both of us lost in our own thoughts.

I have no clue what's going through Audrey's head, but I feel suffocated by the feeling of not knowing. And it's not just being ignorant about what happened to my dad and whether he's going to be okay that has me bothered. I'm still on the fence about whether or not he's a ruthless killer.

With all that to think about, the miles seem to melt away, and before I know it, we're pulling into the parking lot outside Cork University Hospital.

Audrey bolts out of the driver's seat, and I have to run to catch up with her as she enters the hospital lobby through a pair of automatic glass doors. She must already know which room he's in because she bypasses the front desk and heads straight for the elevators.

My feet seem to sense my heart's hesitation because they start to feel sluggish the closer we get to my father's room. I'm scared of what I might find—terrified that I could lose the father I've only just found.

With a sense of relief that's so overwhelming my knees nearly give out from under me, I see Ian sitting up in bed. There's a bandage wrapped around his head, but he's wide-eyed and alert.

"There's my little girl," he slurs his words as he beckons me over with his hand. The handcuffs attached to his wrist rattle against the metal bedframe. "Come over and tell me what you want Santa to bring you for Christmas."

My heart lurches. It's April. And I haven't believed in Santa for two decades. I turn to the nurse, "Has he had a stroke?"

"Not at all. That's just the drugs talking," the nurse assures me. "He needed some stitches in his head, and he has a slight concussion, but other than that, he's grand."

Audrey places her hand on her heart and lets out a deep sigh. When she sees me watching, her hand drops. "How did he get the concussion? Did he fall and hit his head?"

The nurse, a pretty young woman with dark skin and a hijab covering her hair, seems reluctant to go into detail. "You really should wait and speak to the doctor."

"There's no need for all of that. Sure, you're practically a doctor yourself," Audrey's flattery makes the young woman blush. "And I've been so worried about my poor brother on the drive up here. Knowing what happened to him would ease this old woman's mind."

"Of course, it would," the nurse softens, glancing at the door to ensure our privacy. "Don't tell anyone I told you, but it appears your brother was coshed on the back of the head with something blunt and heavy. He was unconscious when the guards brought him in here."

"So it happened to him in jail?" I ask, instantly wondering why anyone in jail would have reason to want to hurt my dad.

"So it did," the nurse confirms, warming to the subject now that she's decided to spill the beans. "I overheard the guards asking him about it when he came to. They wanted to know if he'd seen who'd hit him, but he said he didn't know anything."

"Why are you talking about me like I'm not in the room?" Ian asks petulantly. "And where are my pants? I'll need them if we're going to the pub."

"You're not going to any pub," Audrey tells him. "Do you even know where you are, Ian?"

He looks around, a motion that seems to make him dizzy because he leans his head back against the pillow and closes his eyes. "Are we on a merry-go-round? Sure, we must be because the room is spinning."

Audrey turns to the nurse. "How strong are these drugs you have him on?"

"Just what the doctor prescribed," the nurse assures her. "I have to attend to some other patients, so I'll give you a few minutes alone with him. But he probably just needs some rest."

"Of course." Audrey pats the nurse's arm as my dad begins to snore lightly. "Thank you for looking after him. We won't be staying long."

"We won't?" I ask Audrey after the nurse has left us alone in the room.

Audrey shakes her head. "No. We need to go back to Inbetween and see what we can find out. And we don't have much time. Your dad is probably safe here in the hospital, but…"

She doesn't finish her sentence. There's no need. I already know what she's thinking. If someone at the jail wants to hurt my dad, we have to clear his name before he gets sent back there. Or next time, he might not live to tell the tale.

CHAPTER 25

Frustration that's been building inside me ever since that fateful phone call about Kevin Donnelly's murder finally erupts when Audrey and I settle into her car outside the hospital.

"Aaaaah!"

My scream bounces off the car windows and startles an elderly man walking by so much that he drops the bouquet he'd been carrying. I quickly jump out of the car to pick it up so he doesn't have to bend over. "Sorry about that. I'm just havin' a real bad day. I didn't mean to scare you."

"No bother." He smiles as I hand him his bouquet. "Sure, I have days like that all the time, meself. Better out than in, that's what I always say."

His kindness toward me when I'm acting like a lunatic makes me want to wrap him up in a hug. But I don't. I've already given him one fright for the day. I shoot him a quick wink instead.

Audrey says nothing when I slink back into the passenger seat. She just starts the car and drives us out of the parking lot.

It's not until ten minutes later when we're on the main road out of town that she finally speaks. "So, then. Do you want to tell me what all that was about?"

"I'm sorry, Miss Audrey. I'm just feeling real frustrated," I admit. "It's like every time we have a lead—like the blackmail note, or the article about the cows, or overhearing the cafe owner Mary talkin' about bein' arrested, or the explodin' car—somethin' else happens that sends us off in another direction. And now, someone's trying to hurt my dad in jail? I can't make sense of how it all fits together!"

"I wouldn't be disagreeing with you. This case has more threads to pick at than an Aran jumper." For my sake, she promptly corrects herself, "Sweater. Sorry, I keep forgetting that's what ye Americans call it."

I ignore her comment about culturally different fashion terms to continue my rant. "And don't get me started on suspects! Every day, we're findin' someone new that wanted Donnelly dead. It's like tryin' to find a needle in a pile of needles!"

"Take a breath, dear," Audrey instructs me in her signature cool-as-a-cucumber tone. "If you let yourself get all worked up, you won't be able to spot the real clues when you see them."

"Yeah, but what do we do now? How do we choose?" I ask. "We should probably go check out Rebel County Prestige Autos. From what I overheard at the wake, somethin' funny's goin' on there. Or should we be tryin' to nail down people's alibis? And have you heard anythin' back from your source that was trackin' the bank account?"

"Rein in your horse, Nancy Drew. I'm getting a headache just thinking about what it's like to be inside your head at the moment." Audrey pats me on the leg to soften the blow. "We've just got to focus on what's right in front of us."

I stare out the front windshield. "The road?"

Audrey laughs. "No, smart arse. I mean, we deal with what we can when we can. My source is still chasing down the owner of the bank account, so there's nothing we can do about that yet. But while we wait, we're going to go see a man about his cows."

"Oh, that reminds me…" I pull out my phone and run a Google search for 'Martin Walsh' and 'dead cows.' I see a digital version of the article I found in Donnelly's office, but nothing else comes up. "If the guards did look into what happened to Martin's cows, they didn't bother passin' it along to the press. Should we reach out to that sergeant mentioned in the article—Gerry O'Toole?"

"I already tried," Audrey, who always seems to be five steps ahead, says. "I made a quick call this morning while you were getting ready. Did you know Sergeant O'Toole was the first officer on scene after Donnelly was murdered? I thought that was a bit of a coincidence that he's the one who arrested Ian. Anyway, he's off duty for the next few days. So, Martin is our best bet for information. And here we are."

I glance up as Audrey turns the car onto the pebbled driveway in front of The Spinning Wheel pottery studio. The sandwich board sign is nowhere in sight, and the bright yellow door is closed.

"It doesn't look like Mona's here," I observe. "But the way she made it sound, Martin doesn't leave the house much. We'll probably find him back there."

"Alright, so. Let's go." Audrey gets out of the car quickly and starts marching down the stone walkway that leads to the house in the woods. I rush to keep up with her.

As we pass the side of the pottery studio, a field comes into view with a pen for goats and a chicken coop off to our left. A flash of hi-vis orange catches my eye, and I watch as a solidly built man with an excessive amount of gray facial hair ducks behind the hen house.

I nudge Audrey with my elbow and whisper, "Did you see that?"

"You mean the large man in a fluorescent jacket hiding with the chickens? Nope, I must have missed it." She winks at me. Then, with a finger over her lips, she tilts her head to indicate we should try and sneak up on him.

We walk slowly and carefully across the field, fanning out in different directions when we get close to the chicken coop. The man, whom I assume is Martin, sees Audrey first because he wheels around to run away from her and crashes into me.

"Oomph!" I struggle to reclaim the breath he's just knocked out of me.

"I'm sorry. I didn't mean to hurt you," he apologizes with one frantic eye on the refuge of the house behind me.

Audrey takes up position to the side of Martin so that he's essentially trapped between the two of us and the hen house. "Were you trying to hide from us, Martin?"

He seems confused by her use of his name. "Do I know ye?"

"No," I admit. "But I met your sister the other day. She's real nice."

His eyes twitch, jumping between my face and Audrey's. "Mona's away until tomorrow, but I'd be happy to let her know you dropped by."

"We were actually hoping to speak with you, Martin," Audrey tells him. "We wanted to know more about your cows."

"What are you interested in them for?" He asks, clearly spooked by Audrey's curiosity.

There's no easy way around it, so I decide to be honest with him. "We're lookin' into the murder of Kevin Donnelly—"

"I had nothing to do with that!" He quickly chimes in, holding his hands up in surrender.

"We're not saying you did," Audrey assures him. "We only want to know what evidence you had, if any, that Donnelly killed your cows to get you to sell your land. We read that the guards were looking into it."

He drops his hands and spits on the ground. "They're useless, the lot of them. I had a guard come out to the farm. I gave him vials of blood from me cows. I knew Donnelly had poisoned them. I just couldn't prove it on me own."

"Sergeant O'Toole? Was that the guard you gave the blood to?" I ask.

"Yeah, that was him," Martin confirms. "He came back to me about a month later, after I'd already sold the farm. He said he didn't find anything. But sure, I didn't believe it. He probably just wasn't looking for the right poison."

For Martin's sake, I find myself disappointed that the guards didn't uncover any evidence of foul play. That's probably because I'm beginning to suspect Donnelly wouldn't have been above killing some livestock if it got him what he wanted. And he *was* being blackmailed for something. I wonder if those blood samples are related to why

Sergeant O'Toole's name was circled in the article I'd found on Donnelly's desk.

Audrey's voice interrupts my thoughts. "That must have been difficult. I mean, if you really believed that Donnelly killed your cows, you must have been savage angry to see him getting away with it."

"Sure, I was steaming like a kettle on the boil!" then, seeming to realize the implication of his words, Martin quickly adds, "But I would never hurt your man. I only wanted to see him held to account for what he'd done."

Despite his protestations, Martin clearly had a solid motive for wishing Donnelly harm. It remained to be seen whether he had the opportunity.

"Do you mind me askin' where you were early Tuesday mornin'?" I inquire.

Martin doesn't take offense to the intrusive question. He merely shrugs. "Same place I am every morning. I was in me bed until five o'clock sharp, then I went downstairs to make a pot of coffee before coming out here to feed the chickens."

"Did you happen to see your sister that morning?" Audrey asks. "Could she vouch for you, like?"

Martin shakes his head. "Naw, she's not in the habit of waking up early. She likes to lie in, so she does."

Audrey and I exchange a look, silently acknowledging that Martin —as forthcoming as he might seem—has no alibi.

Sensing our suspicion, Martin says, "If you don't believe me, you can see for yourself. Me sister, Mona, had cameras set up all around the place. She was worried about somebody breaking into the pottery studio. Look at the videos! You'll see I was in the house all night."

"Can we take a look at those videos?" I want to know, excited by the prospect of being able to prove at least one suspect's guilt or innocence.

"Sure, I wouldn't be able to help you with all that. I'm not so good with all this modern technology," Martin admits. "But Mary Hannigan's boy, Oisin, installed them. He could probably sort you out."

The cafe owner's name makes me cringe. I'm not exactly Mary's favorite person after she found out that I'm a journalist. Helping me get access to those tapes probably won't be high on her priority list.

Martin shoves his thick hands in the pockets of his well-worn quilted jacket. "But you'll just be wasting your time. It's plain as the nose on your face who killed Kevin Donnelly."

My eyes open wider in surprise. "It is?"

"Sure, everyone knows it was Clíodhna," he says.

The name sounds vaguely familiar. "Does she live here in town?"

Audrey sighs, then turns to me to explain. "No, dear. Clíodhna lives in the Otherworld. She's the Queen of the Banshees."

"And she's likely to be in a right state after old Donnelly moved her fort," Martin declares.

Audrey's forehead creases with uncertainty. "Sure, now. You don't actually believe that."

"I do!" Martin exclaims. "I saw her myself as clear as I can see the two of ye—back when I still had the farm. She was standing in the middle of the fairy fort late one night. The most beautiful creature I'd ever seen, so she was. I tried going outside to get a closer look, but by the time I made it out the door, she was gone."

"Are you sure she wasn't a real person?" Audrey persists. "You do know that fairies don't exist."

Martin gives Audrey a pitying look. "Believe what you like. But don't tell me they're not real. I've lived alongside one of their forts me whole life. I've seen things. And all I'll say is this: doubt their power at your own peril. Now, if you'll excuse me."

Martin moves toward me, and I step aside to get out of his way. As I watch him disappear inside the house, I only have one thought.

I need to see this fairy fort for myself.

CHAPTER 26

"This is it?" I point to a circular wall of stones that doesn't rise any higher than my calves. It looks like the base of Rapunzel's tower after she was freed—and then took a wrecking ball to it. "This is the fairy fort everyone's been goin' on about?"

"What is it you were expecting?" Audrey wants to know. "A magical castle with twinkling lights and little, winged creatures with pointy ears?"

I shrug, not wanting to admit out loud that the reality leaves me feeling a little underwhelmed. "I was just thinkin' the rocks'd be taller or somethin'."

"Some people do lump dolmens and standing stones into the fairy fort category. But they aren't the same thing." Audrey glances at her cell phone. "Although, they all have one thing in common—they're all in rural areas with terrible reception. I only have two bars."

"Are you expectin' a call?" I ask.

Audrey holds her phone above her head, squinting at the reflective screen. "My source told me this morning that he was close to getting a name associated with that blackmail bank account. I was hoping that would point us to where we should go next."

"Well, there's no reason to hang around here, waitin'. There's nothin' to see." In frustration, I almost kick one of the stones at the base of the fairy fort. I stop myself in the knick of time. It's probably best not to tempt fate.

Audrey continues to walk around the circle of stones, searching for a better signal. "What do you propose we do next? Do you want to head into town and talk to the cafe owner's son—the one who installed the cameras at Mona's pottery studio?"

"Yeah. We could do that." Then I remember something else I'd been meaning to check out. "And there's a guy who works in the museum we should talk to. His name's Domhnell. Rose—the woman who runs the dress shop—told me she saw him and Mary sneakin' out of the museum late at night, not long before the murder. And they were carryin' somethin' that looked heavy."

"Any idea what it was?" Audrey asks the same question I'd earlier asked Rose.

I shake my head. "Naw, and it may be nothin'. But Rose thought it was odd, so it could be worth lookin' into."

She shrugs. "Might as well, seeing as how we're already in the neighborhood."

"Also, I was wonderin' if we should try to track down Sergeant O'Toole. I know you said he's not workin' the next few days, but maybe if we could find out where he lives—"

Audrey cuts me off. "We won't be doing that now. Sure, everybody deserves their days off. We're going to leave the poor man in peace, at least until we see what's on the videotapes from Mona's cameras."

But something has been bothering me about that article I found on Donnelly's desk. "I hear ya, but you don't think there's any way O'Toole was the one blackmailin' Donnelly, do you?"

"I won't say it isn't a possibility," Audrey concedes. "That would explain why Donnelly circled the guard's name in the newspaper story."

"Which means Donnelly probably *did* poison Martin's cows, right? I mean, O'Toole would only be able to blackmail Donnelly if he found somethin' in the cow's blood."

"That's supposing a lot. We don't have any proof O'Toole was involved. We don't even know for certain that the dead cows are tied to the blackmail note," Audrey points out.

Audrey's right. In my haste to solve this case and exonerate my dad, I might be drawing conclusions that don't exist. "Alright, I guess let's go find Mary's son. But you're gonna have to be the one to talk to Mary. She wasn't real happy with me the last time I saw her."

"Why don't you go to the museum and chat with your man, Domhnell, while I go to the cafe? It'll save us some—" Audrey is interrupted by her ringing phone. She looks at the caller ID. "It's my source. I had better reception closer to the road. I won't be a minute."

As Audrey walks away, I turn my attention back to the fairy fort. It's hard to believe that moving this rather unremarkable pile of stones caused such a furor in the village. Not seeing any mortar holding the rocks in place, I can only imagine they had to move it one stone at a time. But how on Earth did they get all the pieces to fit back together?

Leaning forward to get a look at the inside of the ring fort, I notice chalk markings on the stones. It looks like they're some kind of instructions for putting all the pieces back together. The structure has been moved recently, so the elements haven't had ample time to wash away the remnants of its relocation. On the other side of the circle, I see the numbers on the top layer of rocks go from 'A9' to 'A11' to 'A10.' It looks like someone made a mistake in the final stage of the reassembly.

While I'll admit to going out of my way to avoid black cats and walking under ladders, I wouldn't necessarily describe myself as superstitious. But something about all the whispered tension surrounding the fairy forts has me spooked. I figure I might as well rearrange the stones. It can't hurt. Not that I believe that imaginary creatures are wreaking havoc on the village because their fort wasn't put back together perfectly. That would be crazy…right?

Trying not to overthink it, I walk around the circle to where 'A9' and 'A11' touch. I lift 'A11' off the top, unprepared for how heavy the boulder will be. It looks a lot smaller than it feels. Unable to manipulate two of these bad boys simultaneously, I set 'A11' on the ground while I prepare to shift 'A10' into the proper position.

But before I lift the stone, I notice something poking out from underneath the rock. It looks like some kind of strange moss, except instead of being green—as all other vegetation in Ireland seems to be—this moss is a combination of gray and reddish-brown.

I pick up 'A10' and almost immediately have to jump back so the falling stone won't crush my toes. I'd accidentally let go of the rock when I realized what was stuck to the sharp edges on the bottom—clumps of hair and some kind of pinkish-gray gelatinous mass that I assume is a piece of brains all glued in place by dried blood. A whole lot of dried blood.

I look up and, with enormous relief, see Audrey walking toward me. Her face is set in a determined line, but I barely notice her preoccupation.

"Miss Audrey! Miss Audrey! Come quick!"

Concern erases the hard lines on her face. "What is it, dear? Are you alright? Did you hurt yourself?"

"I'm fine," I reassure her. "But I think I mighta just found the murder weapon."

Audrey hesitates. "Say again?"

"Donnelly was hit in the head before he was run over, right?" I don't bother waiting for her to confirm the fact. "Well, I think whoever killed him used one of the fairy fort rocks to do it. Come take a look at this."

Audrey strides toward me purposefully. Her knees pop as she kneels to get a closer look at rock 'A10' on the ground. "Hmmm. I think you might be right. That's definitely blood."

It suddenly hits me what the discovery means. "We need to call Detective Mulhaney right away. If this rock did kill Donnelly, there's no way my dad woulda been able to bring it back here to the fort. They arrested him too quick. He has to be innocent."

"That's not the only reason we need to get in touch with the detective," Audrey says, standing up. "I was just chatting with my source on the phone. He had one hell of a time trying to track the bank account's owner. Whoever set it up was good, but my guy just happens to be better."

She pauses for a minute, increasing the pressure on my frayed nerves.

"You're killin' me, Miss Audrey! Who does the account belong to?"

"As it turns out, you were right about having to disturb Garda O'Toole on his holidays," Audrey says. "He has a hundred thousand Euros worth of questions to be answering."

CHAPTER 27

"Any particular reason you wanted me to meet you in a field?" My dad's lawyer, Cormac McGill, says while using a nearby rock to scrape mud off his Italian leather shoes.

Audrey had called him to say he needed to drop everything and meet us at the fairy fort. Then, she'd waited ten minutes before ringing Detective Brian Mulhaney. Then we'd waited, protecting the evidence until they arrived.

"Sure, I didn't want to go over the details on the phone. But we think we have proof that Ian didn't kill Kevin Donnelly," Audrey quickly fills him in on my discovery. "We wanted you here when we show the evidence to Detective Mulhaney."

Cormac frowns. "You want me to be a witness? Why? Are you worried that Mulhaney's bent?"

Audrey and I exchange a knowing look.

She tries to be tactful. "Now we don't want to be casting aspersions on anyone—"

When I cut her off, I'm not so charitable. "Let's just say he wouldn't be the first crooked cop we've come across today."

"Care to explain?" Cormac asks. "And ye better hurry because an unmarked car just pulled up by the side of the road."

Sure enough, I see Detective Mulhaney climbing out of a nondescript dark blue sedan. Drawing his wool peacoat closed, he begins walking toward us.

"Sure, I'll tell you the whole story later," Audrey promises Cormac. "But we have reason to believe a garda sergeant named Gerry O'Toole was blackmailing Donnelly."

"We think Sergeant O'Toole caught Donnelly poisonin' Martin Walsh's cows," I interject.

Audrey swiftly corrects me. "Sure, we don't know that for certain. There could be any number of reasons he would have been blackmailing Donnelly. Let's face facts. The man was about as pure as the driven snow."

Cormac looks like he's struggling to keep up. "Poisoned cows? I'm sure I have no idea what you're on about now."

"Never mind the cows. They're dead. They can't be helped anyway," Audrey glances over her shoulder, realizing we only have a few seconds before Mulhaney and the uniformed guard with him move into earshot. "I wanted you here because we need to get Ian released before he has to go back to jail."

Now, Cormac really looks confused. "Before he goes *back* to jail?"

"Did you not listen to the voicemail I left you this morning?" Audrey demands.

"It was ten minutes long!" Cormac complains. "I figured I would listen to your podcast *after* I worked out the petition to get your brother released on bail."

Audrey is slightly mollified. "Ah! Did you finish all the paperwork, so?"

"No! You told me to stop whatever I was doing and meet you here," Cormac reminds her. "Where is Ian if he's not in jail?"

"He's in the hospital," I tell him. "Someone at the jail did a real number on him last night. But the doctors say he's gonna be alright."

"For now," Audrey huffs. "But our main priority is making sure Ian doesn't get sent back to jail, alright? Lord knows what might happen."

Cormac nods, pastes on a suave smile, and addresses the

approaching guards. "Good morning to you, Detective Mulhaney. Thanks for meeting us out here on such short notice."

"No bother," Detective Mulhaney says in a way that lets us know he's definitely being inconvenienced. "Anybody want to tell me why I'm here?"

"I think we mighta found the murder weapon," I say. He looks directly at me, and his sultry gaze awakens the butterflies in my stomach. "Not the, um, excavator. Obviously. But, you know, the thing that Donnelly was hit in the back of the head with."

The detective's dark eyes focus on the rock circle behind me. "You better not have brought me all the way out here to tell me the fairies killed Donnelly."

"Sure, we're not daft," Audrey scolds him. "No, Savannah found a stone that appears to have part of Donnelly's skull still attached to it."

Detective Mulhaney's eyes narrow in disbelief. "You're joking me?"

"We are not!" I exclaim. "Murder ain't nothin' to be jokin' about."

Audrey rests a hand on my forearm. "It was just a figure of speech. And he wasn't actually doubting us, were you, Detective?"

"I wouldn't dream of it," he says. "Where is this stone, so?"

"It's over here." I walk over to where I'd dropped the stone earlier. Audrey and I decided to leave it where it was so we didn't contaminate it any more than I already had.

Detective Mulhaney follows me, donning a pair of rubber gloves. "This is where ye found it?"

"Well, no," I admit. "It was in that empty spot there in the circle."

He kneels beside the big rock. "You moved it?"

I can feel my cheeks getting warm, wondering how to explain my actions without sounding like a nut job. "It was in the wrong place. The chalk numbers were out of order. I was just trying to put them back in the right place."

"And why would you do that?" He's gazing up at me, but somehow, it feels like I'm being looked down on.

"Um…" My mind races, trying to come up with an explanation that doesn't involve trying to placate a bunch of nonexistent fairies.

The more I struggle to fabricate an excuse, the harder it becomes to think. "I just thought, um, it should be done right."

His lips curve upwards in the hint of a smile. "Oh, you're one of *those*, are you?"

"I am not!" I have no idea what he means by 'those,' but I do know it's not a compliment.

Audrey rolls her eyes. "Who cares why she moved it? As soon as she saw the blood, she dropped it, and we left it where it fell."

Detective Mulhaney slips on a pair of rubber gloves before picking up the stone and examining it. "The hair does look human. But we'll have to compare it to Donnelly's DNA to confirm it's related to the case."

"How quickly can you do that?" Cormac enters the fray. "I'm asking because, after the events of last night, I'd like to petition for the release of my client *before* he gets sent back to an unsafe jail. After all, if this is the murder weapon, there's no way Ian was involved. Sure, he wouldn't have time to move the stone after Donnelly was killed."

Detective Mulhaney stands, holding the stone out for the uniformed guard to put in an evidence bag. "Let's not get ahead of ourselves, shall we? And as for last night, what happened to Ian Murphy was very unfortunate indeed. But we've dealt with the situation."

"You know who did it?" I ask.

He hesitates, but only for a second. "We do. But we're handling it."

"Well, who was it?" Audrey demands. "And how are you *handling* it?"

Detective Mulhaney lets out a long breath. "You'll be finding out sooner or later, so I suppose there's no harm in telling you. It was a guard that hit Ian. Now, the guard's saying it was self-defense—"

Audrey interrupts him with a snort of contempt.

"—But, we're investigating," Detective Mulhaney continues. "And while we do, the guard in question has been suspended."

Cormac pulls a notebook and pen out of his inner coat pocket. "I'll ask you for the name and badge number of the guard involved in the incident."

"You really should speak to the commissioner for that information," Detective Mulhaney says before turning to the uniformed officer. "Take the evidence to the car. I'll be right behind you."

"Name and badge number," Cormac repeats after the guard has walked away.

"Look, I don't know the man's badge number offhand," Detective Mulhaney tells us, "but his name is Sergeant Gerry O'Toole."

I must have heard him wrong. "Did you say Gerry O'Toole?"

The detective frowns. "Yeah. Do you know him?"

My eyes meet Audrey's, and I can tell she's thinking the same thing I'm thinking. It can't be a coincidence. We need to speak to the guard, even if it is his day off.

"You were right, Savannah. We need to go." Audrey begins walking quickly toward our car, then turns to make sure I'm following. "Well, what are you waiting for?"

Detective Mulhaney looks at me with a questioning look in his sensual eyes. "What were you right about? And where exactly are ye going?"

"I'll tell you later," I call out over my shoulder as I chase after Audrey. "But we really need to find Gerry O'Toole. Preferably before he gets another chance to kill my dad!"

CHAPTER 28

"Stop, Savannah. I can't let you do this." Detective Mulhaney stands in front of me, blocking the walkway that leads to Gerry O'Toole's front door. "Don't make me have to arrest you."

He'd refused to give us the address to the guard's house, but Audrey had called one of her contacts and gotten it anyway. Detective Mulhaney, it seems, followed us to this semi-detached house in a quiet Cork suburb.

"What do you care?" I ask.

"I don't care. What makes you think I care?" It could be my imagination, but I think he's blushing. "I just don't want to see anything bad happen to you."

"But you were just talking about arresting me!" I remind him.

"Only as a way to protect you," he insists.

"Protect me from what?"

"From going to jail!"

I rub my forehead, trying to massage out the building pressure. "You do realize that makes no sense. You're gonna arrest me to protect me from going to jail? What in the heck are you talkin' about?"

"I don't want you to have a criminal record," he pleads. "If you assault O'Toole—who is a Guard, may I remind you—I won't be able to protect you from the consequences."

I'm so shocked by his words my brain nearly gets whiplash. "Assaultin' O'Toole? Who said anything about wantin' to assault him?"

His eyes roll so far back in his head all I can see are the whites of his eyes. "Let's not play games. We both know you're here to get revenge on O'Toole for hurting your auld fella. But trust me, this isn't the way."

"Have you lost your dang mind?" I demand, my hands firmly planted on my hips. "We didn't come here to do anythin' to O'Toole! We just wanted to find out why he was blackmailin' Donnelly?"

"What? O'Toole was blackmailing Donnelly?" It's Detective Mulhaney's turn to be surprised. "Where did you hear a thing like that?"

Oops! I don't think Audrey will be too pleased with me for blabbing, especially since I have no way of explaining how we stumbled upon that note without getting caught red-handed for trespassing.

Think, Savannah!

As if by magic, a safety net appears.

"We didn't hear about it," I start slowly, working out the details in my brain before saying them out loud. I try to stick to the truth as much as possible. "I got a picture of the original note. Don't ask me from whom. Reporters have a right to protect their sources. Anyway, we didn't know who was doin' the blackmailin', but Audrey traced the bank account back to O'Toole."

His pale face turns red so fast that I worry he might be having a heart attack. "Why didn't you tell me about this note? You do realize I could arrest you for impeding an official Gardai investigation."

I can feel my own face getting hot. "Would you stop already with the threats of havin' me arrested! I haven't done anythin' wrong."

"Nothing wrong?" he snorts. "You've been hiding information that could be critical in an ongoing murder investigation."

"We weren't hidin' it," I scoff. "I mean, Audrey only just found out O'Toole was the blackmailer when we were waitin' for you at the fairy fort."

As if suddenly remembering that I didn't come here alone, Detective Mulhaney turns to the left and then to the right, trying to get eyes on Audrey.

"Where *is* Audrey?" he demands. "If she went into that house without me…"

He lets the thought trail off, but it's clear from the enlarged vein throbbing in his neck that he plans to give Audrey a piece of his mind.

He moves toward a gate by the side of the house that hangs open like an invitation. I follow him down a narrow alley into the backyard, not even bothering to hide what I'm doing. I skirt past a plastic green trash bin, its lid kicked back against the fence, revealing an astounding collection of empty beer bottles.

As we round the corner, we catch sight of Audrey standing in front of a set of glass double doors that lead into O'Toole's living room. She's leaning forward, using her hand to block the sunlight so she can peek inside. She seems to sense our approach because she straightens her spine and spins on her heels to face us.

"Ah, Detective, I'm glad you're here. You need to—"

Detective Mulhaney stops her by putting his hand in the air. "Oh no, I don't *need* to do anything. You're the one who owes me an explanation for why you neglected to mention you had evidence of extortion against a murder victim."

Audrey glares at me. I pretend to look at an expensive looking new motorcycle that's parked in the weed-choked back garden.

She lets out a loud sigh. "I understand that you're upset, detective. And I will fill you in on everything I know in due time, but—"

"But nothing," he interrupts. "You can fill me in right now."

Realizing that Audrey doesn't know I lied about how we got the note, I jump in before she accidently blows our cover. "Like I was tellin' you out front, someone sent me a picture of the note. It just said, 'I know what you did. My silence will cost you one hundred thousand Euros.' And then there were a bunch of numbers. We were just tryin' to figure out if the note was real or not."

"You thought it was real enough to run a crosscheck on bank accounts," he points out. "How did you even do that, anyway? That kind of information is supposed to be confidential. You know what? Never mind, I don't want to know. I just can't help but wonder what else the pair of ye are hiding from me."

"We're not *hidin'* anythin'," I fire back at him. "And you should be thankin' us! We're havin' to do *your* job because you won't even consider that someone other than my dad killed Donnelly."

"Excuse me," Audrey chimes in, "there's something you both should really—"

"And *you* refuse to consider that your auld fella might be a murderer," Detective Mulhaney's voice is raised. "I mean, he was practically standing over Donelly's dead body when the guards arrived! And how do you explain the blood on his shirt?"

I can't believe I ever found this man appealing. He's got to be the most exasperating person I've ever met. "How do *you* explain the blood on the rock at the fairy fort? If it weren't for us, you never would have even found the murder weapon."

"If it *is* the murder weapon. You're jumping to a lot of conclusions and—"

Audrey whistles, a sound so high-pitched I have to put my hands over my ears to keep the drums from rupturing.

Detective Mulhaney's anger shifts from me to Audrey. "What in God's name did you do that for?"

When Audrey speaks, her voice is calm. "To stop you from wasting any more time. You need to call in some backup."

Detective Mulhaney shakes his head at Audrey's gall. "You really think I'm going to go barging in on a fellow guard in his own home based on the word of two meddling amateur detectives?"

"No," Audrey concedes. "But I do think you'll want to get someone inside to examine Gerry O'Toole's dead body."

It takes a moment for Audrey's words to sink in.

Then, almost as one, the detective and I rush over to the glass doors and see the suspected blackmailer lying on the kitchen floor in a large pool of his own blood.

CHAPTER 29

"No, really? You don't say," Jamie speaks into the phone held up against his ear. He pauses, listening as the person on the other end of the line responds. Then he says, "I agree. That does sound mighty strange."

Waiting for Jamie's conversation to end has me wriggling like a worm on a hook. My legs bob up and down under the table, and the dinner I cooked to lure Jamie and his mother over to Audrey's house sits, uneaten, on my plate.

After finding the body earlier in the day, Detective Mulhaney evicted Audrey and me from the crime scene, threatening to arrest us if we didn't go home. So, we decided to invite the local Guard over for supper, thinking he might be able to tell us more about the death of his fellow officer, Gerry O'Toole.

But, much to our dismay, Jamie didn't know anything.

He'd initially balked at our request to call one of his work friends, but after we filled him in on O'Toole assaulting my father and blackmailing Donnelly, he agreed to help us.

"And there were no signs of forced entry?" Jamie asks his colleague.

I wish—not for the first time—that Jamie had been willing to put his phone on speaker.

Audrey must be as anxious as I am to hear the latest on the investigation into O'Toole's murder. She's just better at hiding it. She and her neighbor, Deirdre, make small talk between bites of fried chicken and mashed potatoes. I barely hear a word they exchange.

Absentmindedly, I rub the top of Fergal's head, completely oblivious to the fact that he's stealing food from my plate.

After what feels like an eternity, Jamie finally utters the words I long to hear. "You'll let me know if you hear anything else? Thanks, buddy. Talk soon."

"Well, what'd he say?" I demand the moment Jamie slides his cell phone into his pants pocket.

He runs his long fingers through the mop of blond curls on his head. "Sure, I really shouldn't be telling you any of this. I could get in serious trouble. Not that I'm worried about that. I'm more concerned about the two of you getting yourselves caught up in another murder."

Deirdre sets her knife and fork on the placemat. "Jamie, darling, that ship has already sailed, and we're all on board. So be a good boy and skip to the part where you tell us what happened."

"You're incorrigible, the whole lot of you," Jamie complains. "But sure, who am I to stand in your way? Gerry O'Toole was stabbed once in the back. There were no defensive wounds, so chances are he never saw it coming."

I wait for him to elaborate, but he doesn't. "That doesn't sound strange. On the phone, you said somethin' sounded strange."

"I should have known nothing was getting past you. Ears like a bat," Jamie teases me. "The guys on scene don't know what to make of it yet, but when they found O'Toole, he was lying on his back."

"So he was," Audrey confirms. "I saw him myself."

Deirdre looks perplexed. "I'm sorry, but I don't understand. Why does it matter how they found the poor man? God rest him."

"Because he was stabbed in the back," I say aloud, drawing a nod from Jamie. "He should have fallen forward, away from the blade, not onto it."

"Maybe whoever killed him turned him over?" Audrey suggests.

"It's possible," Jamie acknowledges. "But the coroner said there are bruises around the wound consistent with the handle being pushed into his back with a lot of force."

"As if he fell onto the knife?" Audrey asks.

Jamie inclines his head in agreement. "More or less."

I raise my hand as if waiting to be called on in class. "One other thing, I heard you askin' your friend if there were any signs that someone broke into the house. Were there?"

"No. Either O'Toole left his door unlocked, or he let the killer into his house."

Deirdre leans forward in her chair. "What about fingerprints or DNA? They're always gabbing about how important those things are on those true crime programs."

Jamie shakes his head. "I knew I shouldn't have set you up on my Netflix account. But to answer your question, they're still analyzing all the evidence. It could take a couple of days."

My heart lurches. "A couple days? We don't have that kind of time."

"I didn't realize solving murders had a deadline," Jamie quips.

"My dad'll probably be out of the hospital in a couple days, and he can't go back to jail," I try to explain. "We still don't know why my dad was attacked. What if O'Toole had a partner, and that person is gonna try to finish the job?"

Audrey nods. "Savannah's right. We might want to consider the possibility that O'Toole wasn't alone in his blackmail scheme."

"*Or*," Jamie stresses the syllable, "O'Toole was blackmailing someone else, and they killed him for it."

"All this murder and blackmail." Deirdre makes a tsking noise with her mouth. "And the guards involved, too! What's the world coming to?"

"Nothing good, Deidre," Audrey gives a rueful shake of her head. "But since we know at least one guard was crooked, I'm not sure who we *can* trust. Which means, if we want to help Ian, we're going to have to solve this thing ourselves."

Jamie groans. "I was afraid you were going to say that."

"Quit your whinging, Jamie," his mother orders. "You know Audrey's right. And, sure, you've known Ian all your life. You can't just let him rot away in jail, knowing he's innocent."

"Sure, I know he's innocent. That's not the point," Jamie argues. "If that stone you found at the fort turns out to be the murder weapon, they'll have to release Ian and start investigating other suspects. Mulhaney's got a solid reputation. He'll do the right thing. No way he's on the take."

While it's somewhat reassuring to know that Mulhaney's seen as a good cop, his recent threats to arrest me haven't endeared him to me. "Yeah, but how long's it gonna take to confirm the rock killed Donnelly? Anythin' could happen to my dad between now and then."

Jamie rests his hands against his forehead as if trying to massage away a sudden headache. "Now, this isn't to say I'm totally on board with this plan, but if ye were to investigate, how would you go about it?"

The muscles in Audrey's cheeks twitch as she struggles to suppress a smile. "Well, first, we need to establish alibis for some potential suspects. Savannah overheard a lad from Donnelly's dealership talking about not wanting to take the fall for something. I can look into that."

"And I'll try talkin' to Domhnell to find out what he and Mary were doin' at the museum late at night right before Donnelly was murdered," I offer. "But someone should try talkin' to Mary, who owns the cafe. She's hidin' somethin', but she's not gonna tell *me* what it is."

Deirdre claps her hands. "Oh, can I do that? I've heard such good things about her pastries. It couldn't do any harm to try and get some recipes in addition to her alibi."

"Sure, she could learn a thing or two from you in the kitchen," Audrey flatters her friend before circling back to the topic at hand. "Someone also needs to talk to Mary's son, Oisin. He set up cameras on Mona Walsh's property. We need to look at that video to confirm that her brother, Martin, didn't leave the house on the morning of the murder."

When Jamie notices that all eyes are focused on him, he sighs. "The three of you are going to be the death of me. Alright, fine. I'll take a look at the video."

"That'd be great, Jamie. Thank you." I smile at Jamie as a blush rises on his cheeks. "That just leaves Donnelly's ex-wife, Ayleen, and his new wife, Aoife."

Fergal, who settled at my feet after cleaning my plate, suddenly sits up, and a low growl rumbles in his throat. Seconds later, there's a knock at Audrey's front door.

A thick blanket of tension falls over the room as we wonder who'd be calling at this hour of the night.

In a soft voice, I ask Audrey, "You're not expectin' anyone, are you?"

"I most certainly am not." Audrey removes the napkin from her lap and sets it on the table before rising to her feet. "Which means it's either the guards, Donnelly's killer, or the Jehovah's Witnesses."

"Let's hope it's just a couple of misguided missionaries here to save your soul," Deirdre whispers. "Sure, they always turn up when you least expect them."

Jamie falls in step with Audrey as she strides to the door. Deirdre and I follow at a distance, hoping to glimpse the late-night caller, while Fergal stays behind to scrounge what remains of everyone's dinner.

Audrey inhales deeply, then quickly turns the handle and pulls the door toward her. Her voice betrays her surprise. "Deborah?"

Donnelly's youngest daughter stands on the stoop, her blond hair tucked up in a knit cap and her blue eyes screaming uncertainty when she sees the group of us gathered at the door. "I'm sorry to be calling on you so late. But I just saw on the news that someone who worked for my da has been murdered."

I draw in a sharp breath at this unexpected development.

"Gerry O'Toole worked for your father?" Audrey asks the question that's on all our minds.

"I think so," Deborah raises her shoulders slightly. "I was never introduced to him, like. But I saw him with my da a couple of times in the past few months, and it looked like they were talking business."

Why would Donnelly be working with his own blackmailer? Could it be possible Donnelly didn't know that O'Toole was the one who'd been shaking him down for cash? It seems unlikely, seeing as he'd circled the guard's name in the article about Martin's dead cows.

But the more immediate question rattling around in my brain is why news of O'Toole's murder brought Deborah to my aunt's door. I sense that Audrey is similarly puzzled, but she's too polite to broach the subject.

"I can see how news of another killing would be distressing to you," she commiserates with the young woman at her door. "Do you want to come in and talk about it?"

Deborah hesitates, and for a minute, I think she might turn around and run back to her car. Instead, she gathers her courage. "Not meaning any disrespect, but I'd rather get straight to the point. The whole village is talking about how you're doing your own investigation into my da's murder."

"*Investigation* might be too strong a term—" Audrey attempts to downplay our involvement.

Deborah cuts her off. "My da is dead, and now so is someone who worked with him. I need to know what happened, which is why I'm here."

Audrey sighs. "I wish I had answers for you, dear. But we don't know any more than you do."

"Alright, then," Deborah says, pulling the cap off her head and surprising us all by stepping into the house. "I want to help find the killer. What do you need me to do?"

CHAPTER 30

"Are you sure it's a good idea to have Deborah helpin' us?"

Something's been bothering me about the strange visit from Donnelly's daughter the night before. Why, all of a sudden, does she seem so eager to help us catch the killer? Now, speaking to Audrey on speakerphone as I make the journey to Inbetween, I can no longer keep my thoughts to myself.

"Hear me out," I continue, "we still don't know who's gonna be inheritin' all of Donnelly's money. And remember the intruder who broke into Donnelly's office durin' the wake?"

"One could argue that *we* were the intruders," Audrey points out.

I'm tempted to remind her that *she* was the one who physically broke into the office and the safe, but I don't want to lose my train of thought. "We weren't the ones who destroyed evidence, though—the person who *did* left right before us. And who did we find standin' right there in the hallway? Deborah. It can't be a coincidence."

"Sure, I can see why you might have concerns, but I've known Deborah since she was in nappies. You'll have to trust me when I say there isn't a murderous bone in her body." I can hear Audrey's patience being strained over the phone line. "And don't forget, she has a much better chance of finding out if her mother and her old friend, Aoife, have alibis."

"She also has more reason to lie about whatever she finds out," I reason. It's not a stretch to imagine she would want to protect her mother and penalize the former friend who destroyed her family.

While waiting for Audrey to respond, I drive past the fairy fort on the outskirts of Inbetween. Several Garda vehicles are parked on the side of the road, and blue and white crime scene tape encircles the field. I wish I knew if they'd confirmed the stone was the murder weapon, but it's not like keeping me in the loop is high on Detective Mulhaney's list of priorities.

"For now, let's just stick to the plan. We can talk more about this later." Through the car's speakers, I can hear Audrey's turn signal clicking. "I'm just pulling into the lot at Rebel County Prestige Autos, so I have to hang up. Mind how you go at the museum."

Before I can wish her luck digging up information at the dealership, the phone line goes dead.

"Well, Fergal, you heard her. We stick to the plan." My Irish wolfhound pulls his head in from the open window in the back seat, only long enough to see that I don't have any treats for him. Then he returns to enjoying the feeling of the wind through his fur.

He won't be happy about being left in the car while I do my snooping, but what choice do I have? Fergal has all the grace of a baby elephant on ice skates. Even if he were allowed into the museum, he'd have the place looking like a scene from a disaster movie in no time flat. But I couldn't leave him home alone either. Not again. I've barely spent any time with him in the past few days, and he's starting to climb the walls.

His tail thwacks against the back seat when I stop the car in the museum's parking lot. He's so excited by the prospect of a new adventure he doesn't notice when I roll up the windows, keeping them open just a crack to let in fresh air.

I grab my shoulder bag off the passenger seat and sling it across my body.

"I'm real sorry, buddy, but I can't take you with me." I avoid looking into his puppy dog eyes. He rests a paw on my shoulder, and I unwittingly meet his imploring gaze. "This won't take long. I'll be back before you know it, and then we'll go for a long walk, okay?"

As if to make me feel even worse, he lies on the back seat and hangs his head in the footwell.

Before allowing guilt to wear down my resolve, I climb out of the car and lock all the doors. I have a job to do, and I can't let anything stop me.

If not for the sign hanging from a pole affixed to the building, I would almost think the museum was someone's house. The weathered stone walls with ivy creeping up the sides exude an air of coziness, a far cry from the more sterile museums I'm used to from back home.

A small brass bell clangs when I open the door, drawing the attention of a man in his late sixties dressed in a button-down shirt, khakis, and a blazer. He's sitting behind a desk in the small front room to the left of the entrance. His face is etched with deep smile lines, and he wears his silver hair swept back with gel.

"Welcome, welcome! Thanks for stopping by our humble museum," he greets me enthusiastically in a voice weathered by decades of smoking. "Feel free to have a poke around. My name's Domhnell. I'm happy to answer any questions you may have."

I glance around, taking in the framed black and white photos on the wall and glass display cases filled with what looks like broken pottery and old books. All of the items are labeled with handwritten notes, likely describing the artifacts' origins. Though I am curious about the contents of this bizarre little museum, I'm not here as a tourist. I need to get this man talking.

"Nice to meet you, Domhnell," I smile, getting the strangest sensation that we've somehow met before. "This is some place you've got here."

"High praise indeed coming from an American. I'm guessing that's where you're from, based on your accent," his piercing blue eyes twinkle beneath their canopy of bushy eyebrows. "And, if I'm right, you've seen far grander museums than what we have here in our little display. Sure, everything's bigger in America."

"Naw, I like it here. It feels real homey," I try to put him at ease. "Did you start this museum yourself?"

His gravelly laughter echoes off the cavernous ceiling. "Good Lord, no. The community started the museum. I just look after it now that I'm retired. It seemed like a good fit, I suppose, given my affinity for digging up old, dead things."

I subconsciously take a step back toward the door. "I'm sorry, did you say you like diggin' up dead things?"

His eyes widen, and he raises his hands in a placating gesture. "No, no! I didn't mean it in any kind of psychopathic way. You see, I was the local council's archaeologist for thirty-odd years before putting in for my pension last year."

Deborah's friend from the wake, who said he had a similar job, springs to mind. "You wouldn't happen to know Aidan Boyle, would ya?"

"Aye, he's the young lad who took over my post when I traded in my trowels for golf clubs." Then, his eyelids squeeze together in suspicion. "But aren't you a dark horse? How do you know Aidan, so?"

"Oh, I've met him once or twice. He's the friend of a—" my head thinks *murder suspect*, but my mouth says, "—friend. Do you know him well?"

Is it my imagination? Or did his shoulders tense ever so slightly when I asked about his acquaintance with Aidan? And why does his voice sound familiar?

Domhnell's Adam's apple bobs as he swallows. "No. Sure, why would he take any interest in an old fossil like me?"

"Aren't fossils kinda like buried treasure to an archaeologist?" I gently press him with a smile.

"Buried treasure," he repeats, laughing and wagging a bony finger in my direction. "Fair play, young lady. You've got our number, so you do."

I'm trying to think of a casual way to circle the conversation back

T.E. HARKINS

to Aidan—and why Domhnell seems not to want to talk about him—but the museum director outmaneuvers me.

"Getting back to why you're here," he says pointedly, "we have a load of artifacts in the museum, all discovered in the local area. Our ancestors have lived off this land for thousands of years, so those of us who go looking have stumbled across some very interesting ceramics and the like."

Like a lightning bolt from the sky, it strikes me why Domhnell's voice sounds so familiar. He's the man I overheard talking to Mary in the cafe on the morning of Donnelly's murder! From the sounds of it, the two of them had been conspiring to cover up some kind of crime. Knowing that he and Mary snuck something out of the museum late at night, I have to wonder if the two things are connected. And how it might relate to the murder.

While Domhnell may have successfully steered our chat away from Aidan, I won't be so easily dissuaded from getting answers about what he and Mary have been up to. But I must proceed carefully so I don't arouse his suspicion.

"Do you ever find anything valuable?" I ask. The first thought that pops into my mind is that Domhnell and Mary may have been stealing priceless antiques. Maybe Donnelly caught them in the act, and that's why they had to kill him.

Domhnell shakes his head. "Only to us, really. Ireland is littered with similar riches, none of them worth anything in a financial sense. But there's something special about knowing that these things came from *our* people, if you know what I mean."

I don't, not really. But I nod along all the same as I consider the possibility that he and Mary may have been engaged in some perfectly legal activity the night Rose from the dress shop spotted them. "Do you ever loan anything out to, like, other museums in the area?"

He frowns. "That's an odd sort of question. And one I'd never really thought about. Probably because there aren't many museums like ours around these parts. No one's ever asked us for anything, and we've never offered."

In my head, I strike through the various options. Theft? Strike.

Traveling exhibit? Strike. So, what had they been doing? And how do I get him to tell me without blowing my cover?

Before I can devise a plan to elicit the information I need, Domhnell clears his throat. "Would you listen to me going on? Why don't you have a little wander, and I'll make us a nice cup of tea, yeah?"

"That'd be real nice," I lie. I hate tea. I can only hope it puts him in a talkative mood.

As he drifts off into a back room, I peruse the items in the museum's collection. Sauntering past cabinets full of oddities like a wooden trumpet, fractured ceramics, and bronze jewelry, I finally halt beside a countertop display case.

Thick, dark velvet lines the bottom of the display, and metal arms hold up a collection of long, brittle bones. The presence of bones in a natural history museum seems pretty commonplace, but something about this particular display feels wrong.

A handwritten sign informs me that this corpse was unearthed from a local field over fifty years ago.

Which begs the question, if these bones were discovered so long ago, why are they covered in a thin layer of fresh mud?

CHAPTER 31

Well, that's forty minutes of my life I'm never gettin' back, I think when I finally exit the museum.

While Domhnell remained stubbornly tight-lipped about anything that would have been useful to our investigation, he was willing to share the history of nearly every artifact the museum owned. And when I tried pointing out the dirt on the bones, he did his best to convince me it was just fifty years' worth of dust.

I'm not sure if he thought I was thicker than a concrete wall or if he was just too startled to cook up a better lie. Either way, I got nothing more out of him.

It started raining while I was inside. The raindrops are small—too small to even see. But they're there all the same, soaking through my clothes and chilling my bones as I walk to my car.

Fergal must be able to smell me approaching through the open window because he stands up on the back seat, wagging his tail with such enthusiasm that the entire car rocks from side to side.

"Sorry I was gone a while, buddy," I say, attaching a leash from my purse to his collar before releasing him from his vehicular prison so he can empty his bladder. "What do you say we go find some nice woods for a walk?"

Fergal replies with a happy bark, and after finishing his business, he allows me to guide him back into the back seat with minimal fuss.

I slide into the driver's seat, retrieving my phone from my purse to look up nearby parks. But before I can open the home screen, the device buzzes in my hand. It's a text from Jamie.

Hey, Savannah. Just letting you know I'm heading back to Ballygoseir. Oisin is up north today, so I can't watch the video. But we're meeting up first thing tomorrow. Will keep you posted.

It's disappointing I'll have to wait another day to confirm Martin's alibi, but it's starting to feel like nothing more than a formality. I'd be shocked if Martin turned out to be the murderer. Maybe I'm wrong, but a man who hides from two women behind a chicken coop doesn't seem like the type of guy who would bash another man's head in.

I'm about to reply to Jamie's text to ask how his mother is getting on with Mary at the cafe when my phone rings. The call is from an unknown number. I answer.

"Hello?"

"Savannah? It's Deborah. Do you have a moment?"

Having promised Fergal a walk, I know I won't have long before he starts getting antsy. "Yeah, I got a minute."

"I'm in Fermoy, chatting with Aoife, and we were wondering..." her voice trails off.

"Wonderin' what?" I prompt her.

"Well, it's just that Aoife wanted a word, but not over the phone," Deborah explains. "Would you mind driving up to the house so we can have a proper chat? You won't regret it."

She's wrong. I already do regret being unable to say no, even though part of me suspects I'm being led into some kind of trap. As I tried to tell Audrey, I don't entirely trust Deborah.

"I'll be there within the hour," I tell her, against my better judgment. I hang up and type Aoife's address into my GPS. "Sorry, Fergal, you're gonna have to wait a little longer for our walk."

His tail droops, and he lowers his head but quickly perks up when I crack the rear window and start driving. Fergal's head is still hanging out of the side of the car when I pull up in front of Aoife's creepy mansion forty-five minutes later.

Reaching into the back seat, I attach Fergal's lead to his collar. "Alright, buddy. I just need you to be a good boy for a little while longer. I promise I'll make it up to you later."

He lets out a loud snort, his feet dancing on the back seat in anticipation. His enthusiasm dampens when, after letting him out of the car, I march him to the front door instead of allowing him to chase a squirrel that bolted across the front lawn.

I ring the bell and wait.

Just as I'm about to ring the bell again, Deborah opens the front door.

"Savannah, thanks for coming so quick—" she stops speaking, and her eyes widen when she sees Fergal standing beside me. "Oh, no! You brought your dog with you. Sure, I hope you're not expecting to bring him into the house."

"Sorry, we were in Inbetween when you called. I didn't have time to take him home," I explain. "But I'll keep him on a real short leash. I promise I won't let him break anythin'."

Deborah shakes her head. "No, it's not that. Aoife's allergic to dogs, you see. Her eyes will go all puffy, and she'll be sneezing for days. Seeing as how the funeral's tomorrow, there's no way I can let you bring him in here."

"Oh, I didn't realize she was allergic," I say, frowning. When Audrey and I were here last, Aoife told us there were dogs upstairs. But I suppose she has those designer hypoallergenic dogs. When you're rich, it seems, you can even buy your way around allergies. "You know what, I'm sure he'll be fine stayin' outside. There are plenty of squirrels for him to chase."

Relief floods Deborah's eyes. "I sure do appreciate it. We'll close the front gate. He won't be going anywhere."

I kneel and unhook the leash. Fergal stares back at me, almost in disbelief. "Go ahead and run around. Just try not to get into any trouble."

Fergal bounds off toward the nearest tree before I even have time to stand up.

Deborah takes my hand and pulls me into the foyer. "Come on through to the front room. Aoife's waiting. She has something she wants to tell you."

My curiosity outweighs the trepidation I feel at being lured, alone, to the home of one of my lead suspects. I wonder what she could want to tell me.

As we enter the front room, a black-clad Aoife rises from one of the room's many sofas and comes over to greet me. Despite the awkwardness of her enormous baby bump, she looks remarkably poised and put together for a woman preparing to bury her husband the following day.

"I'm so grateful to you for coming on such short notice," she says in her husky, breathless voice. "Deborah says you're a good sort and, I'll be honest, at the moment, I'm not too sure I can trust the police with what I know."

She has my rapt attention. "I can understand that. What is it you wanted to tell me?"

She glances over my shoulder at Deborah, then shifts her focus back to me. "Why don't we sit down? Can I get you anything to drink?"

"No, I'm good. Thanks," I say, eager to cut to the chase. As I walk to an expensive-looking antique chair, I notice for the first time that we're not alone in the room. Donnelly's body is still lying in its casket by the large bay window. An involuntary shiver worms its way up my spine.

Aoife perches on the edge of the sofa nearest me, her spine straight and one perfectly manicured hand resting on her belly. "I don't suppose there's any point in beating around the bush. I asked you here because I know who killed my husband."

It's a good thing I didn't accept her offer of a beverage. If I had, I probably would have spit a mouthful straight into her face. "You do? Who is it?"

Aoife leans closer. "That Garda sergeant they just found murdered in his home. Gerry O'Toole was his name. He killed my poor Kevin."

"Really?" I can hear myself stretching the word out, trying to buy time to think. It hadn't crossed my mind that O'Toole would have killed Donnelly. I mean, why would he shoot a goose that was blackmail gold? But I can't divulge anything about the blackmail to the dead man's wife, not yet. Instead, I turn to face Deborah, who's still standing in the doorway. "Didn't you say O'Toole was workin' for your dad? Why would he kill him?"

Aoife doesn't give Deborah the breathing space to answer. "Oh, he was doing work for my husband, but he was also a kind of double agent."

She's completely lost me now. "You're sayin' O'Toole was a spy? Who was he sellin' his secrets to?"

"No, no. O'Toole wasn't selling any secrets." Her bottomless blue eyes narrow. "He was being paid to get close to Kevin—so he could kill him."

I scratch my head. Her theory is about as clear as the Mississippi River after a bad storm. "And who do you think was payin' him to do that?"

Aoife looks down at her swollen stomach. "Please understand, I'm not telling you any of this because I want to cause harm to anyone. I only want justice for the child I'm carrying who will never get a chance to meet his dad."

I nod, then realize she can't see me with her head bent. "I understand. I want justice, too. For my dad."

Aoife's mesmerizing eyes fly to my safe. "That's just the thing. I can't go to the guards with what I know because they think your father killed Kevin. They won't listen to anything else. And now, knowing that O'Toole was crooked as a corkscrew. I just didn't know what to do or who to tell."

"You can tell me," I appeal to her. "Who killed Gerry O'Toole?"

In a whisper that seems to fill the whole room, she finally tells me. "Mona Walsh."

"Mona?" I hadn't expected her to point a finger at the pottery instructor. Mona just seems so...so harmless. But I suppose she did have a reason for wanting revenge on Donnelly. Or, at least, her brother did. "You're thinkin' she paid O'Toole to kill your husband as payback for killin' Martin's cows?"

Hot blue flames spark in her eyes. "That was never proven. Kevin told me he didn't poison any cows, and I believe him. But there's no talking sense to anyone in that village. They hated poor Kevin for building his shopping center. And they blamed him for every little thing that went wrong in their lives."

Putting the theory of Mona being the mastermind of the plot aside, there is a certain logic in thinking O'Toole killed Donnelly. He was the first guard on the scene after the murder, and he assaulted my dad in jail—maybe because he was worried about what my dad might have seen.

But it does feel like a bit of stretch that O'Toole would have both been blackmailing Donnelly for killing Martin's herd *and* being paid to take Donnelly out as revenge for the same dead cows. Greed can be a strong motivator, but it seems like an unnecessarily complicated and risky plan.

"Do you have any proof that Mona was behind it all?"

Deborah takes a step forward. "That's what we were hoping you could help us find."

Sensing my hesitation, Aoife seeks to sweeten the deal. "I am offering a very generous reward for information that leads to a conviction. If you find us proof, I'll make sure you get that money."

As tempting as that sounds, given the financial nightmare I find myself in over the inheritance tax on my cottage, her offer doesn't factor into my decision. The only thing I care about is clearing my father's name. The sooner I get to the bottom of Donnelly and O'Toole's murders, the safer my dad will be.

As if the universe is trying to remind me of the urgency of that mission, my phone suddenly buzzes with a new message from Audrey.

Your father needs you. Get to the hospital. Now.

CHAPTER 32

By the time I arrive at the hospital in Cork, my nerves are more frazzled than a chihuahua in a room full of vacuum cleaners.

I lost count of the number of times I tried calling Audrey on the drive. I wanted her to tell me nothing bad had happened to my father. That everything was fine. But her phone went straight to voicemail every time.

In the absence of any news, my train of thought went entirely off the rails, imagining the worst. My dad must be dead, and Audrey isn't answering her phone because she wants to tell me in person. Or he's in a coma, and I'm the one who'll have to decide whether to pull the plug on his life support.

With these horrible thoughts taking up all the space in my brain, I don't even know how I have the presence of mind to find the room where I'd last seen my father.

I take a deep breath outside the closed door, mentally preparing myself for whatever I may find on the other side.

Twisting the handle, I push open the door to find…nothing.

The room is empty.

I sink into a cracked faux leather armchair, resting my head in my hands as I fight a tidal wave of nausea.

"Savannah!" a man's voice breaks through my stupor. "Didn't you hear us calling out to you downstairs? You barreled past us as we were ordering drinks."

Looking up, I see my father standing in a hospital gown, a cup of coffee in each hand. Audrey stands beside him, taking a sip from her own cardboard cup.

Without hesitation, I launch myself off the seat and fling my arms around my father's neck. "Thank goodness you're alright!"

"Whoa, careful! This coffee's hot," he warns me. "Of course I'm alright. Why wouldn't I be?"

Relief coursing through me, I struggle to complete a coherent sentence as I let my arms fall back to my side. "Audrey's text message. Sounded bad. Couldn't reach you. No answer."

"Oh, dear," Audrey cringes. "I wasn't thinking about how bad that message might have sounded. Sure, my phone battery was dying. So I just typed whatever popped into my head first."

"This is a hospital. Somebody here must have a charger you coulda used," I point out, feeling slightly miffed that I'd been made to worry for no reason.

"Well, Ian and I got to talking, so…" her sentence trails off. "But everything's grand now. You're here, and everyone's alright."

I study the lines I don't remember noticing before on my dad's face. "You're lookin' better than when I saw you last. How're you feelin'?"

"Sure, I'm grand," he shrugs off my concern. "Even better now I know that O'Toole fella won't be coming back to try and do me in again. God rest him."

"So you knew it was him that hit you?" I want to know.

"I did, of course. The brute was asking me questions while doing his best to beat out of me what little brains I have left," my dad winks at me.

I ignore his attempt at humor. "What was he askin' you?"

"He kept asking me what I saw that morning. He wanted to know if I'd seen a car."

I frown. "A car? What car?"

My dad lifts his shoulders slightly. "I have no idea. He wouldn't say anything more about it. He just kept asking if I'd seen *a* car. And when I said I hadn't, he just hit me again and called me a liar."

I rock back on my heels, thinking. Why would O'Toole ask about a car? If he'd killed Donnelly, why didn't he just ask if my dad had seen *him*? The car must be significant in some way. I just don't know how.

"There's more, too," Audrey's voice pulls me from my silent reflection. "Go on, Ian. Tell her about what happened today."

"You think it's important, do you?" my dad asks.

Audrey nods. "Sure, I do. I'm not exactly sure how it fits in yet, but I have a feeling it's a clue."

My gaze flits back and forth between their faces. "Anybody care to share what y'all are talkin' about?"

"We will indeed," Ian assures me. "But first, take one of these coffees off my hands before the blasted things scald my fingers."

I oblige, taking one of the cups and waiting as he settles himself on the hospital bed.

"I had a visitor come by this morning," he finally says. "A fellow I've worked with on a bunch of jobs. Goes by the name Big Red. Now, that's not his real name, but it's what all the fellas on the sites call him. Come to think of it, I don't even know that I remember his real name."

"Is it Niall Fitzpatrick?" Audrey asks. "He's the only one of your construction friends that's a ginger, as far as I know."

Ian shakes his head. "No, no. Niall took a job out in Saudi Arabia. The pay would set him up to retire early, or so he said."

"He's in the desert with that fair skin of his?" Audrey makes a tsking sound with her mouth. "I hope he packed plenty of sunscreen."

Their small talk is gnawing away at the last ounce of my patience. "His name doesn't matter! What did Big Red say when he came by?"

"I was just getting to that," Ian says. "You see, Big Red was working out on the site of the shopping center. And he happened upon something the afternoon before Donnelly was murdered. As soon as he found it, he went straight to the big man. He knew himself he didn't have the authority to deal with a problem like that on his own."

"No, he wouldn't, would he?" Audrey chimes in.

I throw my hands up in frustration. "Guys, I have no idea what y'all are talkin' about. Would you just tell me what he found already?"

Ian looks at Audrey. She nods, biting her lower lip in anticipation of my response.

"He found bones in the dirt they'd dug up." My dad looks at me expectantly.

My skin tingles. "As in somebody buried a body there? Like a murder?"

"No, nothing like that," Ian quickly corrects me. "The bones were old. Probably from hundreds of years ago. But they were on the construction site."

"Okay. Is that all?" I ask, not understanding the significance. Based on what I'd learned from Domhnell at the museum, old bones were buried pretty much everywhere in Ireland.

"Is that all?" Ian repeats incredulously. "It might have shut down construction for weeks if not years. There would have been a full archaeological exploration of the area, and if they'd uncovered some kind of ancient settlement, Donnelly would have either had to abandon the site or completely rework his construction plans."

"Seriously?" Initially, I'm surprised, but then I remember that conversation I heard between Deborah's friend, Aidan, and a guard on the morning Donnelly was killed. Aidan had said that, as the council archaeologist, he'd only have been able to stop the construction if Donnelly had died a thousand years ago. Now, it all makes sense.

"We're supposed to take it very seriously," Ian tells me. "Sure, in Dublin, the Council Offices in Wood Quay had to build around a city wall dating from 1100 A.D., and a grocery store built glass floors over Viking ruins discovered during excavations. Shoppers walk over an 11th-century settlement all the time."

"Ian, you're too busy counting the leaves to mind the tree!" Audrey chastises her brother. "Tell Savannah what Donnelly did."

Ian glares at his sister. "I was just getting there. Would you ever let me tell the story?"

Audrey shrugs. "We don't have all day, like."

"Donnelly knew about the bones bein' found?" I interrupt, trying to get the ball rolling.

"So he did," Ian confirms. "Big Red said he told Donnelly himself."

I sit on the edge of the hospital bed, drawn in by the story. "And what did Donnelly do about it?"

Ian smiles, relishing the attention. "That's the thing. Donnelly told Big Red not to mention it to anyone. Said he'd take care of it. But now the bones are missing. And there was a freshly dug hole in the foundation where they were supposed to pour concrete later that morning."

A light goes on in my head. "Donnelly was trying to bury the bones so they would never be found under the concrete. That's why he was there alone so early in the mornin'."

Audrey nods. "The question is, where are those bones now? The guards haven't found them at the site. They seem to have just vanished."

Thinking back on the fresh mud coating the relics in the museum, it occurs to me the two things might be connected. Audrey and I may need to pay another visit to Domhnell.

He doesn't strike me as a killer, but I'd bet my last penny he's involved in all of this one way or another.

CHAPTER 33

"Where's that dog of yours?" Audrey asks while retrieving a tiny umbrella from the pocket of her trench coat.

While we were in the hospital, the gray skies made good on their threats of rain. Rivers have formed against the curb, and swollen drops hammer down in an unstoppable barrage. I tug uselessly at the hood of my thin windbreaker, not looking forward to stepping out from under the relative safety of the hospital's front awning.

"He should be back at the cottage by now." I have to speak loudly so Audrey can hear me above the downpour. "Deborah offered to take him home for me, seein' as how I was in such a race to get here."

If Audrey picks up on my not-so-subtle reminder that her text message scared the living tar out of me, she doesn't let on. "Oh really? Just this morning, you were telling me you didn't trust Deborah as far as you could throw her."

My mouth falls open. "I never said I thought she'd do anythin' to hurt Fergal. She might be a murderer, but she's not a monster!"

"That's where you draw the line, is it? Killing *people* is alright, so?"

"I didn't say that," I point out. "People give you plenty of reasons to want to kill 'em. Dogs, not so much. That's all."

"Anyway," Audrey says, stretching the word so long she's doubled its syllables. "I did manage to solve one of our little mysteries today."

Preoccupied with my dad's welfare, I'd completely forgotten about Audrey's trip to Donnelly's dealership. "Did you find out somethin' about the car explosion?"

"I did, sure," she confirms. "But you're not going to like what I discovered."

"What'd ya mean?"

"Only that I'm now certain the car blowing up had nothing to do with Donnelly's murder."

"How can you be so sure?"

There's a twinkle in her eye when she shouts back. "Because Donnelly torched the car himself."

Her explanation makes no sense, and I wonder if I heard her correctly above the rain. "No, he didn't. Why would he do a thing like that?"

"Turns out he was a bit overextended on his line of credit with the bank," Audrey loudly explains. "The mall project was over budget, and he'd invested a tidy sum in electric vehicles that nobody around these parts wanted to buy. And, sure, why would they? The nearest place to charge them is California."

That could shed some light on why a man who owned car dealerships was driving last year's model. "You're tellin' me he couldn't sell the car, so he just blew it up?"

"Not just the one car. Apparently, he did it a number of times. To the point the insurance company was starting to sniff around," Audrey tells me. "That's what that conversation you overheard at the funeral was about. The managers were starting to get worried they'd be left to carry the bag for Donnelly's nefarious business dealings."

Audrey was right. I don't like that a promising lead has just gone up in smoke. No pun intended. But at least we won't waste any more time on something that's not relevant to our investigation.

"Alright. Well, I guess we should focus our efforts on those old bones. It sounds like it coulda been a real problem for Donnelly if anyone found out about 'em."

Audrey nods. "And we know now that Donnelly was under tremendous financial pressure to build that shopping mall. So much of his capital was tied up in the construction; any delay could have proven disastrous for him."

"I mean, you saw that mansion of his. Couldn't he just sell that big old house if he was havin' money problems?" I wonder, trying not to think about the taxes I can't afford on my own small cottage. "That seems a heck of a lot more practical than buryin' bones and blowin' up cars."

A gust of wind partially carries away Audrey's sigh. "My dear, you clearly don't understand anything about Irish men. They'd cut off their toes to buy a pair of shoes if it meant not having to go barefoot to church."

I don't always understand Audrey's analogies, but I think she means to say that Irish men are too proud for their own good. Which could explain why Donnelly came up with a bunch of hair-brained schemes to protect his fortune rather than just selling part of it off.

Thinking of crazy schemes, I can't help but think about the dirty bones in the museum. "There's one still thing I don't understand."

Audrey raises an eyebrow. "*One* thing?"

I ignore her sarcasm. "You said the bones went missin' from the construction site. And it can't just be a coincidence that I saw bones today in the museum that looked like they'd just been dug up."

Realization dawns behind Audrey's hazel eyes. "You're thinking the bones Donnelly was trying to bury are the ones now on exhibit at the local museum."

"Maybe. But I can't figure out whether they were in the museum beforehand?" I ask. "I mean, do you think it's possible someone planted bones that had already been discovered at the construction site to stop Donnelly's crew from pourin' the concrete?"

"I wouldn't put it past the locals to find their own solution to the problem. Sure, their livelihoods were at stake," Audrey's voice carries a suggestion of grudging admiration. "And you did say the owner of the dress shop saw Domhnell and Mary sneaking something out of the museum not long before Donnelly was killed."

"That reminds me. Have you had any updates from Deirdre?" She was supposed to have been spending the day at Mary's café in Inbetween.

"No, I've had too much on today to check in with her." Audrey checks the watch on her wrist. "It's too late to be calling in on her now, but if you pick me up before Donnelly's funeral in the morning, we can pop in next door to see if she's found anything out."

"What time's the funeral?"

"Ten o'clock at St. Fin Barre's Cathedral in Cork."

That won't leave us enough time to stop at the Inbetween museum before the service. We'll have to wait until after the funeral to confront Domhnell with our suspicions about the bones. Not that I'm actually expecting him to spill his guts to us.

Because as Audrey and I race against the rain to get to our respective cars, something occurs to me. The police were on the scene of Donnelly's murder almost instantly after my dad found the body. And there's been a police presence on the site ever since.

So if Domhnell—and possibly Mary—planted the bones and Donnelly died while trying to bury them, how on Earth did they get back to the museum?

CHAPTER 34

I take one last glance at my outfit and sigh. Audrey is not going to be happy with me.

With all the murder and mayhem, I hadn't had time to shop for a black dress.

So, I had to make do with what I had—a black sweater and a pair of black pants that barely graze my ankles after a temperature mishap while I was still figuring out the strange settings on my European washing machine. Coupled with my black ballet flats, I'm hoping people just think I'm channeling Audrey Hepburn.

My aunt must have been watching for me from the front window because she opens the door before I even have a chance to knock. She looks refined in a collared A-line belted dress and black, pointed pumps.

She eyes me up and down. "You look very…funereal."

"Don't even start with me," I beg her. It took me ten minutes with a lint roller in the car this morning to get all of Fergal's hair off my dark clothing.

"So I suppose you're not in the mood for me to complain about you being five minutes late?"

I open my mouth to protest until I see the smile on her face. She's just trying to mess with me. "Very funny, Miss Audrey."

"Well, come on, so." She pulls the door shut behind her and locks it. "I phoned over to Deirdre to let her know we were coming, and, lucky for us, she said she'd put a batch of her scones in the oven. Best to get them while they're hot."

Audrey takes the lead as we walk the short distance to Deirdre's house. The grass, still soggy from last night's downpour, tickles the tops of my feet and sends little rivulets of cold water down the sides of my shoes.

When we arrive at Deirdre's front door, Audrey knocks but doesn't wait for an answer. She breezes into the house and marches straight into the kitchen, where the scent of fresh pastries makes my mouth water.

"Good morning to you both," Deirdre greets us warmly. "I thought I'd try out a new recipe I learned from Mary yesterday."

I glance at Audrey at the mention of Mary's name, but she's too busy peering into the stove to notice. "They smell heavenly. But you shouldn't have gone to all the trouble."

"Nonsense. It's my pleasure," Deirdre says, though she looks a bit frazzled, and I can see a few beads of sweat dotting her hairline. "What else can I get for you? Would you like a nice cup of tea? Or some coffee for the American?"

"I'd love a cup of coffee, Miss Deirdre. But only if it's not too much trouble," I quickly add.

"No trouble at all," she assures me. "Though, all I have is instant. I hope that's alright."

I nod. I've gotten used to people preferring tea in this part of the world. No one seems to like coffee very much. If they did, they certainly wouldn't all be stocking their pantries with bottles of Nescafe.

"So you're off to Donnelly's funeral, are ye?" Deirdre asks while filling the kettle.

"We are indeed," Audrey confirms. "I didn't really know your man.

God rest him, but I'll be interested to see if Ayleen turns off to give her ex-husband a proper send-off."

"I'd be more than a little surprised if she did," Deirdre says. "There was no love lost between those two after the divorce. She's just as like to dance on his grave than utter blessings over it, I can tell you that."

The sound of my stomach rumbling fills the brief gap in the conversation, making me blush. It occurs to me that after I got home and walked Fergal last night, I forgot to make myself anything for dinner.

Armed with potholders, Deirdre opens the oven and lifts out a tray choked with golden scones. She sets it on a hot pad next to a tub of butter, a jar of jam, and some clotted cream. "Go on, then. They won't eat themselves."

Not needing any further encouragement, I slide one of the sweet-smelling pastries onto a plate. Steam rises from the center as I cut it in half, and I can see little dots of red fruit. "These smell delicious. Do you mind me askin' what's in 'em?"

Deirdre smiles. "Candied rhubarb. I've never made rhubarb scones before. But Mary says they're one of her bestsellers."

"All went well with Mary yesterday, so?" Audrey asks nonchalantly while smoothing a thin layer of butter over her breakfast treat.

"Sure, we had a grand time. She even invited me into her kitchen, and we did a little baking," Deirdre gushes. "Some might say she's a tad rough around the edges, but I found her to be quite pleasant."

"I'm glad to hear you had a nice time," Audrey says. "I don't suppose she happened to mention whether she had an alibi for early Tuesday morning."

Deirdre leans in conspiratorially. "I tried to coax it out of her. She got to gossiping about the village, so I asked about the murder. And where she was when Donnelly was killed. God rest him. But she got real cagey, like, and changed the subject."

"Do you think she was hidin' something?" I ask between bites of my scone.

Deirdre contemplates the question for a moment before answering. "I definitely got the sense she didn't want to talk about it. So, I left it be. I'm afraid I'm not a great one for the subterfuge."

"Sure, you're a better woman than me, Deirdre Reilly," Audrey chuckles. "Did she volunteer anything at all you found interesting or possibly helpful to our murder investigation?"

Deirdre shakes her head. "Sorry, no. But I *do* suspect something is going on between Mary and the man who runs the museum. She's sweet on him, I can tell you that. You'd said someone saw them together late at night. Are you sure it wasn't some kind of secret tryst?"

"I don't think so," I reply with a frown. There didn't seem to be anything romantic about the conversation I overheard them having earlier in the week. She'd been telling him to keep his mouth shut if he wanted to stay out of jail. Then again, Deirdre just said Mary was a little rough around the edges. Who knows how she would talk to prospective suitors?

Audrey's voice silences my thoughts. "You said Mary was gossiping about the village? What kinds of things was she saying?"

Deirdre strokes her chin and stares into the middle distance. "Nothing that would be relevant to your investigation, I wouldn't think. She said Mona should give up on the pottery and go into commercial photography. Apparently, she has a way with a camera. Also, she told me that Rose from the dress shop is quite the local busybody, always nosing into other people's business. Oh, and she said that her son, Oisin, could have done much better than her daughter-in-law, Saoirse."

Having met and been rebuked by Saoirse a few times myself, I wouldn't disagree with Mary's assessment. But the mention of Oisin's name brings another thought to mind. "Have you talked to Jamie today? He sent me a text sayin' he was supposed to be meetin' with Oisin this mornin'."

Deirdre nods. "So he is. He called about an hour ago saying he was on his way to Inbetween to look at some security footage."

Out of the corner of my eye, I catch Audrey glancing at her phone and smiling. Then she tucks the phone into her purse and rests a hand on my shoulder. "Well, we best be off if we want to make it to the funeral on time. Thank you for the marvelous scones, Deirdre. You've outdone yourself."

Deirdre reddens with pride. "Not at all. They're just something I whipped up quickly. I need to be off myself. Mary invited me back to try out some new savory recipes."

While I am a little disappointed Deirdre didn't get any useful information out of Mary, it can't hurt that the two women are spending more time together. It might help soften Mary up if I need to speak with her again.

Based on the conversation I'd overheard between Mary and Domhnell and the suspicions I have about them planting bones on Donnelly's construction site, I imagine I will need to talk to Mary again.

And soon.

CHAPTER 35

*A*s the last notes of the organ's dirge echo off the lofty arches of Saint Fin Barre's Cathedral, I feel a strange combination of awe and unease.

I haven't spent a lot of time in churches. Sure, my grandma used to take me to services when I was little, but back home in Alabama, the Baptist church we went to also doubled as the senior's bingo hall. The only thing there capable of taking your breath away was the smell of mothballs and Vick's VapoRub.

This church, on the other hand, can only be described as magnificent...and a little creepy.

Brightly colored saints stare down in judgment from the soaring ceiling, while the mosaic floor dances with multicolored bursts of light cast by sunlight filtering through the enormous stained-glass windows.

I shift on the hard wooden pew, trying not to choke on the cloying aroma of incense as the priest walks past, swinging a thurible. Behind him, pallbearers carry Donnelly's coffin out of the cathedral toward the waiting hearse. Aoife, dressed in a designer black sheath dress that clings to her baby bulge, follows the procession. She wears a look of calm resolve under the veil of her stylish hat.

It's the first glimpse I've had of her today. Audrey and I had struggled to find parking near the cathedral, so we'd arrived just as the service was getting underway. We sat in the back, where we practically needed binoculars to see the other end of the church.

Around me, mourners start to rise and move into the aisles. Before Audrey and I make our exit, there's one thing I just have to ask her.

"Hey, do you see that thing hanging from the wall above the altar? Is that a cannonball?"

Without even glancing in the direction my finger is pointing, she says, "It is, of course. That cannonball was fired at the church during the siege of Cork in 1690. The church has been rebuilt since. But it's important to keep the old history alive."

I don't bother mentioning that the projectile is older than the whole United States of America. I know it's what Audrey is already thinking.

Outside, surrounded by a massive crowd of mourners, I finally feel like I can breathe again.

I recognize a few of the people milling about. Donnelly's lawyer stands beside the hearse, speaking with a man I assume is the funeral director. Deborah and her sister, Caitlin, are off to my left, accepting condolences from an older couple. Detective Mulhaney has also made an appearance, though he is standing off to the side and doing his best to remain inconspicuous.

There are even a couple of faces I know from the newspapers, the main one being Eoghan Gallagher. He's the elected head of the Irish Republic's government, what the Irish call the taoiseach. Not surprisingly, he's flanked by a small group of burly men with earpieces. Donnelly had friends in very high places, indeed.

The one person I don't see is Aoife.

Audrey, as if reading my thoughts, points out another person absent from the crowd. "Deirdre was right about Ayleen not coming to the funeral. But I suppose that's to be expected from the ex-wife. Either way, we should go pay our respects to Deborah and Caitlin before we head off."

Though the public was welcome to attend the funeral, the burial is for immediate family only. Not that I mind skipping it. It's already approaching noon, and I'm anxious to speak to Domhnell at the museum in Inbetween.

"I'm ready whenever—" I pause, taking stock of the items I brought to the church. "Oh, shoot! I left my purse under the pew. Hang on a minute. I'll just run in and grab it."

"No bother. But don't dawdle," Audrey instructs. "The day's not getting any younger."

As if I would want to linger alone in the big, empty church.

Quickly climbing the steps that lead back into the church, I head for the pew where Audrey and I had been sitting. It only takes me a minute to locate my forgotten purse. I'm about to exit the church when I hear the whisper of voices coming from a chapel tucked off to the side of the altar. I can't hear what's being said. The people speaking are too far away. But I can tell from the tone of their voices that they're arguing.

Curious to see who's fighting in a church after a funeral, I tiptoe toward the side wall. I won't be any closer to the sparring couple, but I will have a better line of sight to witness their altercation.

Hiding behind a large stone pillar, I peek out and nearly gasp when I see a stoic Aoife standing rigidly in front of a man leaning forward from the waist, gesturing toward her with clasped hands. He looks like he's pleading with her.

I squint my eyes to get a better look at the man. Is that Aidan? The archaeologist from Inbetween? What is he doing here? And why does Aoife look furious with him?

She raises her arm and points toward the door as if telling him to get lost.

Not wanting them to catch me spying, I race to the exit and allow myself to be swallowed up by the large group of Donnelly's grieving friends outside.

It doesn't take me long to spot Audrey, a look of sympathy on her face as she chats with Deborah and Caitlin. I make my way over to them.

"Thank you again for coming," Caitlin is saying to Audrey. "It means a lot to us."

'Don't mention it," Audrey replies. "I suppose you'll be heading off to the graveyard soon. We don't want to keep you."

Caitlin rolls her eyes. "We will be whenever we can find Aoife. Unfortunately, we can't leave without her."

Deborah frowns. "Where is she, anyway? I haven't seen her since the service ended."

I clear my throat. "She's inside the church. I saw her talkin' to Aidan."

"Aidan?" Audrey's eyes widen. "The archaeologist from Inbetween? I didn't realize he and Aoife were acquainted."

"Sure, we all went to school together," Deborah informs us. "They were friends long before I met either of them."

"You don't say? Well, he's a good friend to be here for the both of you in these dark times." Audrey's words sound genuine, but I can tell she's as surprised as I am by the connection.

"I should probably go inside and hurry her along," Deborah tells us. "If you'll excuse me?"

"Of course, my dear. We'll leave you to it," Audrey says. "And, again, you have our deepest condolences on your loss."

Moments later, as Audrey and I emerge from the throng, she has some questions for me. "Are you going to tell me what you saw inside? I can tell something's on your mind."

Before I can answer her, Detective Mulhaney steps in front of us, blocking our path.

"What now?" I demand. "Are you gonna threaten to arrest us again?"

"Don't tempt me," he fires back. "For your information, I was stopping you to let you know that we have officially cleared your father in Donnelly's murder."

Audrey blows out a deep, relieved breath, then quickly regathers her composure. "It's about time, too. Will you be releasing him today, so?"

"Ultimately, that's up to the hospital…and yourselves," he says cryptically.

I'm in no mood to puzzle out his ciphers. "Up to us? What'd you mean?"

"Surely it's crossed your mind that whoever killed O'Toole is still out there," his tone borders on condescending. "And we have no idea if Ian is still in any danger. I'm merely proposing to you that he might be safer in the hospital than he would be at home."

"Sure, anyone can walk straight into the hospital," Audrey argues. "How's he any safer there?"

"With your permission, we'd be happy to put a guard at his door to make sure he's safe," Detective Mulhaney offers.

This is probably the first time I've thought of Mulhaney as a good cop. "You'd be willin' to do that?"

"Without hesitation. After all, we're here to protect and serve," he actually smiles as he says it. A slightly self-deprecating smile.

I'm tempted to smile back, but I don't. "I'm okay with it if you think that's what's best."

He opens his mouth to answer, but his phone begins to chirp. He pulls his cell out of his pocket and reads the newly arrived text message. He stares down at the phone, a frown creasing his brows.

"I'm sorry. I have to go," he finally says.

"Has there been a break in the case?" Audrey asks.

"Maybe," he admits. "But I can't be sure. As for your father, try not to worry. I'll arrange for a guard at the hospital right away. But I do have to leave. Have a nice day, ladies."

As his long strides carry him away, I want to chase after him to see what he's learned. But Audrey's hand on my arm stops me.

"Come on, so. We have our own inquiries to make," she reminds me.

She's right. Whatever lead Mulhaney is chasing, I'm convinced it's somehow connected to the bones found at the construction site.

And to get to the bottom of that mystery, we can't waste time in Cork. We have to go back to the scene of the crime.

CHAPTER 36

The little brass bell above the door jangles as Audrey and I enter the museum early that afternoon. I glance to my left, expecting to find Domhnell seated behind the desk where I first saw him yesterday.

But he's not there. And, wherever he is, he doesn't seem to have heard the bell.

Sensing an opportunity, I whisper to Audrey, "The bones I was talkin' about are over there. Let me show you."

She follows me past a row of meticulously curated glass cases to the countertop display in the center of the room. Audrey stares down at the ancient remains while I keep watch for Domhnell. Out of the corner of my eye, I see her lean closer, her breath fogging up the glass as she peers at the yellowed skeleton.

After a few moments pass, she asks, "Sorry, dear. What am I supposed to be looking at?"

Nervous that Domhnell could appear at any moment, I murmur impatiently, "What? Don't you see all the mud on the bones?"

"Not really," she replies. "They look pretty clean to me."

"Maybe if you put on your glasses—"

"I don't need glasses," she cuts me off angrily. "There's nothing wrong with my eyes. Sure, they get tired sometimes when I'm reading. But that happens to everyone."

"Of course it does," I try to keep a neutral tone, so she doesn't think I'm being a smartarse. "Any chance your eyes are tired right now?"

Audrey straightens her spine so we're at eye level when she glares at me. "No, they are not! Why don't you take a look for yourself? Sure, you can tell me what my blind eyes aren't seeing."

Sighing deeply to ensure my frustration has been effectively communicated, I turn to inspect the bones. It only takes me a second to realize something is very wrong. The mud I'd seen on them yesterday is gone. Domhnell must have cleaned them after I left!

"Can I help you ladies?" A raspy male voice asks.

Audrey and I had been so focused on the mudless bones neither of us noticed Domhnell entering the room. Once we're facing him, a look of recognition dawns on his face.

"I know you," he points a long finger at me. "You're the American that was in here yesterday. I'm pleased you fancied the museum enough to return for a second visit. And I see you brought a friend."

There's a smile on his face, but I detect a hint of wariness in his demeanor.

Since he caught us staring at the skeletal remains, it hardly seems worth the effort to try beating around the bush. "What'd you do to 'em?"

"What did I do to what?" he asks with a straight face, but his lack of confusion convinces me he knows exactly what I'm talking about.

"The bones I was askin' you about yesterday," I tell him, even though I know that he knows that I know he's being evasive. "You've gone and cleaned all the dirt off 'em."

He tries to chuckle, but it sounds more like the croak of a startled frog. "The cleaners were in last night. Sure, you've no idea the amount of dust that gets into these display cabinets."

"If that was dust, I'm a pig in a prom dress!" I exclaim.

Audrey rests a calming hand on my arm before addressing the museum's curator. "You're called Domhnell, yes?"

His eyes swing wildly between Audrey and me. "So I am. Who's asking?"

"My name's Audrey Murphy. You wouldn't know me, but I'm guessing you know of my brother, Ian. He was arrested for the murder of Kevin Donnelly."

Domhnell's Adam's apple bobs frantically as he swallows.

"Sure, I know he's innocent," Audrey continues. "But that leaves the question of who did kill Donnelly. God rest him. And we happened to hear the strangest rumor that, right before he died, Donnelly stumbled upon some old bones out at the construction site."

Suddenly pale-faced, Domhnell quickly replies, "I wouldn't know anything about that."

"Is that so?" Audrey asks, taking a step in Domhnell's direction. "It's only that those bones have now gone missing. They just vanished into thin air. Poof! But then, my niece comes into your museum and sees an old skeleton covered in mud. A day later, we return and the bones are polished shinier than an Army sergeant's dress shoes. Do you not see how that might seem a tad suspicious?"

"It was only dust," Domhnell tries to convince us, but the inflection at the end of his sentence makes it come off as more of a question than a statement of fact.

"Even so, I hope you understand why we have to inform the Guards about this," Audrey gently threatens. "We were hoping we could resolve this amongst ourselves, like. But if you aren't able to tell us what happened, we'll have to find someone who can."

"Ye can't go to the Guards!" Domhnell begins to panic. "You've got nothing on me."

"We have a witness who saw you carryin' a big bag out of the museum late at night a few days before the murder," I interject. I don't mention Mary's possible involvement. Not yet. I get the sense he'll be more prone to confess if he thinks he's keeping his lady friend out of trouble.

"Who told you—" he abruptly shuts his mouth, but it's too late. His whole body seems to shrink in defeat.

Audrey walks over to Domhnell and puts a hand on his shoulder.

"You planted those bones at the construction site to stop the shopping mall from being built, didn't you?"

With his eyes on the ground, Domhnell slowly nods.

"But then Donnelly tried to cover up the discovery," Audrey continues, her voice soft. "He was going to bury the bones under a layer of concrete, where they'd never be found again. You couldn't let that happen. You had no choice but to kill him."

For a man of his advanced years, he moves surprisingly quickly to shrug off Audrey's hand. There's a look of terror in his eyes. "No, no, no! I never killed anybody! Sure, I came up with the plan to plant the bones. But I never touched Donnelly. You have to believe me!"

"We want to believe you, Domhnell," Audrey insists. "If you tell us everything, we might be able to help you."

"How did the bones get back to the museum?" I ask the question that's been bugging me since last night. "Did you bring 'em back after the murder?"

He shakes his head. "There were too many guards around after your man was killed. I couldn't get anywhere near them."

Audrey's eyebrows draw together. "So, how did they get back here?"

"I can't rightly say." There's a puzzled look on Domhnell's face. "I came into the museum the day after the murder, and they were just sitting there by the back entrance. I don't know who put them there. Sure, I didn't know what to do, so I just brought them inside and put them back in the display case."

"Were you working with anyone else on this plan of yours?" Audrey asks him.

For the first time since confessing, Domhnell raises his eyes to meet Audrey's gaze. "Absolutely not. I planned the whole thing myself. No one helped me. I assume whoever it was just wanted to preserve the artifacts. A concerned citizen, like."

"Someone like Mary Hannigan?" I push. "That witness I mentioned earlier says they saw Mary with you that night, movin' the bones."

"I don't know who you've been talking to, but they're wrong. Dead wrong," he insists. His eyes plead with us to believe him. "I mean it. Mary had nothing to do with anything. I moved the bones. Just me. But that's all I did. I never killed anyone."

Even though he'd lied initially about the mud on the bones, I believe he is being truthful when he says he didn't kill Donnelly. While he may have been willing to go to extraordinary lengths to protect his community, I don't think his commitment went so far as to commit murder. Still, he is holding out on sharing Mary's involvement, most likely because he wants to protect her if he can.

But protect her from what? Does he suspect his girlfriend might be a murderer?

If he does, there's no way he's telling us.

Audrey seems to share my opinion that Domhnell has said all he's going to say. "We'll leave you be, so. The Guards will likely want a few words with you, but we'll do our best to help you if we can."

Domhnell, lost in his own thoughts, doesn't seem to notice when Audrey and I leave. But as we step outside into the overcast afternoon, we hear the door to the museum lock behind us.

Once we're back in the privacy of my car, I say, "We should probably get over to Mary's café. Domhnell is probably callin' to warn her as we speak."

Audrey reaches for her seatbelt. "I agree. Let's go. Deirdre is there with her. I hope to God we haven't put her in any danger."

Before I can start the car, I feel the phone buzz in my pocket. I go to check it and see I have ten missed calls from Deirdre's son, Jamie. And he's just texted me. It's a short message. All it says is: *Call me.*

Just then, an ambulance with its siren blaring speeds past us on the main road.

Audrey turns to me, concern in her hazel eyes. "Follow that ambulance."

CHAPTER 37

With my foot heavy on the gas pedal, I chase the ambulance through the village.

Audrey's head rotates as we fly past Hannigan's Hideaway Cafe. She's probably hoping to catch a glimpse of Deirdre inside with Mary, but the car is moving too fast.

Seconds later, we've passed all the shopfronts on the main street, and we're headed into the countryside. I'm starting to think we may have acted too hastily. After all, we have no idea where this emergency vehicle is going. The odds that it's related to Donnelly's murder are probably relatively low.

Audrey seems to be having the same misgivings. "Perhaps we should turn around. There's a good chance this has nothing at all to do with—"

Before she can finish her sentence, the ambulance swings wide into the other lane of traffic. I have to slam on the brakes to avoid crashing into the back bumper as it executes a quick turn into the driveway of The Spinning Wheel Pottery Studio.

Several other Garda vehicles litter the parking lot, abandoned like forgotten toys. Something big has happened here.

Is Martin the killer after all? Could I have been so wrong about him?

But as I wedge my car into an empty patch of gravel beside some hedges, I see Martin standing next to the sunshine-colored door of his sister's studio. All the blood seems to have drained out of his face, and the dirt on his cheeks is streaked with fresh tears.

"Look, there's Jamie," Audrey points to a spot near the back of the recently arrived ambulance. "Blimey, he's talking to Detective Mulhaney. One of us will have to create a distraction so we can get Jamie on his own to tell us what's what."

"Or I could just call Jamie and tell him we're here," I suggest.

"I suppose that would work too," she grudgingly agrees. "Well, what are you waiting for?"

"Alright, alright. I'm callin' already." I resist the urge to chuckle as I reach for my phone. Audrey does enjoy her spy games.

Jamie answers on the second ring. Through the windshield, I see him step away from Detective Mulhaney. "Savannah, I've been calling you all afternoon. There's been a development."

"At Mona's pottery studio?" I ask, watching his brows knit together in a frown.

"Now, how would you know that?" he asks.

I'm tempted to string him along a little longer, but Audrey waves her hand, silently telling me to get on with it.

"Audrey and I are in the parkin' lot," I tell him.

His eyes scan the lot, settling on my Honda CR-V. "Right. I'm on my way."

Jamie exchanges a few words with Detective Mulhaney, then stands aside as some EMTs wheel a gurney past him into the studio. Mulhaney follows the gurney inside while Jamie makes his way over to my car. He opens the back door and slides into the rear seat.

Audrey and I angle our bodies so we can see him better.

"One of these days, you are going to have to loop me in on who your sources are," Jamie says, only half-joking. "MI5's got nothing on the pair of ye."

I don't want to burst his bubble by revealing we're literal ambulance chasers. "What's the gurney for? Is Mona alright?"

Jamie shakes his head. "It's touch and go. She's been poisoned. Though we're not sure yet if it was self-inflicted."

"You think she might have done it herself?" Audrey asks. "Why would she do a thing like that?"

Jamie pauses, savoring the feeling of knowing more than we do for once. "Maybe she was worried we were on to her."

Nothing he could have said would have shocked me more. "On to her? For what?"

"I finally had a chance to look at that home security footage you were on at me about," Jamie tells us. "Oisin met with me in town earlier and showed it to me. The video clearly shows that Martin never left the house the morning of the murder, but Mona did. She left around four o'clock and didn't return until half six."

It doesn't take me long to work out the significance of the timing. "That's around the time my dad found Donnelly's body."

Audrey fixes her gaze on me, looking slightly disappointed. "All that time we spent thinking Martin might have killed Donnelly to get revenge for his cows, and we never even considered that his sister might have been involved."

She's not entirely accurate. There had been a brief period when I considered adding Mona to our suspect list, but she'd been so kind and maternal. Even now, I'm skeptical about the prospect of her being a murderer. "I don't know. It doesn't feel right. And, if we're thinkin' there's only one killer, what reason did she have to do away with Sergeant O'Toole?"

"Maybe she knew he'd taken a bribe from Donnelly to keep quiet about her brother's dead cows," Audrey suggests.

Something still doesn't sit right with me. "And what about O'Toole beatin' up my dad? How does that fit in?"

Jamie takes a minute to consider the question. "Maybe O'Toole saw her at the construction site on the morning of the murder, and he was demanding money in exchange for keeping his trap shut."

I look at the well-loved but weathered studio and the old box van parked closer to the main house. "Martin and Mona don't strike me as the kind of people that have a lot of money to throw around on bribes."

Audrey's joints creak as she swivels to face Jamie. "Tell me this, when Mona came back at half six, was she driving a car by any chance?"

Jamie seems confused by the question. "A car? Why would that matter?"

It hits me then why Audrey asked if Mona drove that morning. O'Toole had asked my dad if he'd seen a car. Not *his* car, just *a* car. "My dad said O'Toole was askin' about a car out at the construction site. It may have been Mona's."

Jamie shakes his head. "If she went to the construction site in a car it wasn't her own. Her old beater was parked beside the house all morning."

Audrey sinks into the passenger side bucket seat, deflated. I know how she feels. That's just one more piece of the puzzle that remains unresolved.

Movement outside the pottery studio catches my attention. I see Mona, strapped to the gurney with an oxygen mask covering most of her face, being wheeled to the ambulance. Martin tries to follow his sister, but Detective Mulhaney steps forward to block his path.

From the shelter of my car, we watch as the ambulance races out of the driveway in a storm of dust and gravel.

"Were you able to get anything out of Mona before ye called emergency services?" Audrey asks.

"Sadly, no," Jamie admits. "As soon as I saw the tape, I called the station to get ahold of Mulhaney. They told him to meet me out here."

That explains the text message the detective received when we were chatting with him outside the funeral. He'd only left Cork a few minutes before we did. He must have come to talk to Mona while Audrey and I were with Domhnell at the museum.

"Mona didn't answer the door when we knocked, so we went around the side of the building," Jamie continues, pointing at the tree lined edge of the property. "Through the windows, we saw her lying on the floor of her studio, unconscious. Luckily, the back door was open, so we were able to get to her real quick, like."

"And Martin?" I ask, keeping an eye on Mona's brother who is currently being led into the studio by Detective Mulhaney. "Was he able to tell you anythin'?"

Jamie shakes his head, his short blond curls flopping. "Nothing yet. But Detective Mulhaney planned on interviewing him right after Mona was taken off to hospital."

Audrey opens the passenger door. "Well, what are the two of ye waiting for, an invitation? We've got to hear what Martin has to say for his sister."

Jamie sighs deeply and I can easily read his thoughts. He knows he's not, technically, allowed to let us on site for an official police interrogation. He also knows there's not a darn thing he can do to stop us.

Shooting him a sympathetic smile, I open my own door and quickly climb out of the car.

Whatever Martin has to say could be the key to finding the killer. I just hope, this time, he doesn't try to blame fairies for all that's going deadly wrong in Inbetween.

CHAPTER 38

"There's no point taking a turn around the maypole, Martin. Your sister could be in a lot of trouble," Detective Mulhaney warns the frightened-looking farmer. "The quicker you talk, the better your chances of not spending the night behind bars."

I roll my eyes in disgust. Detective Mulhaney could be such an attractive man. If only he didn't threaten to imprison someone every time he opened his mouth.

Jamie had followed Detective Mulhaney and Martin into Mona's studio, but not before telling Audrey and me that we needed to stay out of sight. So we're hiding from view, snug against the doorframe that separates the front room from the main studio. They can't see us, but thanks to a compact mirror Audrey had in her purse, we do have eyes on them.

Through the looking glass, I watch Martin's eyes grow wide. "M-m-m-me? Behind bars? But I didn't do anything!"

"You could be aiding and abetting, for all I know," Detective Mulhaney says, shifting his perch on a workbench. "Just tell me where your sister was the morning of Donnelly's murder."

"Sure, I didn't even realize she'd left the house. Not until—" Martin abruptly shuts his mouth.

Detective Mulhaney leans forward, resting his elbows on the worktop. "Until what?"

"Mona would never kill anybody," Martin babbles in a shaky voice. "She's just not that sort of person."

"I'm not asking you to be a character witness, Martin. I just need to know where your sister went when she left the house early Tuesday morning."

Martin buries his face in his hands, clearly torn. A moment later, his hands fall to his lap, and he exhales deeply. "This is all my fault. If only I hadn't told those two nosey women about the security tape, none of this would be happening."

"So you *do* know what was on the tape?" Detective Mulhaney presses him.

"Sure, I had no idea. Not until I told Mona that I'd mentioned it to those two women who cornered me out at the chicken coop. They were fierce pushy, so they were."

I can feel my face heating up. Beside me, Audrey seems completely unfazed.

"I know the women you're talking about. And I can understand how they would do your head in," Detective Mulhaney commiserates. "So what happened when you told Mona that the two women knew about the tape?"

"She got real upset, like. She said you'd probably lock her up, and she wouldn't even be able to say anything in her own defense," Martin says.

"Why wouldn't she be able to defend herself?"

"She didn't want to land anyone else in hot water, now did she?"

Detective Mulhaney frowns. "Why would anyone else get in trouble because Mona went out on the morning of the murder?"

"Sure, she wasn't alone in the planning, was she?" Martin doesn't wait for an answer. "She only went to take pictures of Donnelly burying the bones out at the construction site. And she only did that because they asked her to."

"What bones? Is there another body, Martin?" Detective

Mulhaney's voice sounds tense and urgent. "Did Mona and her accomplices kill someone else?"

"Oh, for goodness' sake. We'll be here all day if we leave this to the detective." Audrey snaps her compact mirror shut and breezes into the studio.

Martin rises from his seat when he sees Audrey. "You again."

"What in the—" Detective Mulhaney also stands, glancing from me to Audrey with a look of growing annoyance.

My eyes meet Jamie's. He shakes his head, letting me know he's not getting involved.

"Yes, it's the two nosey women again," Audrey says. "Come here to me, Martin. We know Domhnell tried to stop the mall construction by planting bones from the museum out at the site. He's already told us as much."

Detective Mulhaney rounds on me. "You didn't bother to tell me about any of this?"

If he weren't being so obnoxious, I might feel intimidated. "Cool your jets. We only just found out before comin' over here. I woulda told you." Eventually.

"You say your sister was going to take pictures of Donnelly burying the bones," Audrey continues, ignoring me and the detective. "Who asked her to do that? Was it Domhnell?"

Martin looks to Detective Mulhaney, who shrugs his shoulders and says, "You might as well answer. Sure, they won't stop asking until you do."

Out of the corner of my eye, I see Jamie struggling to stifle a smile.

"No, Domhnell didn't ask her," Martin tells us. "Mary did."

"Mary from the cafe?" I ask.

"That's the one," Martin confirms. "Mona said that Mary and Domhnell cooked up the plan, but it backfired when Donnelly didn't report finding the bones. They knew Mona was good with a camera, so they asked her to do them a favor, like. One that could help save this community. It was just supposed to be a quick morning jog to take a few pictures. That was it."

"And after Donnelly poisoned your cows and drove you off your land, Mona was probably only too happy to catch him committing a crime. Even if it was only an archaeological one," Audrey reasons.

"So Mona *was* out at the construction site when Donnelly was murdered?" Detective Mulhaney brings us all back to the point.

"She didn't kill him if that's what you're getting at," Martin promptly clarifies.

Detective Mulhaney doesn't look convinced but seems content to play along. "Did she, by any chance, see who did?"

Martin shakes his head. "No. She said she saw Donnelly. She watched him get on the excavator and dig a hole, but then she heard movement out on the road and got spooked. Worried that someone was on to her, like."

Audrey cocks her head. "Was there someone else there?"

"Sure, I asked her that," Martin replies. "Mona, said I, if you saw someone, you need to tell me. Whoever it was could be the murderer. But she swore up and down she didn't see anyone. She heard what she thought was a car and cleared out of there as quick as she could. She even lost the lens cap for her camera. She was in such a state."

"Maybe it was Ian's car she heard?" Detective Mulhaney speculates.

"It couldn't have been. Not if Donnelly was still alive," I argue. "You've already cleared my dad of the murder, remember?"

"So I did." Detective Mulhaney sighs in frustration. "Right. Martin, I'm going to need to see your sister's camera. Maybe there's something in one of her photographs that can enlighten us. Do you know where she keeps it?"

"I don't. But I'm sure I can find it," Martin promises.

"Be quick about it. I'll leave a Guard here with you while you're searching," Detective Mulhaney tells Martin. "Once you find it, the Guard will drop the camera off to me and then take you to the hospital so you can check in on your sister."

Martin nods, tears welling in his eyes at the mention of Mona. "She wouldn't do it, you know. Try to kill herself. Not even if she thought she was going to be arrested for murder."

"That would mean someone wants your sister dead," Audrey

chimes in. "She might not have seen anyone that morning, but that doesn't mean they didn't see her."

Detective Mulhaney turns away from Martin to face Audrey and me. "I don't suppose I can convince the pair of ye to go home and leave this to me?"

Audrey plants her hands on her hips. "I think we all know that's not happening. And besides, if Mary's involved in all of this, I need to make sure Deirdre's okay. She's with Mary at the cafe as we speak."

"Now, who's Deirdre?" Detective Mulhaney doesn't even try to keep the exasperation out of his voice.

"That'd be my mother, sir," Jamie interjects. "She's been trying to get close to Mary. You see, Savannah overheard Mary talking about committing some kind of crime. We thought Mary might let something slip to my mum while they were baking together."

Detective Mulhaney shakes his head, trying to make sense of everything he's hearing. "We? You're all in on this together? And why is your mum baking with a possible murder suspect?"

"I asked her to," Audrey volunteers. "She's my neighbor. We do each other favors from time to time."

"Lord, give me patience," Detective Mulhaney mutters. "I can't believe I'm saying this, but fine. Miss Marple and Nancy Drew, you go over to Mary's cafe. Boy Wonder, you're coming with me to pick up this Domhnell fellow from the museum. We'll all meet up at the cafe where, hopefully, we can make some sense of this daft business."

As soon as he finishes barking out his orders, Detective Mulhaney storms out of the room.

The rest of us quickly follow him outside. We all know time is of the essence.

There's a murderer on the loose who's showing no signs of stopping. We have to catch them before they have another opportunity to kill again.

CHAPTER 39

If looks were weapons, Mary would have already killed me.

When she saw me waltzing into her cafe with Audrey at my side, she'd instantly launched into a tirade about her right to refuse service to any low-life journalist she chose. Mary would probably still be raging if she hadn't threatened to call the guards on me.

At that, Audrey had told her not to worry. The guards were already on their way. And they wanted a word with Mary.

That silenced the cafe owner. But it hadn't stopped her from glaring at me as if I'd just gone number two in her latest batch of brownie batter.

So, it's a massive relief when Detective Mulhaney strides through the door with Jamie and a subdued-looking Domhnell in tow.

Mary breaks her one-sided staring contest when she sees her friend from the museum sporting a set of shiny handcuffs. All the blood seems to drain from her face.

"Good, we're all here." Detective Mulhaney strips off his trench coat and throws it over the back of an empty chair. "And we're not leaving until you all tell me what I need to know."

"Sure, I already told you. I'm the one you want," Domhnell says. "I won't let anyone else take the fall for what I've done."

"Shut your mouth, Domhnell," Mary hisses. "Say nothing."

"No, my lov—Mary. A man takes responsibility for his actions." Domhnell gives Mary a bittersweet smile. "It was me who planted the bones, detective. It was all my idea, so you might as well take me away now."

"All in good time." Detective Mulhaney circles Domhnell like a lion ready to pounce on a wounded gazelle. "First, I want you to describe to me how you killed Donnelly."

"I didn't—" Domhnell blurts, then quickly clams up. He looks at Mary with a question in his eyes. She shakes her head in return. His shoulders sag. "Fine. I hit him over the head, and then I ran over him with the excavator."

Mary shifts her considerable weight faster than I would have thought possible, flying to her feet. "Domhnell, no!"

Deirdre rests a calming hand on Mary's arm.

Detective Mulhaney ignores the outburst, keeping his focus on Domhnell. "Care to tell me why you killed him?"

"Sure, you already know," Domhnell replies. "Donnelly was going to destroy this town with his fancy, new shopping center. All the decent, hard-working shop owners who've been here for decades would have gone out of business. I couldn't let that happen."

"And that's why you killed him." Detective Mulhaney doesn't frame it as a question.

Domhnell swallows. "I mean, I didn't want to kill him. I'm not a murderer."

Detective Mulhaney tilts his head, a look of exaggerated confusion on his handsome face. "I thought you just told me you were a murderer."

"Well, yes. But no," Domhnell stammers. "I did try to resolve the situation without resorting to violence."

I shift uncomfortably in my seat, trying to figure out why Domhnell is lying. While I do believe he's guilty of trying to sabotage the plans to build a mall, I don't think for one second he would have had the nerve to actually kill Donnelly.

"But when your little plan with the bones didn't work, you decided

Donnelly needed to die." Detective Mulhaney takes a step closer to his prey. "So, you bashed in his skull with a hurling stick."

"Yes, just so," Domhnell confirms. "That's exactly what I did. I coshed him with a hurl."

Detective Mulhaney sighs. "Grand, so. There's just one thing. Donnelly wasn't killed with a hurl. The murderer—the real murderer—clocked him with a stone from the fairy fort."

I find myself grinning. It's inappropriate, I know. But I can't help but be impressed by how Detective Mulhaney tripped up the false confessor. Maybe, just maybe, I haven't been giving him enough credit.

Mary, still on her feet, begins to sway. Deirdre has to help her back into her seat to keep her from fainting.

Domhnell stands rigid, looking like he's about to cry. "I'm so sorry, Mary."

"Now, why would you be apologizing for *not* being a murderer?" Audrey wonders aloud. Then, realization dawns on her face. "Oh, I see. You confessed to protect Mary. You think she killed Donnelly."

"What?" Mary thunders.

"No, I never said that!" Domhnell exclaims.

"But did you think it?" Audrey asks.

Domhnell looks frantically from Audrey to Mary and back again. "I mean…"

"Domhnell!" Mary shouts. "How could you even think that? Sure, I thought I was protecting you!"

"Me?" he barks. "I could never kill anyone! And can you blame me for being a little suspicious? You wouldn't tell me where you were when Donnelly was killed, and I know you weren't home because I stopped by at six to bring you coffee."

'I was at Oisin's house, looking after his wee girl. She's been sick, and I was up half the night tending to her," Mary explains. "Saoirse was in another one of her moods and stormed out of the house. That's why I didn't want to say anything. I didn't want to embarrass Oisin."

Domhnell walks over to where Mary is sitting, drops down to his knees, and, still wearing handcuffs, awkwardly takes her hands in his.

"Oh, Mary. I wish you had told me. I've been going half mad worrying about you."

Mary clasps his hands tightly. "And I've been losing my mind thinking you might be carted off to jail any day. I can't imagine my life without you."

"I can't imagine mine without you, either," Domhnell gushes. "Mary, would you make me the happiest man alive and say you'll be my wife."

"Oh, Domhnell." A schoolgirl grin appears on Mary's rotund face. "Yes, yes, yes!"

"No, no, no!" Detective Mulhaney cries out. "I realize I'm ruining a moment here. But there's still the matter of a dead man who you both plotted to put out of business with your little scheme."

"Yes, we did do that." Domhnell's face is a mask of contrition. "But we didn't kill him. We just wanted to slow down construction so we had enough time to hire a proper lawyer. And Donnelly broke the law when he tried to hide evidence of an archaeological find. So, really, he's the one you should be going after."

Detective Mulhaney's face is red, and the veins in his neck are engorged. "He's dead!"

"Well, yes. There is that," Domhnell concedes.

Sensing the situation is rapidly sliding out of control, I decide to take the lead. "What about Mona? Did you ask her to go to the construction site on Tuesday mornin'?"

"Mona?" Domhnell's smile fades. "She has nothing to do with any of this."

I struggle to rein in my impatience. "We already know she was involved. She told her brother about it all right before someone tried to poison her. So would you stop tryin' to protect people and just tell us what happened?"

"Mona's been poisoned?" Domhnell looks like he might be sick.

"Yeah, she has," I say. "So, let's try this again. Did you tell her to go out there?"

"No, that was her idea," Mary answers, looking slightly less annoyed with me now that she's engaged to be married. "After the bones were planted, Mona kept a lookout. She said she wanted to see the look on Donnelly's face when his dreams of a shopping center went up in smoke."

"Except Donnelly decided not to report finding them," Audrey interjects.

Mary nods. "Just so. Mona saw Donnelly put them in the boot of his car. And she knew he was going to try to cover the whole thing up. So she decided to try and catch him in the act, like."

"I need to ask you something, and I only want to have to ask once," Detective Mulhaney speaks through gritted teeth. "Did anyone else in town know about your plan? Because it seems to me the only reason Mona would be targeted is if someone knows she was at the construction site on Tuesday morning."

Mary and Domhnell exchange a look, but before they can say anything, the door to the cafe flies open, and a uniformed Garda officer walks in looking for Detective Mulhaney.

"Sir, I have that camera you were looking for."

CHAPTER 40

"Maybe try hitting that button there," I suggest.

"No, no. I think you're supposed to twist that knob at the top," Jamie corrects me.

"Are you sure the film doesn't need to be developed before you can look at the pictures?" Deirdre asks.

"Don't look at me." Audrey puts her hands in the air. "I have no idea how these fancy new cameras work."

After the uniformed guard handed Detective Mulhaney Mona's camera, we'd all circled around him, anxious to see what clues might be hidden on the device's memory card. The only problem is that it's a professional DSLR camera with more functions than a space shuttle control panel, and none of us could figure out how to use it.

Detective Mulhaney jerks the camera away from our prying eyes. "Would you all just back off for a minute so I can work this out?"

"Do you want me to call my son Oisin?" Mary offers. "He's good with the technology. I'm sure he can talk you through it."

"No, I don't need any help. I just need a little peace and quiet for *one* minute," Detective Mulhaney shouts. I get the sense he doesn't like being unable to do anything.

He turns his back to us, and we all fall silent. We remain utterly

CURSED GROUND

still, afraid any movement might risk his ire or, worse, further delay getting a glimpse of what's on that camera.

"Alright, I think I've got it working again," Detective Mulhaney says as if the issue was with the camera and not our operation of it. "Yep, here we go. There's Donnelly walking toward the excavator."

I rush to Detective Mulhaney's side, jostling with Audrey, Deirdre, and Jamie for the best position. Domhnell and Mary hang back, holding hands and waiting for us to tell them if Mona caught the killer with her camera.

It feels wrong to be so eager to look at images of a dead man in the final moments of his life. But we're not focused on Donnelly. We want to see if we can spot who killed him so we can stop them from killing anyone else.

"Can you make the pictures any bigger? I can't make out a thing," Audrey complains.

"Are your eyes tired again?" I tease her.

"That's enough out of you," she grumbles. "I don't need glasses. That screen's too small, and I'm too far away. Just tell me what I'm looking at."

"Donnelly is moving to his car," Deirdre, who is wearing glasses, tells Audrey.

Jamie points to the next photo in the sequence. "Look, he's getting the bones out of the boot of his car. That confirms what Mona told Martin, at least."

"And there he is, puttin' the bones in the hole he dug," I say, mainly for Audrey's sake so she knows what's happening.

Detective Mulhaney flips to the next image and those of us who can see lean in closer, squinting our eyes.

"Well, what are you all looking at?" Audrey demands.

"Sure, I have no idea," Deirdre says. "Can anyone else tell what we're looking at?"

Nobody answers right away for the simple reason that none of us knows. It just looks like a blurry picture of blades of grass shot at ground level. But why would Mona have taken this particular shot? Is

205

there something she wanted to record that we just can't see because the LCD screen is too small?

"Can you zoom in at all?" Jamie asks Mulhaney.

"Give me a second. I think I can with this little dial over here." Detective Mulhaney turns the dial, and the blades of grass grow before our eyes. "I still don't see anything useful."

"Wait a minute," a thought occurs to me. "Didn't Martin say Mona lost the lens cap?"

Audrey nods. "That does sound familiar."

"What if she dropped the camera after she heard the car out on the road?" I pose the question. "Maybe when she went to pick it up, her finger slipped, and she accidentally took this picture."

Detective Mulhaney glances at me in a way that makes me think he might be impressed by my reasoning. "That's as good a theory as any."

"Skip to the next picture, so," Audrey orders, drawing a look of warning from the detective, which she ignores. "Well, what do you see?"

It's another blurry picture, probably taken by accident, as Mona was frantically trying to escape after being spooked by a noise on the road. On the far righthand side of the image, Donnelly wields a shovel as he attempts to bury the bones. But it's what's in the left corner of the picture that draws my attention.

Pointing with my finger, I ask, "Can you zoom in there?"

Detective Mulhaney obliges, and a car comes into focus. A man dressed all in black is standing beside the open driver's side door.

"Now, who is that?" Deirdre wonders aloud.

I lean in closer, catching a hint of Detective Mulhaney's sandalwood-scented aftershave. "That's Aidan Boyle."

"The council archaeologist? Are you sure?" Detective Mulhaney asks before handing the camera to Jamie and wheeling around to look at Domhnell and Mary. "Do you two know anything about this?"

"Of course not!" Mary exclaims.

Detective Mulhaney seems skeptical. "Was he involved in your plot to stop the construction?"

Mary isn't as quick to deny this latest allegation.

In the end, it's Domhnell who responds. "Aidan came to me for advice after Donnelly skirted the council and illegally got the fairy fort relocated. He was furious, saying people like Donnelly were destroying our national heritage. We seemed to be of a like mind, so I told him about our plan."

"What part did he play in your little scheme?"

Mary sighs. "He volunteered to plant the bones at the construction site. Sure, Domhnell and I aren't as nimble as we used to be. And, in his professional capacity, Aidan had every right to be nosing around at the construction site. So, it would be easy to explain away if he'd been caught. So, we took him up on his offer."

"And when you just confessed to the plot? Why didn't you say anythin' about Aidan then?" I ask. I can understand why Domhnell and Mary want to protect each other, but why are they loyal to Aidan? "Has he threatened you?"

Domhnell glances at Mary before speaking. "Not in so many words. But he made it pretty clear he wanted us to stay quiet about his role in our little partnership."

Detective Mulhaney stares at the pair with ice in his eyes. "You do realize Mona might die because you chose to say nothing."

Mary's eyes grow wide. "You don't think Aidan had anything to do with Mona being poisoned, do you?"

"Did you happen to mention to him that Mona was out at the construction site that morning taking pictures?" Audrey asks, searching for the connection.

Mary and Domhnell's guilty silence answers for them.

"Detective?" Jamie's voice cuts through the quiet. "I think there was someone with Aidan in the car."

"What?" Detective Mulhaney looks down at the screen as Jamie holds the camera out to him. "Is that a woman?"

I move in for a closer look at the pixelated screen. "It sure looks like it. But I can't make out who it is."

"Do you have any idea who that woman might be?" Detective

Mulhaney demands of Mary and Domhnell. "Did anyone else know about your plan?"

"No," Mary emphatically states. "We've told you everything we know."

"Are you sure now this time?" Detective Mulhaney presses.

Domhnell has the good sense to look chastened rather than offended. "We're sure. Only myself, Mary, Mona, and Aidan were in on the plan. You have my word."

"I suppose that'll have to do. For now." Detective Mulhaney reaches for his coat on the back of the chair. "Right, I think it's high time we had a wee word with Aidan Boyle. Jamie, you're coming with me. The rest of ye, return to your homes and we'll be in touch."

I take a step toward Detective Mulhaney. "But—"

"Go home," he orders me before turning on his heels and striding out of the cafe.

CHAPTER 41

"Well, that's a fine how do you do," Audrey gripes from the passenger seat of my car as we travel back to Ballygoseir. "We practically cracked the case for that detective and how does he thank us? By sending us on home like errant schoolchildren."

Though I, too, feel the sting of Detective Mulhaney's casual dismissal, I'm somewhat relieved. I've faced off against more than my fair share of psychopaths in the past few months. As far as I'm concerned, let someone else catch the killer for once.

Met with my silence, Audrey continues to think aloud. "But sure, arresting Aidan is only the half of it. Someone else was with him in that car. At the funeral, didn't Deborah say that Aidan and Aoife had been thick as thieves in their university days?"

"Yeah," I concede. "But Aidan is Deborah's friend, too. She could just as easily be the woman in Mona's photo."

In my peripheral vision, I can see the whites of Audrey's eyes as she rolls them. "Would you ever ease up on poor Deborah? She can't have had an easy time of things at home, not after being the one to bring the cuckoo into the nest."

I assume she's referring to Aoife. "That's exactly why it was probably Deborah. Especially if she knew her dad was thinkin' about changin' his will. Can you imagine how much worse it woulda been for her if he'd left everythin' to Aoife?"

"Deborah wouldn't have been as bothered about all of that as her mother, Ayleen, would have been," Audrey says. "Come to think of it, Ayleen probably would have known Aidan, seeing as how he's Deborah's friend. Maybe we should consider the possibility it was Ayleen in the car."

I'm not sure whether she genuinely suspects Ayleen or if this is just another attempt to divert my attention away from Deborah.

"It wasn't Ayleen who was lurkin' around in the hallway after someone broke into Donnelly's study," I remind Audrey of the encounter at Donnelly's wake. "And remember, Aidan appeared just seconds after we bumped into Deborah."

Audrey waves off the insinuation. "Sure, that hallway had the nearest toilet to the front room. It's no surprise people were wandering about."

"And Deborah's sudden interest in our investigation?" I press. "You can't tell me it wasn't odd that she just showed up at your door all of a sudden wantin' to help out."

"It was the poor girl's father that was killed," Audrey argues. "She just wanted our help finding answers, like."

I do my best to muzzle my frustration. "I don't mean no disrespect, Miss Audrey, but why're you refusin' even to consider that Deborah might be in cahoots with Aidan?"

"I'm telling you, Deborah's not the sort that would kill her own father. I'd bet my life on it," Audrey insists. "Why are you so unwilling to entertain the notion that Deborah is blameless in all of this? What did she do to make you dislike her so much?"

Audrey's words strike a nerve, prompting a painful bolt of self-realization. The problem isn't that I dislike Deborah. It's that I do like her. Under different circumstances, I think we could be friends. But I've been betrayed once by someone I thought was a friend, and I guess my subconscious isn't eager to repeat the experience.

I figure if I assume the worst, it won't hurt as much if I turn out to be right.

Rather than admit all this, I decide to tell a different truth. "I just want to catch whoever told Sergeant O'Toole to hurt my dad."

Audrey pats my knee under the steering wheel. "I know you do, dear. That's what I want, too."

I swallow a lump of emotion. "Alright. If not Deborah, who do you think was in the car with Aidan?"

"Maybe Aoife? She probably wasn't thrilled being hitched to a man twice her age," Audrey muses. "Sure, most wives have some form of buyer's remorse after tying the knot. And she'd have got more money if he was six feet under than in a messy divorce."

"Wouldn't she have at least held off until their baby was born?" I ask. "I mean, her little boy was the one that was gonna inherit the whole shebang."

"Perhaps she couldn't be bothered waiting. From what we know of Donnelly, he was the sort of man to make a saint toss off their halo and pick up a pint," Audrey points out.

"You're sayin' she killed him just 'cause she didn't like him anymore? As a motive, that's thinner than the gravy on a Yankee's biscuit."

Audrey holds up a finger as if to punctuate the point she's about to make. "It's never wise to underestimate the simmering resentment of a bored, rich housewife. Especially a young and beautiful one. Maybe she went looking for excitement elsewhere. Your man Aidan is handsome enough. His attention might have been too tempting to resist."

Having witnessed their clandestine meeting earlier in the day, I'm not convinced. "Naw. He might be into her, but Aoife wanted nothing to do with him. At the church today, she looked mad enough to rip his head clear off."

"Lovers often fight with a fierceness that puts enemies to shame," Audrey quips.

I shake my head, careful to keep my eyes focused on the road. "She wouldn't scheme to kill her husband to be with Aidan, then kick him to the curb. That doesn't make a lick of sense." The problem is nothing much does. "And why would either of 'em want to kill O'Toole? Or Mona?"

Audrey ponders the question as we drive past the crumbling ruins of Castle Doyle on the outskirts of Ballygoseir. "Remember the note you pulled out of the fire in Donnelly's office? It said, 'your car.' What if O'Toole saw Aidan's car at the construction site that morning and blackmailed him to keep it quiet?"

I can't deny the logic of her thinking. But it doesn't answer all of our questions. "And Mona? Only Mary and Domhnell knew she was goin' out to take pictures."

"Sure, you know yourself. Villages keep secrets about as well as a sieve holds water."

As we round the bay approaching Ballygoseir, the sun sets, painting the horizon with a dazzling display of vibrant pink and violet. Silhouettes of the fishing boats that dot the tranquil bay fade like ghostly apparitions into the gathering darkness.

I yawn, only just becoming aware of how exhausted I am from the day. "Well, none of it's our problem anymore. We proved my dad's not a murderer. Detective Mulhaney can handle it from here."

I can feel Audrey's eyes on me, but it's too dark in the car to read her expression. "You really aren't interested in finding Aidan's accomplice?"

"I'm too tired to be interested in much of anythin' at the moment," I admit before smiling and adding, "but try me again tomorrow after I've had some sleep."

Audrey smiles and nods as we pull up in front of her house. "I could do with a good night's sleep myself. Get some rest, dear. We'll chat in the morning."

"Good night, Miss Audrey."

I wait until she's safely inside her house before pulling onto the backroads that lead to Raven's Wing. Fergal has been alone in the cottage all day, which means he'll be bored, hungry, and in desperate need of a wee when I get home. I don't have the energy to take him walking in the woods tonight. He'll have to make do with a quick outdoor potty break before bed. He won't be impressed, but I'll take him out for hours tomorrow to make up for it.

All the windows are dark when I ease the car into my driveway. In the light of the high beams, I search the windows for Fergal's eager face. But he's nowhere to be seen. I've been frightfully neglectful of him lately. He might be punishing me.

I unfold my weary limbs from the car and walk quickly to the front door, drawing my coat closer around me against the cold. Unlocking the front door, I step inside and flick on the lights. Under my feet lies a pile of mail. On top is a letter from the Office of the Revenue Commissioners. An angry red stamp warns me that this is my final notice.

Groaning, I kneel to pick it up when, from the other room, I hear the sound of someone sneezing. Before I can turn my head to investigate the source of the sound, I hear footsteps rapidly approaching me.

Then something heavy collides with the back of my head, and I suddenly, blissfully, and terrifyingly lose consciousness.

CHAPTER 42

My head hurts. That's my first thought as the veil of unconsciousness begins to lift.

I try opening my eyes, but it feels like lead weights are attached to my lashes. When I'm finally able to crack them open a sliver, the overhead lights send shards of pain straight to my brain.

The living room of my cottage slowly comes into focus, with all its pleasant familiarity. Only now, there's nothing enjoyable or normal about being here. I'm sitting on a kitchen chair with my hands tied behind my back.

How did I get here?

I remember hearing a sneeze in the living room, then something heavy collided with the back of my head. After that, everything is a blank.

I'm alone, but I can hear people chatting in the kitchen.

I strain my ears to hear their voices. A man is speaking. His words freeze my blood.

"Why wouldn't you just let me kill her? Sure, there's no need to be dragging this out."

"We don't know what she's been telling other people, do we? That's why we're here. To stop her from sniffing around anymore," a woman says as if speaking to a toddler. "If you're right, and she's pinned the whole lot on Mona and her idiot brother, we know we're in the clear."

"But Mona's in hospital," the man, who I assume is Aidan, points out. "If your one here is murdered while Mona's laid up, they'll start looking for other suspects."

I hear the woman sigh. "We won't make it *look* like a murder, will we? She and her dog will just take a little fall off the cliff. A terrible accident, nothing more."

Fergal! What have these monsters done to my dog? If they've hurt him, they'll be the ones going over the cliff, not me.

Brave words, I know, for someone tied to a chair with what feels like Fergal's leash. I have to find a way to free myself before Aidan and the woman know I've woken up. Lifting my right shoulder, I try yanking my hand out of the noose on my wrist.

The rope doesn't budge, but my weight shifting causes the chair to squeak. I wince, hoping the couple in the other room didn't notice. No such luck.

"Did you hear that?" the woman asks.

Shoes clack against the tiled kitchen floor, and a woman appears in the doorway—a very pregnant woman.

Aoife! She is Aidan's accomplice.

I groan out loud. Not from the pain in my head, which is considerable, but because Audrey was right. I have been way too hard on Deborah.

"Well, well. Look who finally woke up," Aoife waddles into the living room, one hand under her baby bump as if trying to fight gravity.

"Where's Fergal?" I demand. "What have you done with him?"

Aoife raises one meticulously groomed eyebrow. "Your stupid dog? That's what you're worried about?"

"If you've hurt him, I'll—"

Before I can finish the sentence, Aidan flies across the room and gives me a smack upside the head.

"Don't you dare threaten my Aoife," he warns me.

Maybe they jiggled something loose in my brain when they clobbered me earlier because I don't feel scared even though I probably should. All I care about is that Fergal is alright. "Did you hurt my dog?"

"Good Lord, enough about the dog," Aoife complains in her smoother-than-honey voice. "Your mangy mongrel is fine. We just had to put him out the back. I'm horribly allergic to anything with fur."

"But don't you have your own dogs?" I ask, remembering the bang from upstairs the first time Audrey and I visited Aoife's house. Then it dawns on me, "That wasn't pets upstairs knockin' things over, was it?"

Aoife glares at Aidan. He responds defensively, "I already said I was sorry. Sure, you know yourself, the corner of that rug in your bedroom is always tripping me."

Her bedroom? It looks like Audrey was right about them being in a relationship, too.

"Oh, I get it," the realization hits me like a firecracker on the Fourth of July. "So, tell me. Did Donnelly know he wasn't your baby's father?"

Aoife's eyes flash like lightning in a winter storm, and she clutches her stomach protectively. "Has anyone ever told you it's rude to be so forward? But I suppose that cleverness of yours will be your undoing. Just as it was for my poor, late husband, he might still be alive—if only he hadn't insisted on getting a paternity test."

"Aoife!" Aidan cries out in alarm. "You can't be telling people that. Not if we want to collect on the inheritance."

Aoife hangs her head, slowly shaking it back and forth. "Aidan, what does it matter if she knows? It's not like she's going to live to tell anyone, now is she?"

"Oh, right," Aidan puffs his chest out. "And sure, I do like being able to admit that I'm going to be a father."

"I'm glad you're happy, sweetheart," Aoife appeases him like she might a child. "Now, do you mind if we get back to the matter at hand?"

I don't wait for Aidan to answer. There are a few things I want to know before they follow through on their threats to kill me. I also need to buy a little more time to try and loosen the knot on my wrist. "If you wanted to kill Donnelly, why didn't you just cut the brakes on his car or somethin'? Why run him over with an excavator?"

"We needed someone else to blame, obviously," Aoife seems offended that I hadn't worked it out. "So, when Aidan heard about the plot to plant old bones, it was like a godsend. There was no way my husband would let a few little bones stop his grand plans for a shopping center. We knew he would try to bury them when no one was around. All we needed was someone to take the fall for the murder."

"So you texted my dad to make sure he was there." It's not a question.

Aoife shrugs. "I mean, after breaking my husband's nose, you have to admit your dad was the perfect patsy."

"And sure, worst-case scenario, those idiots in the village are all so superstitious," Aidan contributes. "It wouldn't take much to convince them the fairies had killed him for moving their fort."

Aidan's not wrong. Some of the locals did believe the fairies had gotten their revenge on Donnelly.

"Sounds like you put a whole lotta thought into this," I say.

"I—we, me and Aidan, did. It was the perfect plan. All Sergeant O'Toole had to do was arrest your father as soon as he got out to the site," Aoife explains. "I knew O'Toole could be bought after the incident with Martin's cattle."

"So, Donnelly *did* poison the cows? And that's why O'Toole was blackmailin' him!" I exclaim. It's not much, especially considering the circumstances, but it is nice to know I was at least right about one thing.

"Well, of course," Aoife's nonchalance takes the wind out of my triumph. "O'Toole would sell his own soul for a payout. And he was greedy. We'd already settled on a price for his…shall we say, services. But he wanted more. He slipped a note through the door, saying your dad might have seen my car at the construction site that morning. He said he would deal with it—for a price."

That's why O'Toole beat up my dad—to try and squeeze more money out of Aoife.

"It was never going to stop," Aidan chimes in. "Sure, when we went to your man's house to have a little chat with him, he wanted even more money. I had no choice but to stab him."

"I just wish you hadn't stabbed him in the back," Aoife complains. "I barely had the strength to push him off when he started to fall on me."

"I did apologize for that," Aidan reminds Aoife. "And we were really hoping it would all end there. But before he died, O'Toole told us there was another potential witness running by the side of the road that morning."

"Mona," I say, fitting the pieces together. "That's why you got Deborah to bring me round your house. To blame Mona before she could point the finger at you. But then, why did you poison her? Were you hopin' we'd all assume she did it if she wasn't around to defend herself?"

Aoife glances at Aidan. His cheeks flush with color. "That's on me. When I heard that Mona was there that morning, I thought it best to silence her about anything she may have seen. Sure, I didn't know at the time that Aoife had her own plan for dealing with it."

The scene of them arguing in the church earlier today springs to mind. It's clear now they were fighting about Aidan's impulsive decision to try and kill Mona. That's why Aoife had seemed so angry.

All of the puzzle pieces are now in place, and the complete picture makes me realize the precariousness of my position. Aoife and Aidan were willing to kill three people to keep their homicidal secret. I highly doubt a sudden bout of conscience will prevent them from adding one more body—mine—to their tally.

I have to keep them talking.

"I hate to break it to you, but Detective Mulhaney already knows you were there when Donnelly died," I tell Aidan. "Mona got a picture of you when she was runnin' away."

Aidan's eyes widen slightly, but he otherwise remains stoic. "You're bluffing."

"Cross my heart and hope to die," I say, belatedly regretting my choice of words. "I mean, I don't want to die. I just meant I'm not lyin'. The guards are on to you. It's only a matter of time before they lock you up and throw away the key."

"No, no, no!" Aidan cries. "They can't have figured it out. We were so careful. Aoife, you said this plan would work. I can't go to prison! What would my mother tell the neighbors?"

Aoife ignores his outburst, taking a step toward me. "Do they know about me?"

"If that was you in the car with Aidan that morning, they'll know soon enough," I tell her. "We just couldn't see your face on that tiny little camera screen."

Aoife sucks in a lungful of air, then slowly blows it out. I can practically hear the malicious wheels of her warped mind spinning.

To my left, Aidan paces, muttering to himself about the injustice of being a suspect in the murders he just admitted to committing.

With her back to me, Aoife walks slowly to the fireplace.

"We're going to have to run, Aidan," she says calmly. "Our baby can't be born behind bars."

I see her bend at the waist, and for a minute, I wonder if she's going to be sick. Then she spins around, a poker in her hand and a wild look in her eyes.

"But first, we have one last loose end to clean up."

That's when the fear finally settles in. I'm about to die!

There's nothing left to do but scream.

CHAPTER 43

*A*oife strides toward me like a wild, pregnant banshee from the depths of hell.

But as she approaches, raising the poker above her head, something on the other side of the window catches her eye. She hesitates and halts her advance, squinting outside into the darkness.

"No, it can't be," she mutters, sidestepping me to creep closer to the window.

"What is it?" Aidan demands, joining Aoife near the window. "Is it the guards? Have they found us already?"

Eager to take advantage of their distraction, I twist in the chair, trying to loosen the rope around my wrists. I can feel it giving slightly. Fergal has a habit of chewing through his leashes. He's had this one for two weeks now, so there's probably already a tear in it somewhere. I just need to tug on the right spot.

As I work to free myself, my eyes remain glued on Aoife and Aidan.

"No. I thought I saw lights. Fairy lights." Aoife's voice sounds shaky. "I could have sworn they were headed this way."

"Come here to me, Aoife. Neither of us believes in fairies. Do we?"

Aidan doesn't seem entirely clear about where he should stand on the issue. "And why would the fairies be coming for us, anyway?"

"Have you forgotten that you insisted on using one of the stones from the fort to bash my late husband's head in," she reminds him, caught somewhere between fear and blame. "You called it the perfect symmetry—that moving a historical site would be the thing that killed him. But I warned you, it's never wise to mess with the fairy folk."

Aidan wraps his arm around Aoife's shoulder. "There's nothing out there, Aoife. Are you sure it wasn't just your imagination? What with the baby and all the murdering, you've been under a lot of stress lately, sweetheart."

"Go away. It was not my imagination!" Aoife shrugs off his embrace. "There was something out there. I swear it."

As they chat, my fingers search the rope, finally landing on a frayed section. My heart pounds with anticipation as I grip the leash and jerk my arms apart. The leash snaps in half with a satisfying little rip. I'm free!

Now, what do I do?

Looking around, I don't see anything within reach that would act as a weapon against two people intent on killing me. Even if one of them is eight and a half months pregnant.

"There!" Aoife cries out suddenly, making me jump. Her free hand, the one not gripping the poker, wraps around Aidan's arm, squeezing so hard her fingers turn white. "Just under the windowsill. There's something there."

"I don't see anything," Aidan tries to reassure her. His face hovers so close to the window his breath starts to fog the glass. "There's nothing—"

Just then, Fergal's face appears out of nowhere. His paws land hard on the other side of the glass above the windowsill flower box. A string of solar-powered lights my father had recently strung around the back patio hang from Fergal's mouth.

Aoife lets out a shrill shriek and stumbles backward. The poker falls from her hand, and she bends forward, her fingers digging into her thighs. For a second, I think she might be having a heart attack.

What happens is actually far worse. Her water breaks all over my living room floor.

"Aoife!" Aidan rushes to her side. "Are you having the baby?"

"No, Aidan. I just took a wee all over the floor for no reason," she replies through clenched teeth. "Of course, I'm having the baby!"

"Oh, Good Lord. This is really happening." Aidan runs his hands through his hair. "What do I do? Tell me what to do!"

"How would I know?" she screams. "I've never done this before! Owwww!"

Aoife sinks to the floor, and Aidan kneels beside her.

My first inclination is to want to help in some way. Then, I remember that not two minutes ago, Aoife was prepared to bash my brains in. I think, in this instance, the standard social niceties can be ignored.

My mind jumps to planning my escape.

They're so caught up in the imminent birth of their child that they seem to have completely forgotten that I'm in the room. Of course, that would probably change if they noticed me fleeing. They just confessed to multiple murders. They can't let me walk out the door. And Aoife's labor could take a while. She'd probably have plenty of time to kill me between contractions.

The poker is on the floor near Aidan's feet. If I could just get to that, at least I'd have some kind of weapon to defend myself if they came after me.

"Why is this so painful?" Aoife wails. "Aidan, I'm never letting you touch me again!"

I shift forward in the seat in preparation to stand. Just that slight movement sends my head spinning. I probably have a concussion. If I try to stand up, the motion could knock me out again, making me an even easier target. But what choice do I have?

Using my arms to propel my body off the chair, I launch myself toward the poker lying on the floor as Aoife lets out an ear-splitting scream.

Aidan covers his ears and turns away from Aoife. Surprised that I'm no longer tied to the chair, he watches as my fingers close around the shaft of the poker. He scrambles to snatch it away from me before I can get a proper grip.

If it comes to a contest of strength, I know Aidan will win. Not only will he be armed, he'll also be angry. My odds of getting out of this alive are shrinking by the minute.

Then glass shatters behind me, and cold liquid soaks the back of my shirt.

"Stay where you are, Aidan, or I'll slash you to ribbons," a female voice says above me.

I grab the poker and shuffle backward on my knees. Only when I'm a safe distance from Aidan do I look up to face my rescuer.

"You?" I whisper.

Deborah stands glaring at Aidan, holding a broken wine bottle with the jagged edges aimed at her old friend. "What's going on here?"

Silence descends, broken only by the odd drop of wine landing on the wooden floor and Aoife's quick, aggressive breaths.

"Deborah, I know this doesn't look great," Aidan finally admits. "But if you just give me a little time, I can explain everything."

I snort derisively. "How about I summarize? These two are greedy, murderin' psychopaths. See now, that wasn't so hard to explain."

Aidan slowly rises to a standing position. "Don't listen to her. We've been friends for years, Deborah. You know who I am."

She steps toward Aidan, lowering the bottle down to her side.

Oh, no! She's falling for his lies, I think to myself. *Or worse, maybe she's in on it after all.*

With some effort, I force myself onto my feet.

Deborah is so close to Aidan now it looks like she's about to hug him.

"That's true, Aidan. I have known you for a long time," she says. "And I've always thought you were a bit of an arsehole."

Aidan's eyes widen in surprise seconds before Deborah's knee slams into his crotch.

Aidan doubles over in pain.

Deborah shifts her gaze to me. "Jamie and Audrey will be here any minute. I rang them when I saw what was going on. But can you get to a phone and call an ambulance for Aoife?"

"Yeah, I just need to find my purse." I look around the room to see where my attackers might have put it after knocking me out. I find it lying on the ground next to the front door. Walking slowly toward it, I feel a surge of pain in the back of my head. Reaching up to rub it, my hand comes away covered in a warm sticky liquid.

I feel nauseous, and the room seems to spin around me.

I remain conscious just long enough to see the ground racing to meet me as I fall.

EPILOGUE

Two days later

There's not much I remember from the past forty-eight hours.

I vaguely recall being turned into a human pincushion, doctors playing flashlight tag with my eyeballs, and battling a relentless itch at the back of my head.

Apparently, Aidan's whack to my skull landed me with a severe concussion and a gash that needed twelve stitches. Audrey keeps threatening to slap a plastic cone around my neck if I don't stop scratching at them like a dog with fleas.

Because my injury resulted in two bouts of unconsciousness in less than half an hour, the doctors insisted on keeping me in the hospital for a few days.

Audrey never left my side.

Finally, this afternoon, I got the green light to go home.

On the drive back to Raven's Wing, I fill Audrey in on my altercation with Aiofe and Aidan at the cabin on Sunday night. In exchange, she brings me up to speed on the drama I missed during my unscheduled blackout.

She tells me that, two days ago, Deborah came around the cottage with a bottle of wine, hoping to squeeze some juicy details out of me about Mona's poisoning. Instead of what she expected to be a cozy chat, she'd seen me tied to a chair and called Audrey in a full-blown panic.

If Deborah hadn't come by, who knows what might have happened? But it's fair to say Deborah saved my life.

I'll need to get her flowers or take her to dinner to thank her and, honestly, to ease my guilt over accusing her, behind her back, of being the murderer.

"Aoife had her baby. She named him Kevin, supposedly after his late father," Audrey scoffs. "As if the whole world doesn't know that Aidan's the father of that baby."

"She's in jail, though, right?" I wonder if Aoife is vengeful enough to do something as stupid as coming after me again.

"Oh, yes. Sure, there's not a judge in Ireland who would give her bail after being accused of killing two people and trying to kill two more," Audrey assures me. "She insists she's not guilty, mind you. But Detective Mulhaney reckons he has a strong case. And with your testimony, it'll be rock solid."

"You've been talkin' to Detective Mulhaney?" I ask, struggling to keep my voice neutral.

"Sure, he arrived at the hospital desperate to know you were alright." Audrey takes her eyes off the wheel just long enough to give me a suggestive glance.

"I'm sure he just wanted to know what Aidan and Aiofe said to me," I quickly reply, eager to take some of the wind out of her sails. "And knowin' that man, he was probably fixin' to find some other reason to threaten to arrest me."

There's a twinkle in Audrey's eye when she says, "He does seem to take pleasure in thinking of you at his mercy."

"Miss Audrey!" I exclaim, feeling my face getting hotter.

"Alright, alright. I'll keep my thoughts to myself, shall I?" she smirks. "Oh, I don't think I mentioned it before. Jamie stopped by the hospital with that beautiful bouquet of flowers in the backseat."

I try to cast her a stern look but struggle not to laugh. "So this is what you not meddlin' looks like?"

"Meddling?" She gasps in mock horror. "And me only trying to bring you up to date on all you've missed."

After a few silent seconds, we both burst out laughing.

Before anything more can be said, Audrey steers her car into the driveway of my cottage.

A wave of sadness washes over me as Raven's Wing comes into view. Despite nearly being murdered there, I love this cottage that my mom bought when I was just a baby. Even though she never mentioned this place while she was alive, I feel closer to her, somehow, when I'm here.

But it won't be mine for much longer. For all that I've forgotten about what happened two nights ago, I do remember that right before Aidan knocked me out, I'd seen a final notice for the inheritance taxes I owe. Short of robbing a bank, there's no way I'll be able to come up with the money in time.

It vaguely occurs to me that there are several cars I don't recognize in the large driveway. But thoughts of who they might belong to disappear when I see my dad's smiling face as he emerges from the cottage, Fergal close at his heels.

"Welcome home, Savannah!" my dad calls out as I open the car door.

Despite the lingering tenderness of his own recent injury, he lunges forward and envelops me in a tight embrace. Not wanting to miss out, Fergal rises on his hind legs and rests his paws on our shoulders.

We chuckle, rubbing Fergal on the back.

"Ian, what are you doing on your feet? The pair of ye should be resting and taking it easy," Audrey chastises both of us.

"Calm yourself, Audrey. I've been in bed all day, just as the doctor ordered," Ian tells her. "But sure, I couldn't turn away visitors, now could I?"

"Visitors?" I ask, immediately assuming the worst. "What's wrong? Did somethin' else happen?"

My dad slings an arm across my shoulders and guides me toward the front door. "Come inside and find out."

Stepping into the living room, I see a crowd of familiar faces. Deborah, Deirdre, and Jamie rush over to hug me as my eyes take in all the other smiling faces.

Colin and Neve from the hotel have come bearing bottles of champagne to welcome me home, as have Ayleen and Caitlin. Domhnell and Mary brought a full spread of sandwiches and pastries. And on the sofa, I see Martin and Mona—who looks much healthier than the last time I saw her—unpacking a full set of pottery wine goblets! I'm delighted by the stunning gift, but I'm even happier to see she's recovered from Aidan's poisoning attempt.

"Everyone pitched in to get things cleaned up before you got home," my dad tells me proudly. "And we've changed all the locks and installed doorbell cameras at the front and back, so you'll always get an alert when someone comes near the house."

"I don't know what to say. Thanks ever so much." Tears well up in my eyes, both in gratitude for what they've done and out of sorrow, knowing they've only added value for the cottage's next owner.

"It's the least we could do for catching the savages that murdered my dad and very nearly killed Mona," Deborah says. "And for showing me who Aoife really is. I found out that she and Aidan had only become my friends so that Aoife could get close to my father. They were after his money all along."

"I'm so sorry, Deborah," I sympathize. "I know how it feels to be betrayed by a friend. It cuts deep, don't it?"

"It most certainly does," Deborah agrees with a bittersweet smile.

Jamie pops the cork on a bottle of bubbly and calls out, "What do you say we get this party started? Colin, you're in charge of tunes."

I make sure to spend time chatting with all my guests, thanking each of them for helping clean up the mess after Aidan and Aoife's break-in. Their kindness and generosity genuinely touches me. But I also realize this impromptu celebration of friendship will only make it harder when I'm forced to leave Raven's Wing.

As people get pleasantly buzzed and the singsong begins, feelings of loss threaten to overwhelm me. When no one is looking, I slip out front to get a breath of fresh air.

As I step outside, I see Detective Mulhaney opening the door of his car, preparing to leave.

"What? You came all this way to sneak off without so much as a hello?" I call out to him.

He pauses. "I heard that you were out of the hospital. I didn't know you'd be having a party. I don't want to interrupt."

"Don't be silly. Come on in if you like—" I give him my fiercest imitation of Audrey's stern look, "—but only if you don't try and arrest any of my guests."

He laughs—a deep, husky sound—and closes the distance between us. "I wouldn't be able to make any guarantees."

A tingle dances up my spine at his closeness. "So, why did you come all the way out here? Was there somethin' you needed?"

"Well, we will need a full statement from you at some point," he says. "But that's not why I'm here. I wanted to bring this to you in person."

He hands me a plain envelope with no markings on the outside. I glance up at him, raising an eyebrow.

"Go ahead, open it," he encourages me.

"Alright. This better not be a search warrant or—" I can't finish the sentence because all the air has suddenly gone out of my lungs. "W-what is this?"

He smiles. "What? You don't recognize a check for 50 thousand Euros when you see it?"

"Of course I do, but why is it made out to *me*?"

"I don't know if you'd heard, but Aiofe had the gall to put up a reward for finding Donnelly's killer," he explains. "The department figures if anyone deserves it, that would be you."

My heart feels like it's stopped beating. This is far more than I would need to pay off the inheritance taxes on Raven's Wing. It seems too good to be true, which means it probably is. "Are you pullin' my leg?"

He shakes his head. "I swear to you, this is real. That money belongs to you."

Without thinking, I throw my arms around him and squeeze him close to me. A few seconds later, when my head comes out of the clouds, I'm overcome with embarrassment. My arms drop to my sides, and I take a step back.

"Sorry about that," I say, suddenly feeling very warm. "It's just, well, you have no idea how much this means to me."

"In that case, I'm glad I made the trip," he says in a breathless, throaty voice. "But I best be on my way."

"Are you sure you don't want to come inside for a while?" I ask.

"No. Go on, get back to your party. But I'm warning you, the next time I see you, there better not be another dead body coming between us," Detective Mulhaney teases.

"Trust me, I never want to see another dead body for as long as I live," I assure him. "And if I do, I promise I'm running in the other direction!"

But like they always say. Promises were made to be broken.

END OF CURSED GROUND

RAVEN'S WING IRISH MURDER MYSTERY SERIES BOOK 2

I hope you've enjoyed your time in Ballygoseir!

From the coast of Ireland to the beaches of Florida, continue your cozy mystery adventure with a preview of the first book in my Egret's Loft Murder Mystery series, ***Unnatural Causes***.

THANK YOU!

If you enjoyed *Cursed Ground*, I'd be incredibly grateful if you could leave a quick review. Even just a few words can help other cozy mystery lovers find my books.

Thank you so much for your support and for being a part of his journey. I can't wait to bring you along on the next adventure!

And don't forget to join me on social media for updates and info on new releases!

instagram.com/teharkinsbooks
facebook.com/teharkins.author

UNNATURAL CAUSES

An Egret's Loft Murder Mystery

T.E. HARKINS

BLURB

Retirement can be murder....

Madeline Delarouse always thought growing old would take a lot longer. But when her adult kids move her into an upscale retirement community on the west coast of Florida, she fears her best days are behind her.

ALSO BY: UNNATURAL CAUSES

That is, until her new neighbor is found dead - a golf club stuck in her head.

Against the orders of her sarcastic son and exceptionally well-informed daughter, Madeline teams up with a wisecracking New York retiree to figure out whodunnit. Could it be the Black Widow living across the street? The mysterious Colombian in the colored caftan? Or the ex-Super Bowl quarterback who just can't stand losing?

Against a backdrop of perpetually sunny skies, endless activities and lots and lots of over sixty-fives in golf carts, Madeline has to find out who killed her neighbor and why before her nosiness makes her the killer's next victim.

Grab your copy of *Unnatural Causes* (*Book 1 of the Egret's Loft Murder Mystery Series*) today!

* * *

EXCERPT

PROLOGUE

The day Ritchie moved me into Egret's Loft, I thought that was it, I was done for. In for life, with no possibility of parole. Extradition to a luxurious kind of prison where I, and all my new neighbors, were just waiting to die.

That might sound a touch melodramatic, but there's a pretty compelling reason people joke about Florida being God's waiting room.

Not the parts of the state furthest south, like the Florida Keys or Miami, where it's all surf, sun, and another three-letter "s" word that people of my generation don't like to use in mixed company.

No, I'm talking about the parts of the state where every restaurant has an early bird special and there are no cars on the road after eight

ALSO BY: UNNATURAL CAUSES

o'clock in the evening. The kinds of places where the only children you see around town are the ones visiting their grandparents and the obituaries take up more space than the sports pages in the local newspaper.

A kind of place like Calusa, Florida—a small Gulf Coast town nestled comfortably between Fort Myers and Naples.

Population: 2,473.

Average Age: 75.

And Calusa was going to be my new home.

It was for the best.

At least, that's what Ritchie and Eliza had agreed before even bothering to broach the subject with me—their own mother. By the time I was brought into the conversation, they'd already picked out a high-end, low-crime community with guarded gates, loads of golf, and more activities than anyone over sixty-five could possibly have the energy for. But best of all, they said, I'd be around lots of people my own age.

I remember telling the kids, when they were little, that they should go play outside to be around people their own age. It didn't matter so much to me whom they socialized with, I just wanted to get them out from underfoot. This phrase has now, decades later, come back to bite me.

My outlook and attitude were grim as I packed my bags and prepared for the move to Cypress Point Avenue.

Little did I know then, the day I moved into Egret's Loft was the beginning of the most exciting chapter of my life…and the most dangerous.

Grab your copy of *Unnatural Causes (Book 1 of the Egret's Loft Murder Mystery Series)* today!